W9-CNL-470

THE
RESORT

BOOKS BY SUE WATSON

THE
RESORT

SUE WATSON

Bookouture

Published by Bookouture in 2022

An imprint of Storyfire Ltd.
Carmelite House
50 Victoria Embankment
London EC4Y 0DZ

www.bookouture.com

Copyright © Sue Watson, 2022

Sue Watson has asserted her right to be identified as the author of this work.

All rights reserved. No part of this publication may be reproduced, stored in any retrieval system, or transmitted, in any form or by any means, electronic, mechanical, photocopying, recording or otherwise, without the prior written permission of the publishers.

ISBN: 978-1-80314-256-2
eBook ISBN: 978-1-80314-255-5

This book is a work of fiction. Names, characters, businesses, organizations, places and events other than those clearly in the public domain, are either the product of the author's imagination or are used fictitiously. Any resemblance to actual persons, living or dead, events or locales is entirely coincidental.

For anyone who's ever had a holiday from hell.

PROLOGUE

As I step onto the boat, a sudden breeze catches my hat and though I try to grab it, I'm not quick enough. With tears in my eyes, I watch the beautiful Gucci boater tied with grosgrain ribbon, as it floats further and further away.

I try not to cry as I take my seat on deck, opposite a woman with searching eyes and alarm in her voice.

'Oh no, is that your hat?' she asks.

I nod, avoiding her searching eyes.

'Was it expensive?'

'Very,' I reply, wishing she'd shut up.

I take my phone from my bag in an attempt to avoid speaking to her. I'm surprised to see a signal. We've been shut off from the rest of the UK for the past few weeks, and it feels strange now, almost scary to be able to speak to the outside world. I don't know what to say. What can I say? Impulsively, I decide to call my sister; I'm tired and tearful, I need to hear a familiar voice.

'Hey, you,' she says. 'Are you okay? I heard what happened, it was in all the newspapers. Are you finally coming home?'

I'm moved by my sister's voice, and the sound of home, but

her words are like a hammer in my head – a reminder of how life was before this trip.

'Are you there, are you okay?' my sister's saying, and a wave of huge, loud sobs emerge from somewhere deep inside me. The woman opposite is staring at me.

'No, to be honest, I'm not okay.'

'What? What is it?' My sister's voice has turned to panic.

'Sis, can you do me a favour?' I say. 'My signal's dying. Will you call the police and ask them to meet me on the mainland? I have something to tell them.'

Still clutching the phone to my ear, I move further down the deck, so I can't see my departing hat, or the woman's beady eyes. I stand alone at the far end of the boat, surrounded by the ocean for the last time. I allow the salty sea breeze to ruffle my hair, and cool my cheeks. It has been the hottest summer the UK had ever known.

As the mercury rose, and storms rolled in, secrets were spilled and lives were lost in that beautiful white palace overlooking a turquoise sea. And as the boat cuts through the now choppy waters, I see Fitzgerald's grow smaller and smaller in the distance, until it looks like a glittering diamond standing proud in the middle of the Atlantic Ocean. Only then do I turn to see the mainland, where an uncertain future awaits. I pull my shawl around me and brace myself for what happens now.

ONE

SAM

Three Weeks Earlier

It was our third night at Fitzgerald's, and my new husband and I were having dinner. It was the most luxurious, most expensive hotel I'd ever set foot in, and along with naked swims, couples' massages and every whim catered to, the food was just heavenly. It was the honeymoon I'd always dreamed of. It was also the hottest summer the UK had ever known.

'Are you happy?' I asked, and David smiled, his eyes drifting towards the window, to the sea waiting outside in the oncoming darkness, a storm slowly brewing in the distance.

'Of course I'm happy, I'm with you,' he said, his eyes returning briefly to mine and his hand reaching out across the table, touching my fingers. I took the inevitable bolt of electricity from his touch and shivered with anticipation.

I sipped on my cold water and continued to gaze at him.

He glanced at me briefly, but his eyes seemed unable to tear themselves away from the window and the sun in its last throes of the day, a bright orange rage against the dying of the light.

I followed his gaze and joined him as he stared at the sun slowly seeping into the pale sky, leaving blood-red smears in its wake. The flames were reflected in the sea now, and I turned back to him. 'Hard to imagine something so beautiful being so dangerous,' I said. 'It's like molten gold.'

He shrugged. 'Yeah, the tides can be treacherous. It might look calm, but it can suck you under quite easily, then spit you out.'

'Eww, suck you in and spit you out – that sounds horrible.'

'Very much like a beautiful woman,' he said in a mock-French accent, making me giggle.

I looked around at all the glamorous, wealthy people, who seemed to wear evening clothes with the same ease I wore pyjamas. A woman on the next table was dressed in a glittery dress that twinkled, it was mesmerising, and I tried not to stare. Her hair was a cloud of platinum curls, her make-up flawless and her red lips shone like glass. I wondered if she was a model. I glanced down at my Marks and Spencer's floral maxi dress. It had looked great in my bedroom mirror at home, but now among the designer dresses and sophisticated glitz it seemed decidedly frumpy.

I glanced again at David and waited for the rush, which always came when I looked at my new husband. The now dusky pink light from the window framed his profile, giving him a soft glow. I longed to touch the gently curling hair reaching the nape of his neck, and had this strong urge to lunge over the table and kiss him, full on the lips. I smiled to myself at the prospect of me giving in to my urges here in this beautiful, sedate dining room filled with glamorous people eating teeny tiny things. No, this wasn't the place to be myself. I had to behave, so I placed my sweaty palms on the cool linen tablecloth.

'God it's so hot!' I exclaimed, lifting my hair from the nape of my neck for some relief.

'Listen to you complaining about the heat,' he said. 'You'd be pissed off if it was raining.'

'Oh, I'm not complaining at all,' I said. 'It's perfect, the Mediterranean weather in the middle of Devon, the hotel like a big white palace, the staff...you. No, I'm certainly not complaining,' I said, reaching out my hand to touch his face. 'I've seen it in magazines and on Instagram, but never thought I'd actually *stay* here, as a guest.' I gave a contented sigh.

He slowly turned from the window, his eyes bringing everything back to me, another little rush. 'And this is only the beginning,' he replied softly. He caught my hand and kissed it gently, making me shiver with excitement.

The starter arrived, and as the waitress laid down the plate, I caught David looking at her. She looked back, and I realised it was the same girl who manned the beach bar by the pool.

'*Bonsoir,*' she said to David, who didn't reply, but smiled, in a slightly stand-offish kind of way.

She looked momentarily awkward, and in an attempt to rescue her I said, 'Hi, it's Stella, isn't it? You run the beach bar?'

'Yeah, yeah that's right,' she said with a smile. She was very young, blonde and pretty; even the rather stiff waitress uniform couldn't hide that.

'I thought I might come to your yoga class,' I said. 'Do you have one tomorrow?'

'Yeah, nine thirty in the area by the pool,' she replied enthusiastically.

'She's nice, isn't she?' I remarked to David, as she walked away.

'Is she?' he said, pretending not to have noticed.

'Yeah, well you should know, you were chatting to her today at the pool bar. In French.'

He gave a deep sigh. 'I was ordering our drinks. In French. I wasn't exactly *chatting*.' He looked up suddenly from his plate. 'Sam, I hope you're not playing *that* game.'

'No, no of course I'm not, I was just making an observation.'

'Not a point?'

'No,' I shook my head vigorously. 'She teaches the yoga class, runs the beach bar, I didn't realise she was a waitress as well,' I murmured, almost to myself.

'One job not enough for her?' he muttered, without meeting my eyes.

I shrugged. 'She's young, probably needs the money.' I was now gazing at the line of knives and forks before me, reminded of a police line-up; each one was daring me to choose them and get it wrong.

I discreetly watched David take a fork from the outside to taste his starter, and I did the same. As lovely as it all was here, I was unsure of the etiquette, especially at the table. I'd already made a huge faux pas on the first night there.

'I think she made a mistake,' I'd whispered to David, as I looked round for the waitress who'd just delivered the starters to our table.

'Why do you think it's a mistake? And why are you whispering?' David had said loudly, making me cringe. His eyes were dancing, something amused him.

I leaned forwards and said quietly, 'I ordered the paté.' I nodded at the tiny plate of toast and foam in front of me. 'I'm whispering because I don't want to get the waitress into trouble.'

'It's not the *starter*,' he replied, laughing openly. 'It's an *amuse bouche*,' he said, like this made everything clear.

It didn't. I was mortified, but not sure why, so I just smiled. 'Well, it's very... nice.' My cheeks were hot with embarrassment. I tasted the little morsel on toast, a sort of surprisingly savoury sorbet, which confused me and my taste buds. But David seemed to find it all very funny, and once he explained that an amuse bouche was something served before dinner, like a canapé, I smiled, like it made sense. But it didn't; I was completely out of my depth. And the battery of cutlery gleaming arrogantly at me now was just a reminder that it was very early days, and I still had a lot to learn.

David was now studying the wine menu. Unlike me, he seemed at home here in his black tie, effortlessly demanding attention like he was born to it. As lovely as it was, I couldn't imagine ever feeling quite so at home here in this hedonistic hotel where a Diet Coke cost more than some people earn an hour.

I felt guilty, but reminded myself how lucky I was to be here. Built in the 1920s Fitzgerald's was essentially a big, white, beautiful palace on a rugged island in the middle of the ocean. The building had been renovated over the years, but it remained faithful to the era and the geography, both inside and out. Looking around the dining room, I could see how the interior was a reflection of the sea and rugged cliffs with its ocean-blue, warm gold and rich coffee colour palette.

'This place is a love letter to the 1920s,' David had remarked only that morning as we'd cooled down in the beautiful mosaic pool, created by an art deco designer of the time. Ever since we'd decided to come here, I'd read every blog and magazine article I could find about Fitzgerald's. I savoured each photo, every little morsel of information. The brochure, now dog-eared after my constant rereads, covered the luxury, the history and the beauty of the island, but didn't dwell too much on the darker aspects. There was no mention of the millionaire poisoned by his love rival – the hotel chef – in 1924. Nor did the brochure mention the famous actress who plunged to her death from the cliffs, or the two lovers dying in a suicide pact in the honeymoon suite many years before. The same honeymoon suite David and I shared, which was stunning, in pale blues and golds, a huge bed under a white canopy, and a bath big enough for two. But I didn't sleep well in that gorgeous room. I'd wake in the middle of the night and imagine what happened there.

Despite Fitzgerald's dark history, I'd fallen in love with the place from the moment I arrived. Even after reading about all the terrible things that had happened there, I still loved the way those fronded palms beckoned me inside. On the day we arrived, from the moment I walked into that hushed foyer smelling of jasmine and lemons, Fitzgerald's held me in her embrace and I never wanted to leave.

Back then, eating dinner on the first night of my honeymoon, I was just so happy to be there with him; it was all that mattered to me. I had no idea of what was ahead. My feelings for him were so intense, so passionate, heightened by the heady atmosphere, and the heat. The weather changed from typical British cloudy, rain-threatening coolness, to a whoosh of almost tropical temperatures within hours of our arrival on the island. The guests talked of 'a micro-climate,' but as David said, 'It's a heatwave. It's all over this part of the UK, and it's just bloody *hot!*'

I'd met my new husband just six months before, and we were now married, which had been a lovely and unexpected surprise. As a single thirty-something I'd assumed love had passed me by, and resigned myself to life looking after Mum and working as a hairdresser in a little shop a few minutes from where I was born. I'd spent my days thinking of what might have been as I cut hair and listened to the ongoing chapters of my clients' lives. But my life was just one long chapter; it was all the same until I met David, who was different from all the rest. At forty, he was a grown-up who had a successful property business, a beautiful home and was looking for love. He turned up in my life when I'd just about given up, and even on our first meeting, he looked at me like I was *everything*. No one had ever looked at me like that before and from then onwards, the life I'd led – which consisted mostly of trying to keep a roof over my head and stop my mother from burning her house down – changed. After years of swiping right, hanging around in bars and clinging desperately to men who always dumped me, my prince had come. It sounds like a cliché, but it really *was* like a fairy tale: he bought me flowers, took me to lovely restaurants, for long walks in the country, days by the seaside, and made me feel whole for the first time in my life. Since meeting him I'd had to pinch myself every morning when I woke up, because things like this, men like this, happened to other girls; men like David didn't happen to Sam Richards from Manchester. And not only did David care for *me*, he'd also been supportive of Mum, who's had early-onset dementia for years. It had been such a struggle, but now if I had to work late, he'd pop round to see her, often taking her favourite chocolate bar. He was so kind, he'd sit and listen for hours while she told him her life story, over and over again. He understood that she didn't know who he was – hell, she didn't know who I was most days, and it broke my heart. But David was so thoughtful, he even paid for a nurse to move in with Mum for the two weeks we were away. My sister, Jen, and I were both so grateful to him – it must have cost a fortune, but he didn't mind, he was very generous.

'Can you believe it, this time last year we didn't even know each other?' I said as I embarked on my scallop starter.

'I know – funny how life can surprise you, isn't it?'

'Tell me why you love me.'

He laughed. 'Again?'

'Yes, I like to hear it.' I giggled, taking a mouthful of scallop, which tasted like a seafood marshmallow, spiky with salt, lemon and samphire. It was a small and delicious explosion of the sea.

'Why do I love you?' he asked, and pretended to think for a moment. 'Well,' he started, 'I love your eyes, your sense of fun, your body... but let's not go there,' he added with a twinkling smile, those dimples appearing like sunshine.

'Yes, *do* go there,' I replied playfully.

'I'm afraid that's *not* appropriate over dinner,' he joked, in a posh voice that made me giggle. 'But there are so many things I love about you, they're too long to list while I'm trying to concentrate on my food.' He reached out his hand and touched mine. 'I still wake up each morning, and go to sleep at night, see your hair on the pillow and remember how lucky I am...' I saw his eyes dampen and wanted to hug him.

Abandoning my starter, I moved my chair towards him slightly to reach in and kiss his cheek.

'Do you?' I flushed with pleasure and surprise. Being adored was all very new to me. I'd been unlucky in love, so had he, and I felt like we both deserved this.

'Yeah, you're beautiful when you sleep...' He touched my face before returning to the menu. 'It's when you wake up the trouble starts.'

I laughed. 'You had to go and spoil it, you pig,' I said in mock anger, giving him a light slap on the arm.

David teased me a lot, he was very funny – but I was sensitive, and sometimes took things too much to heart. Our rare conflicts were often about my thin skin but it was because he meant so much to me that what he said went deep. Even a casual remark about my weight (with all the lovely dinners, I'd put on a few pounds since we'd met) or a less than complimentary remark about my hair set me off. But David was very understanding. He said my irrational responses to his remarks were perfectly logical, because I'd been hurt so much in the past. As he pointed out, I was always on the defensive because I was waiting to be criticised or hurt, so even though he didn't *mean* it, I took offence.

We both sat now, holding hands, smiling at each other, and I know it sounds cringey, but I felt like I'd finally been let in on something magical. Until David I'd never been in love, and I used to see couples together and wonder what love felt like. But not anymore.

'I can tell you the exact moment I fell in love with you,' I said.

'Really, when?' he asked, then just as I was about to respond, he frustratingly called a passing waiter over to our table.

'*David,*' I reprimanded him, as the waiter approached, 'don't you want to know?'

'Yes of course I do, but I also want a drink, as I'm sure you do.' He smiled at the waiter who was now standing expectantly at our table, as requested. I watched and waited, and after a very short conflab over the wine list, David decided on a French white. David said the name of the wine in that French accent again, and this time it wasn't jokey, it was real and clever.

The waiter was clearly impressed by David's wine knowledge and the two chatted along for ages in French, just as he had earlier that day with Stella, the waitress. I obviously couldn't join in, so just smiled and looked round the room wishing I'd paid more attention in French classes at school. But listening to him chatting away, it didn't matter that I didn't understand a word; I felt so proud, and still so amazed that he chose me to marry. I'd never been with a man who could speak another language before and I found it very exciting. I wanted to take him straight back to our room and tell the waiter to send the wine after us.

Once we were alone again, I instinctively leaned towards David across the table, and he moved to meet me so our heads were together, our hands entwined. It felt *so* good.

'Go on, you were saying... when did you realise it was love?' he asked, directing his gaze right at me, making my nerve ends tingle.

'It was on our fourth date,' I started, looking up into the ceiling, pretending to remember exactly when, but all the time I knew. I was just finding the courage to say it.

'It was the evening we went to the wine bar in town, and Marie was there... do you remember?'

His face dropped. Of course he remembered, how could anyone forget? The escalation from nought to 100, the screaming, the blind rage. *Marie.* He looked beyond me again, through the window, out to sea. I don't know why I'd felt compelled to bring her into our intimate dinner, to allow her to thrash around the table, to remind him of her. I knew I should have lied, told him I'd fallen in love any other night, but sometimes I couldn't help myself. I felt this uncontrollable urge to do and say things that I felt, even if that tested us. Perhaps because I couldn't believe how lucky I was, I felt this constant need to push at it, like it was a closed door. And now I'd spoiled everything, and a dark shadow was shrouding the table.

'Look, let's not...' he said, no sign of his smiling dimples. I wondered, as I often did, if he still had feelings for her? 'It's all so difficult... painful,' he said, his eye contact waning. I was losing him, and I swear the lights dimmed, the gold filigree trimmings around the beautiful ballroom dulled.

He turned away from me, not wanting to hear what I had to say, but I said it anyway. Like I say, sometimes I just can't help myself and I do and say what my heart tells me, and not my head.

We'd both tried to ignore what happened for too long, but it was time to exorcise her from our lives and free up the space she'd taken up in our relationship. I could feel her sitting between us now.

'David—'

A moment of anger flashed in his eyes. I knew his rage was for her, not me, but still it shook me.

'What I remember most about that night was that I worried you might actually *believe* what she was saying,' he said. His eyes softened, and when he reached out and caressed my hand lovingly, all traces of anger were gone.

I squeezed his hand reassuringly. 'I saw Marie for what she was. Your crazy ex-wife,' I added, the flippancy in my tone contradicting the very real fear I'd felt at the time. That night her anger was visceral, she was driven by fury. Delicate features, small, white teeth like tight little pearls, parting and spitting venom at him. At me.

'*You!*' She pointed at me. 'Standing there like the cat that got the cream. He'll do the same to you,' she'd yelled. 'He sleeps with anyone, *everyone*, and he'll deny it until you think you're going crazy. He's the psycho, but he'll convince you *you're* the one who's mad!'

David had warned me what she was like, but seeing and hearing it for myself was shocking. I shuddered at the memory.

I could still hear her screaming at us as her friend pulled her away from David. 'He's not *worth* it, Marie.' Everyone in the wine bar was staring at her, and as he tried to move away, she hammered on David's back. He didn't retaliate, of course – he wasn't violent or aggressive. He just scrunched himself up as she kept on hammering with both fists. 'You bastard,' she screamed, until the barman ran over and dragged her away from him.

'Look, I'm sorry, I shouldn't have brought all this up,' I said, returning to the present. 'I just wanted you to know that it wasn't all bad that night – because the way you held yourself through it made me fall in love with you.'

He gave a big sigh and shook his head slowly. 'I don't like to think about it.'

'You were so calm, so protective of me,' I went on, trying hard not to think about how her words cut into my flesh. 'She said some terrible things. I find it hard to understand how anyone could feel that way about you, you're so kind and thoughtful, and—'

'I don't know why I stayed as long as I did,' he said over my words. 'Perhaps I thought I could help her, make her better?'

'I doubt *anyone* could help Marie.'

'She wasn't always like that. When we first met, she was gentle, really sweet and funny, you know?' he said, as if to himself. I wondered what rare, 'loving moment' in their dark, twisted union his mind had suddenly alighted on.

'I remember you saying how jealous she was though?' I reminded him.

'Yeah, her jealousy,' he continued to shake his head, like he still couldn't believe it. 'She could kick off any time,' he added, now lost in his own world, one where I couldn't reach him. And despite his words, and everything that happened, I felt insecure – did he still have feelings for her?

'She'd say, "do you think so and so looks good with that new haircut?" Or, "doesn't she look cute now she's lost weight?"' he continued. 'And I'd agree, say, "yeah, I guess she does", or something like that. But then she'd accuse me of secretly fancying them, or *seeing* them. She even said I was sleeping with her best friend, Alice, who never spoke to her again. God, it was awful, everything was always heightened, she was hell-bent on finding me guilty of something, *anything*. She accused me of seeing women at work, looking too long at a shop assistant, a waitress when we ordered dinner.' He shook his head at the memory, and I remembered our previous conversation about him chatting to Stella in French and how he'd reacted. It was clear why he was so paranoid about being accused of cheating.

'Marie was unhinged, but at first I just didn't see it,' he said.

I thought back to that night. She must have followed him, waiting in the shadows for her moment. I'd been so scared and after that episode we'd had some uncomfortable times wondering if and when it might happen again. Even now I sometimes look over my shoulder when I'm alone, just in case.

'You cheating bastard,' she'd shrieked as she was escorted from the premises. But she didn't stop there, she threw her drink at David's head. The glass caught his face, but she continued to scream at us, hurling her words like sharp arrows; her aim was to wound. 'Get out while you can,' she yelled as her friend bundled her out of the door. 'If you don't, he'll ruin your life.'

And after that, she made our lives a misery. Even on honeymoon I felt like she was present. I could have sworn I'd seen her walking on the beach, stopping and looking up at our bedroom, planning her next move. And now, sitting in that beautiful ballroom, about to enjoy a wonderful dinner, my finger ends tingled as I glimpsed a waitress with long, dark hair just like Marie. She wafted through the room, and I felt my whole body spark with fear. For a moment I thought she'd disguised herself in a uniform and turned up on our honeymoon! I imagined I saw her everywhere; she was now standing by the door, gazing at me, and for a few, terrifying seconds, I really thought she was back to take her revenge. I wondered if I would ever be free from those troubling thoughts and visions.

She'd seemed so consumed with jealousy, I was genuinely scared of what she might do to split us up, to take David away from me.

But even his crazy ex couldn't keep us apart, and within weeks David had proposed. For a little while, I allowed myself to forget Marie and her hatred, and concentrated on planning our small but perfect wedding, followed by the dream honeymoon at Fitzgerald's. I would sweep the salon floor while imagining me and David lying by the mosaic pool. I'd cut hair while thinking about us sipping cocktails in the 1920s bar and wandering the beach at sunset. I'd lie alone in my single bed gazing at the online brochure that promised a paradise of 'unparalleled luxury, an indulgent spa and exquisite food'. This was accompanied by the added assurance that, '*once you arrive at this white jewel glittering in the ocean, you'll never want to leave*'.

And I *never* wanted to leave. It was love at first sight when I saw the gleaming white palace from the boat. I couldn't wait to cross the small expanse of ocean keeping me from her. I was beguiled by her beauty and enchanted by what she had to offer me. But there were dark secrets woven into the fabric of Fitzgerald's, and what I didn't see from my parasol on the beach was how the building thrummed with life and lust and revenge. And that summer made us so reckless, we never noticed, but along with the glamorous guests and tropical cocktails something malevolent was unwittingly welcomed in.

TWO

DAISY

'I was told there was no phone signal here,' Daisy said, plucking her phone from her evening bag. 'I wanted this to be our getaway, our chance to regroup, but I'm still getting messages.' She looked up at her husband.

'The signal's intermittent,' Tom replied, checking his own phone, disappointed to see nothing.

'I've got *so* many messages,' she murmured, scrolling down quickly with two fingers.

'Ignore them.'

'I will,' she replied absently. 'Oh I've got *another* message from that girl asking me if there's any work for a trainee on the magazine. She's a photography student. I checked her Instagram, she's good. I'm going to ask her if we can meet up.'

'I wouldn't agree to meet anyone from social media, you don't know who they are. It might not even be a girl, it could be some weird guy?'

'No, she was at art college in London, she's even got some photos of here – they're so good.'

'So she's here, at the hotel?'

'No, the pictures were taken last summer, she used a couple

of friends as models. But it's a great idea to do a shoot out here. I wonder if she was staying here?'

'A student? At these prices?' he snorted.

'Who knows? Perhaps Mummy and Daddy paid for her to come here, or the hotel let her just use the place to take photos. I doubt it, but either way I'm going to make sure there's some work for her when I get back.'

'Stop thinking about work, you're on holiday. And you're too soft, you can't just give random people what they ask for, you're always helping someone. It's time you helped yourself.'

'I don't mind – but I'll message her back when we're home. Sorry, Pink Girl, you'll have to wait,' she muttered at the screen before quickly putting her phone away.

Daisy was trying to enjoy her luxury break with husband, Tom. Fitzgerald's was somewhere they'd always promised themselves they would go, and it was everything she'd thought it would be. From the minute they stepped on the island, Daisy felt like she'd walked into another world. She knew she was lucky to be there, but she'd been through so much, she found it hard to let go, to forget.

'You okay?' he asked.

She nodded. 'I'm fine, just feeling a bit edgy, a drink will help,' she said, turning around to see if she could see someone to bring them something cold. After the heat of the day, a storm was brewing and the air was heavy. The pressure made her headachy and dry-mouthed. 'I'm parched,' she said, her head darting about in search of drink.

Daisy looked like one of the models she worked with as art director for an upmarket glossy magazine. Her curly blonde bob framed her face like an explosion of white sunshine. Very much aware of her beauty, she wore it with ease. She knew what worked, and her glitzy dropped-waist flapper dress was perfect in the art deco setting; the pale silver beaded fabric glittered like the sea and reflected on her skin like diamonds, as she knew it would. She could have been a model once upon a time, but at five feet five inches she was deemed too short, so she'd opted to work behind the scenes instead. So many wannabe models had been devastated when they didn't fit in the fascistic fashion of the late nineties, but Daisy had always made the best of things. Until now. Leaning back in her chair, she allowed the male eyes in the room to land on her like gentle, if persistent caresses. But what had once soothed her, had no effect now. She wanted nothing except one thing. It thrummed through her veins, starved her of sleep, made her cry like a baby. Just like a baby.

Daisy was only too aware that Tom was as lost as she was. Neither of them knew where to go from here, the road ahead that had been waiting on the horizon had suddenly disappeared. This holiday was make or break for them, because everything they'd planned for had suddenly become dust in their hands. The future they'd intended would be a different shape, but did they both fit into that? How she longed for those early days when they first got together and there were so many possibilities – or so she'd thought. They'd met four years before at a glitzy party in London. Tom worked for a big German bank, and Daisy was an art director. Over canapés and champagne, they'd chatted briefly, but Daisy could see he was younger than her, and she'd had enough of party boys, so when he asked if he could take her to dinner she'd politely refused. But as often happens in this age of online friendships and romance, he followed her to the ends of the earth – well, Instagram. Here she posted pictures of herself in glamorous surroundings at fashion shoots with the magazine. From Paris Fashion week to bikini shoots in the Maldives, she lived a glamorous, jet-setting life that all her friends envied. And when the younger, but very hunky Tom began to pursue her online, those friends urged her to take him on, despite the age difference.

'What's eight years when he looks like that?' her friend, Abby, had said. 'Besides, on average women live seven years longer than men, so you're practically the same age!' For a while, they'd flirted in cyberspace, and one weekend, when she was bored and lonely in her flat, she invited him over for drinks. He turned up with flowers – not just any old flowers though; he'd done his research and produced blooms from her favourite florist. He didn't go home that first weekend, and the following Monday over G&Ts in a wine bar off Wardour Street she announced to her girlfriends: 'He's gorgeous to look at, good in bed and I've invited him to Marrakesh to watch the sunrise from a hot air balloon next weekend.'

It was a pretty fantastic second date, and within a month they both knew they'd found the one. He proposed on a mountain in Wales, they married in Italy, and their new home was a gorgeous house in the Cotswolds, with acres of garden for children and dogs to romp.

So when, after just six months of marriage Daisy discovered she was pregnant, it wasn't even a surprise; their relationship had been so perfect, it was all meant to be. A child was something Daisy had longed for, and her chance to put right all the wrongs in her own childhood.

Daisy loved her career, but by then was thirty-five and ready to leave the London life behind, do some freelance work and play house in the Cotswolds. She abandoned the foreign shoots, glittering hotels and life spent on planes flying around the world to create a nursery in lemon and blue with moon and star mobiles and clouds on the walls. She felt privileged to sit in that room chatting to the baby she felt she knew so well but was yet to meet. She'd tell her unborn child all about the life that awaited them, the adventures they'd have together, and how much Mummy and Daddy loved them already. Meanwhile, their friends and Tom's family helped fill their home with toys and baby blankets and things soon-to-be parents don't even know they need. And as the months went on and the bump grew, they discovered it was a boy, and started to think about names. James was Tom's father's name, and they both liked it so the bump became James and they felt they knew their baby even better. He took on a personality. Tom said his eye-watering intelligence meant he would be a brilliant surgeon, and Daisy said he was going to be whatever he wanted to be as long as he was happy. They both talked about how he'd have a happy disposition, and blond hair and blue eyes just like them. Baby James was consulted regularly about this and his kicking became a whole new language.

'One kick for yes, two for no,' Tom would say, when discussing the score from that Saturday's football match. Even Daisy's interior design project on their home was assisted by James. The colour palette of lemon and blue and the clouds on the nursery walls were, according to Daisy, all per James's instructions from the womb.

So when, at eight months, Daisy felt no movement from the baby for a whole day, it was unusual. She called her midwife, who popped in to check all was well. It wasn't.

A day later, James Robert Jones was born, in deafening silence, having never really lived. Babies are not supposed to die. And the days, weeks and months that followed were the most difficult of Daisy's life. She couldn't eat, she couldn't work, she needed pills to fall asleep and pills to stay awake. She couldn't even look at babies, and walls painted with clouds made her cry. She was broken and felt like she would never be able to put herself back together. Later, they tried again, and when nothing happened, they went through the tortuous process of three cycles of IVF, all failed. And now at thirty-eight, Daisy was trying to begin to accept and understand a future without a child of her own. She thought about James every hour of every day, even now, almost three years after losing him.

Sitting in the restaurant of a beautiful hotel, politely eating dinner, he filled her head. She couldn't imagine living without

James, or any other baby, and quite frankly Daisy didn't know if she could get through *dinner* without having a breakdown, let alone the rest of her life. Every time she looked at Tom she saw their baby, and the ones that might have come later. And as she sipped her dirty martini, she knew she wasn't the woman Tom had married, and wondered if this was where their rainbow ended?

'So what now, Tom?'

He took a deep breath. 'The main course?' he said, unsmiling.

'You *know* what I'm talking about.' She felt her eyes welling with tears. She was so bloody emotional these days. What happened to Daisy the tough cookie who never let anything break her?

'I don't know what's next,' he murmured.

She sighed, a deep sigh that made him look up from his drink. 'I don't know what to do, Tom, for the first time in my life, I'm lost.' She swallowed her tears down with the lump of bread. But she knew he didn't know what to do either. She watched as the beautiful young waitress with the long, blonde hair approached them. She must only have been in her twenties. She brought them a jug of water and placed it on the table.

'Anything else?' she asked.

Daisy wanted to say, 'Yes, don't leave it too late to have a baby,' but she resisted. Daisy wished someone would have warned her, but would she have listened? Ambition and long hours and travel had all eaten away at her twenties, and by the time she was ready to give everything up to hold a baby in her arms, age had been against her. Of course she still had her career, but it could only take you so far. Recently she'd won an award for a big fashion campaign she'd worked months on, photographers and fashion editors from magazines all over the world wanted to take her out for lunch. They'd wined her and dined her and said her work was 'amazing,' 'important,' 'a landmark in art directing and fashion photography,' 'visually stunning,'... It went on and on, but it didn't erase the other stuff, the pain that kept her awake at night.

Tom reached out his hand and held hers across the table.

'After James... and the failed IVF, I really didn't think I could carry on,' she said, 'but we have no choice, do we?'

'We *will* carry on, we can get through this together,' he said tenderly. 'There is an alternative, we can live a life – another life without children?'

But Daisy looked back at that sunset, then at the beautiful waitress who was returning with their starter. She continued to watch her as she walked away.

'I wonder if she'll have children?' Daisy murmured, envying her youth, her beauty. This healthy young woman wasn't broken like Daisy.

'Who, Stella?' he said, looking up from his starter.

'You know her?'

'Only from here – she's working for the summer, she's an art student.'

Daisy wasn't usually the jealous type. But after everything that had happened she was feeling insecure and old and beginning to feel she had nothing to offer her younger husband. She'd already lost his baby. She could hear her mother slurring, 'You had one job!'

At thirty, Tom still had plenty of time to be a young father, to blow birthday candles out and play football with another James; all he had to do was meet someone younger, someone who could give him that son. She sipped on her drink while watching Tom watching Stella walk away. And Daisy wondered if she should be worried.

THREE

BECKY

Our day begins gently, the room fills with calming scent and soothing music, no alarm clocks here at the resort, where 'your peace of mind is our peace of mind.'

'I like where they're coming from, but not sure I'm feeling Zen yet,' I say to Josh, who's lying on the blazing white sheets, still half asleep. It's so warm, we don't even need bedding, the sheets are merely cosmetic. The laminated cards dotted around offer advice on 'How to get the best from your stay,' and suggest that 'Nightwear is just another layer, and may impede the emotional peeling process.'

'Emotional peeling?' I read it out loud. 'What the hell is that? Sounds painful.'

'It's a song, isn't it?' Josh replies, with a chuckle.

'It's rubbish,' I say.

'Becks, try, and be more open to this, for me,' he replies, suddenly all serious.

I immediately feel guilty. My husband brought me here because he wants to make me happy again, he's constantly buying me things, taking me places and Fitzgerald's is just another on his shopping list of joy. I should be grateful.

'Shall I order some of that green tea you like?' he asks, rolling out of bed and wandering towards the window where he pulls the curtains wide, causing a shaft of sunlight to spill into the room.

I hate green tea, but to please him I say, 'Yeah, that'd be nice.' I plump my pillow and sit up, watching him stand at the window. 'Your legs look really muscular,' I say, admiring his new silhouette against the bright light. 'Like David Beckham's... sort of,' I add with a smile, envying his firm torso, wrought from his recent obsession with running.

'David Beckham *sort of*? I'll take that.' He flexes his arms in a comical pose.

'You were late back again last night,' I say. 'I fell asleep waiting for you, that's two nights in a row.'

'Is it?' A shadow crosses his face and I wish I hadn't said anything. It doesn't matter. 'Yeah, yeah, I did a few extra laps.' He turns back to look out of the window.

A *few* extra? On both nights I fell asleep about 1am, and he still hadn't returned to the room.

'How do you find your way round the island in the dark?' I ask, intrigued why anyone would even want to run around in the dark after midnight.

He turns away and looks through the window at the sea. 'It wasn't dark, the moon lit up the beach.'

'Yeah, but it wasn't a *full* moon the last couple of nights, it can't have been that bright.'

'Becky, why so many questions?' he says, irritated. 'It was light enough. I go for late-night runs on the beach, I'm *used* to it.'

'It's just that you don't go running at night when we're at home.'

'Well, I do here. I like the beach, the cliffs, the emptiness, it helps me to think.' He tries to hide the exasperation in his voice, but it comes out like a strangled cry. 'You know what I'm like: I worry and I don't want to lay it all on you.'

He's still staring out of the window. I look down and play with my wedding ring in silence for a few moments. The light-hearted morning banter from seconds before is gone.

'All that running's giving you muscles you didn't know you had,' I say, to lighten the mood.

He turns and smiles at me.

'I don't know where you find the time, or the energy,' I say, stifling a yawn. 'I'm exhausted just *thinking* about exercise.'

'You shouldn't *even* be thinking about exercise,' he says in a mildly chastising tone.

'I should do some,' I murmur.

'No you shouldn't. The last time you went running you sprained your ankle.'

'I could come running with you?' I suggest.

'No way, I'm increasing my speed, setting a new personal record every time. You'd never keep up.'

His words gnaw at my insides as I smile and go along with this charade. He thinks I'm fragile, made of glass. But I'm stronger than both of us. I have to be.

'It's beautiful here,' I say, and he just gazes at me. The love on his face blinds me, it's almost *too* much. Is it possible to love someone *too* much?

'I'm not sure about the idea of being cut off,' I add. 'It freaks me out that there's no mobile phone signal, I find it really stress-ful.' I hear the whine in my voice and hate myself for it. But it's true; as always with Josh, I feel trapped.

'It's all part of the process,' he says, wandering over to the bed and sitting down, giving me his full attention.

'Yeah, but there isn't even a landline in the room.'

'Hotel policy. There's no point being here and using the facilities, eating healthy food, swimming every day if your phone's ringing and people are harassing you.'

'It's more stressful *not* to have a phone. I'm worried about the kids. Are they driving my mum and sister mad? And who's fed the cat, does someone need to talk to me about work or life or... anything?'

He sighs. 'I *told* you, the kids are fine. Becky, they're virtually grown-ups.'

'But what about my sister, and Mum? I haven't heard from them for three days.'

'I *told* you,' he says again, clearly trying to push down his irritation. 'Your mum and Liz have the hotel reception number. I've asked them not to call unless it's an absolute emergency, you need a break. We need this time together. Let me look after you, give you what you need, and stop worrying about everyone else.'

I take a deep breath. He can be so insistent. 'I can't change who I am, Josh, I can't just switch off. I'm worried about work too.'

'You've left work, so you can stop worrying about that. Even if there *was* an emergency, they wouldn't be calling you.'

I don't say anything, what's the point? But I wish someone from work *would* call me, even if only to chat. I'm a teacher, and that isn't a job, it's a vocation. I can't just suddenly stop thinking about my pupils, even if I have left. I still think I should have stayed on, but Josh made a big fuss, said I couldn't cope, even spoke to the headmistress about it. I try not to get angry, he means well. I wish Mum or my sister would call – it sounds mad, but I *want* there to be a teeny tiny crisis back home that only I can deal with.

'Now let's get dressed and go down to breakfast,' he says. 'There's a yoga class by the pool this morning, I thought I might go?'

'Really?' I say, suddenly feeling anxious. 'But you always said you hate anything like that ...'

'I just fancy it, that's all.'

'Fancy *it* or fancy the *teacher*?' I try to make a joke of this, but it probably sounds pained, I'm sure.

He shoots me a look, but doesn't acknowledge what I said. 'She makes a better yoga teacher than a barmaid – she's all over the place at the pool bar, you can never get served.'

'She's a waitress too, she must work from early morning until way after midnight,' I say, feeling tired just thinking about it. 'Now come on and get dressed, I don't want you to miss breakfast, or the class.'

I won't be attending class – the downward dog is the last thing I need. The physical effort, coupled with the fact that everyone else is so fit and flexible isn't good for my self-esteem. I think of the woman who was at dinner last night, the one in the beautiful glittery dress, probably vintage. I bet she'll be there looking all tanned and fit. The man she was with is handsome too; as they walked into the dining room all the women were gawping at him, and the men were looking at her.

'The quail was interesting, at dinner last night,' I say, remembering the way the glittery dress woman had picked at hers. 'That woman on the table near us didn't eat it, she gave hers to the guy she was with. He ate the lot, and then he ate her oysters.'

'God, at these prices I don't blame him, too expensive to waste.'

'She was very beautiful, wasn't she?'

'I didn't see her,' he says dismissively, and touches my arm. 'You did well, darling, to eat most of the dinner,' he adds. But I know he did see her, because I saw him watching her, drinking her in like the rest of them.

'It was seven courses and you ate them all, well done.' It's like he's talking to a six-year-old.

'It was a *tasting* menu, the portions were tiny.' I prickle at feeling patronised, aware of that rising panic that hits me these days. I feel trapped again.

'I think the sea air is giving you an appetite.'

'I love being by the sea, but I miss the kids.'

'They're *fine*. I hate to break it to you, love, but they wouldn't want to be here anyway. Amy won't leave Alex, and Ben won't leave his computer.'

I smile at the thought of sixteen-year-old Amy, all grown up with a boyfriend, and my baby boy at fourteen whose voice is now gravelly. My eyes well with tears at the thought of my kids.

'Come on, love, we're supposed to be having a happy time.' Josh hates when I cry, he doesn't know how to handle it. 'The spa treatment was good yesterday, wasn't it? You looked great when you came out of there. Did you feel good?' He's trying hard, too hard.

'Yeah, yeah,' I lie, it was a facial with nice oils, but it didn't change how I feel. 'How much did that treatment cost?' I ask, trying not to spoil his thoughtful gesture of booking me for a pamper session.

He shrugs. 'It doesn't matter.' He gets up from the bed and starts to dress.

'Josh,' I call after him as he disappears into the bathroom. 'We *can* afford this, can't we?'

'Of *course* we can,' he calls back, his words muffled as he brushes his teeth.

'Good,' I say, almost to myself. 'And thanks,' I call, while trying to stop my voice from breaking.

He leans out through the door, toothbrush still in his mouth. 'What for?'

'Everything.' I look around the beautiful room, decorated in pale pink and gold, the standalone bathtub near the window, the luxurious bed linen. 'Thanks for all this.'

He takes his toothbrush from his mouth. 'You deserve it,' he says, before disappearing back into the bathroom. I lie back on the soft pillows that feel like clouds, and drift off into sleepy whiteness. Sunlight and silence fill the room, and I wonder if this is what it feels like to die.

'Hey, sleepy head, are you going to get dressed?' What feels like seconds later, Josh's voice breaks into the whiteness. 'We don't want to miss breakfast.'

I desperately want to curl up. The only rest my mind has these days is sleep. 'I'm not really hungry, and I don't fancy sitting in the restaurant with all those people this morning.'

'Oh, Becky.' He sounds disappointed as he sits on the bed and puts his arms around me for a long hug. I hate disappointing him.

'I'm fine, honestly,' I lie. My life is one big lie now, as I hang on, clinging to the abyss, repeating my constant refrain: 'I'm just tired.'

'It'll do you good to get up, and if you don't fancy watching the yoga, you can come back here after breakfast?'

'I don't want to be stuck in the room again, I sat here all yesterday. Please, Josh?'

'Okay, but you know what you're like.'

'Yeah, I know, I get tired, I fall asleep in public, but it's the tablets.'

Right on cue he goes into the bathroom, then he's back out with a glass of water, his palm open with three pills sitting there.

'I almost forgot,' he's saying, really pleased with himself.

'I don't *want* to, don't make me.'

'You have to, the anti-depressants are almost as important as the painkillers, you'll feel better.'

'They make me feel like I'm sitting in cotton wool!' I'm almost crying now, but he isn't moving. He will stand here with his palm outstretched until I agree to take the bloody pills. So I do. I swallow them down, knowing I don't need anti-depressants, I just need someone to talk to.

'Good girl,' he says, and I want to slap him.

'I was thinking of trying to get some of the other guests involved in sponsoring me,' he says as he climbs into his shorts.

'Oh?' My heart dips slightly.

'We should get chatting to people, so I can tell them about my runs. I could even do a run round the island. People here have got a bit of money, haven't they?' he says, bending over to stretch his muscles.

'Oh, Josh, I don't know. I thought we were here to rest, have some time together.'

'We are, but we've got that trip to the US to pay for at the end of August, the flights alone cost a fortune not to mention—'

'But I thought we had *enough* money for the American trip?'

'We *do*,' he says, not meeting my eyes, 'we do,' he repeats, more quietly. For a moment he seems unreachable, and we're miles apart, then he says, 'But it's not just the flights, the whole thing is going to cost a fortune, and if we run out of money...' He stops himself, then changes the subject and asks, a little too brightly, 'So, breakfast, and yoga?'

'Yeah, let's go to breakfast and yoga,' I say, agreeing like a robot. And later, as we sit down to breakfast, I nod reluctantly again when he insists I have the scrambled eggs. I hate scrambled eggs.

'Coffee please,' I say to the waitress when she asks me what I'd like to drink – but even as I say it, I'm waiting for him to intervene. My heart is pumping.

'Becks?' And there it is. 'No caffeine,' he says, shaking his head slowly, and I want to scream and yell and hurl my glass of orange juice at him. But instead I turn to the waitress, smile and say: 'Sorry, I've changed my mind, I'll have a green tea please.'

I watch Josh carefully pouring water from the table jug like a priest pouring wine at communion. He has this pious look on his face – having been banned from drinking coffee I am more irritated than I probably should be by his demeanour. There's so much I'm not allowed to do. I watch him looking at the attractive blonde woman who was wearing vintage glitter last night. She looks just as lovely this morning. I've seen her around the hotel, she's always so well-groomed, glamorous, like she's thought about every aspect of her clothes, her make-up. She has 'a look' whereas these days I just feel thrown together. This morning, she looks fresh and cool in head to toe coral, while the rest of us melt in the heat.

'It's so warm, and it isn't even 9am,' I say, as the waitress brings my bloody green tea, but Josh isn't listening. He's watching the cool pretty, young blonde, mesmerised.

'She's lovely, isn't she?' I say.

'Who?' he asks.

I don't answer him, I just quietly sip my disgusting green tea and think about the past two nights. I don't believe his story that he came back late because he was running along the beach. It wouldn't be the first time Josh has lied to me.

FOUR

SAM

The next morning I was rather looking forward to the yoga class with Stella. It was now day four on our honeymoon, and I was thinking it would be great to do yoga on a daily basis for the rest of the holiday.

'If I attend Stella's class every day, I might look like her by the time we leave the island,' I joked with David that morning in our room.

'She's twenty years younger and at least two stone lighter, it would take a miracle!' he replied.

I'll admit, I sulked a bit at this, and when he didn't notice I was sulking, I had to say something. 'I know you're only joking, but sometimes you hurt me with the things you say,' I murmured.

He looked at me with genuine surprise. 'Oh, Sam, you're kidding, right?'

I shook my head.

'Wow.'

'What do you mean, *wow*!'

'You really are going to have to learn to take a joke,' he said, climbing out of bed, his back to me.

'I can take a joke, but you know I'm insecure about my looks. I'm aware I'm not beautiful with a perfectly toned body, but I don't want my husband to keep reminding me.'

He turned and glared at me. 'I'm not in the mood this morning, I have a headache and I really don't need it.'

'I'm not surprised you have a headache, you didn't come to bed until 2am,' I snapped.

He stood up and, pulling on his jeans, looked down at me in bed with what I can only describe as disgust.

'Do you wonder why I came to bed at 2am?' he asked, walking into the bathroom.

'Why?' I asked, a familiar feeling of dread filling my stomach.

He slowly moved back into the doorway and stood there glaring at me. David didn't like it when I challenged him, and he retaliated.

'If you want to know why I came in late, look in the mirror. There's your answer.' He shut the door, and I heard water running. I cried a little. This wasn't how honeymoons were meant to be, they were supposed to be the best part of being married, any problems started later, didn't they? David said I was a daydreamer, and no one would ever live up to my expectations. Perhaps he was right, but until the honeymoon I really thought he was perfect. To anaesthetise the pain of his remarks, I told myself he didn't mean it and put his mood down to a late night and a hangover. I'd gone to bed at eleven the previous night and left him drinking in the bar.

Eventually he came out of the bathroom, while I was getting dressed. I didn't speak to him, I felt too wounded. I wanted to ask him why he was so late, why he came in and went straight out onto the balcony like he couldn't bear to be near me. I also wanted to ask him if he'd been talking to Stella, the waitress, just to see what he'd say. But I was scared he might tell me something that would hurt, and I couldn't take that, so I just sat at the dressing table and applied my make-up.

'So you're running with this?' he asked, I could see him in the mirror, he had his back to me and was gazing out of the window.

'Sometimes you really make me feel vulnerable and insecure,' I said, putting on my mascara and telling myself it would all blow over later; it was just part of getting to know each other.

'Oh, I'm sorry if I make you feel like that. Here's an idea, why don't you start taking responsibility for your own weaknesses?' he snapped. 'I have given you everything, I spent a fortune on the perfect wedding, you had everything... didn't you?'

I couldn't answer him, my throat was tight with tears.

'Didn't you?' he yelled.

I didn't respond, just stayed at the dressing table, applying foundation and trying not to cry.

'I hate when women *do* this,' he hissed. I felt the anger laced through his words, and in that moment I felt more alone than I ever had when I was single.

I didn't rise to meet his anger. I just wanted him to calm down, and for things to be like they *should* be on a honeymoon. A few minutes later, I got my wish when he wandered over to where I was sitting and, from behind, I felt both his hands slide around my waist.

'Sorry!' he said into the mirror. 'I shouldn't have lost control like that.'

'You really hurt my feelings, David.'

'I know and I didn't mean it. I had too much to drink last night, I feel rough, and sometimes I lash out.'

'I won't put up with it.'

'I know, I'm really sorry, I love you so much, the last thing I'd ever want to do is hurt you.'

I gave in, and turned around so we could embrace, then we

kissed and made up and I felt a little better. But a seed of doubt was planted in my heart. He was my new husband, and wasn't meant to say nasty hurtful things.

But it was times like this that made me question him, and doubt who he was. After all, I didn't really know him. And that morning, I was slightly wary of my husband, because what he said revealed to me a cruelty that, until then, I hadn't thought him capable of.

'So, are you going to yoga class after breakfast?' he asked me as we continued to get ready for the day.

'Yeah, I think so,' I said, still feeling raw from our encounter, while he seemed completely over it.

'Great! I'll come along too.' He rubbed his hands together in anticipation. He must have seen the look on my face because he said, 'Don't worry, I won't join in, I'll just watch.'

I wasn't sure what was worse: my husband attempting the downward dog, or him on the sidelines comparing me to the other women in their tight lycra. But it seemed he'd made his mind up, because straight after breakfast, he accompanied me down to the pool area where all the yoga mats were laid out.

David took a seat at a table, and I made small talk with the woman on the mat next to mine while we waited for Stella, the instructor, to arrive. But after about twenty minutes, Paulo, the assistant manager, appeared.

'I'm so sorry, ladies, but there won't be a yoga class today,' he said. 'Our yoga teacher isn't feeling very well and has had to cancel.'

'Oh no, I was really looking forward to it,' the woman next to me was saying. I turned to her and realised it was the woman from the previous evening who'd worn the glittery dress. Her hair was tied up, and without all those curls I didn't recognise her.

She was slightly older close-up, but still lovely, and apparently David thought so too. When I looked over at him, he waved, pretending he was looking at me in my big sports bra and leggings. I knew damn well he wasn't. He clearly liked blondes if the previous evening's constant observation of Stella was anything to go by. He'd been joined by the blonde woman's partner, who was as beautiful as her in a manly way – the kind of guy who could wander around in underwear and look like an ad for aftershave. *Designer* aftershave.

'I'm Daisy by the way,' the woman said, holding out her hand. I shook it, introduced myself and tried not to stare. She looked like a model. She had this glow about her and not a drop of sweat despite the already raging heat. On this holiday I was discovering a whole new species of human. Everyone was glamorous and rich, and so at home in these fabulous surroundings.

'That's my hubby, Tom,' she said, pointing over to her gorgeous husband who'd let his long hair down and was listening intently to David. My husband was probably telling him about his new car. I liked nice cars too, but David did tend to go on and on like he was obsessed with it. I hoped they weren't bonding too much, because holiday friendships are always a risk. You meet someone in the first couple of days, then decide you don't click and spend the rest of the fortnight avoiding them.

'Are you here with *your* husband?' Daisy asked.

'Yeah.' I glanced over at David by way of pointing him out, but she was already looking at him. And he was looking at her.

'Well, looks like our men have already met!' she said, waving at both of them, causing her full breasts to bounce enthusiastically in the tiny coral cups of her bikini. She looked fresh and pretty, whereas I was already beginning to perspire again and I'd only just left the shower. So not only was she beautiful, it seemed she didn't sweat either, and the way she was looking at David made me feel uneasy. He was quite charismatic and I didn't blame women for falling at his feet; the previous day it was Stella with her come-to-bed eyes and eager breasts, and now Daisy was bouncing around in a bikini giving him a big, toothy smile. No wonder my honeymoon was rapidly sinking. David was being constantly inundated with gorgeous women giving him the eye, and he didn't exactly ignore them either. I was surprised (and a little flattered) when Daisy suggested we 'join the men.' I liked her, but wasn't sure I wanted to be friends with her on my honeymoon, with David looking at me and wishing I was her.

I was also nervous and not sure I'd know what to say to people like that after the initial small talk. Sitting down with them, I felt like a fish out of water, but David was chatting easily, ordering drinks, just being himself despite the setting. They were all talking now, and Daisy had been swallowed up in the men's banter, leaving me feeling excluded. Just looking at their designer clothes, the way they held themselves, it was clear they weren't from my world. These people obviously took luxurious surroundings and money for granted, whereas I kept worrying about what I was wearing and fretting about how much everything cost.

After a few minutes, we were joined by another guy and a pale, thin woman who seemed very clingy towards him. I'd seen them around the hotel. She always seemed to be walking several paces behind him and would enter the dining room looking scared and anxious. In fact, she was the only other person in the hotel who looked more intimidated than I was. I remembered the previous evening at dinner how the guy had pulled out her chair, laid her napkin on her knee... he did *everything* for her. I'd even remarked to David, 'I'm waiting for him to take her knife and fork, cut it up and feed her dinner to her next.'

I nodded at the pale woman and she sort of nodded back, while Daisy asked the waiter, who happened to be Paulo that morning, for an Aperol spritz. 'With plenty of ice,' she said, unsmiling. He loitered a moment, like he was breathing her in. It was quite uncomfortable, but I think it was only me who noticed. I glanced over at David who was still talking, and clearly settled in for a while making new friends. As Paulo was still loitering, I asked him for the same drink as Daisy. I think I was hoping some of her sparkle might rub off on me.

She was now standing up, her taut, brown tummy on display above tiny bikini bottoms. She held her arms up as she saluted the sun and shimmied into a beach cover-up in a beautiful shade of orange that matched her bikini – and her lips – but barely covered her breasts. I hoped I didn't look too dowdy next to her and tried to catch David's eye for reassurance, but his eyes were on Daisy.

'So where was your teacher this morning?' Daisy's husband, Tom, asked.

Daisy shrugged. 'Apparently she's sick.'

'Oh that's a shame,' David said. 'So much for your plan to do yoga classes every day and look like Stella.' He laughed. I laughed. But I wanted to die. Did he really just say that?

'I *was* joking, David,' I said, as the others smiled politely.

'Running, that's what you should do to lose weight,' the pale woman's husband said. I was mortified; no one, not even David, had said I needed to lose weight, but now a stranger was advising me.

'I can't run, I'm asthmatic,' I said.

'Doesn't stop you from running – my mate has asthma and he runs. I'm out at 6am every morning. I see the sun rise,' he said with a sigh.

'Oh, so it was you I saw this morning at dawn running along the beach,' Daisy exclaimed. 'I said to Tom, "he's a *machine*."' She almost purred the word.

The pale woman's husband blushed slightly, and I swear I saw his chest swell a little. 'I do a run every morning and night. I run a lot for charities. At the moment I run about thirty kilometres a day and then...'

I heard his wife murmur *Josh* under her breath, I think she was trying to shut him up. But it didn't seem to work, he just continued to list his running schedule. I could see Daisy felt the same as me when she stifled a yawn.

'Sorry, I haven't introduced you to my wife,' David suddenly said, cutting in over Josh's list of kilometres and marathons. David was good with people. He didn't tolerate annoying or boring ones, but always made everyone else feel at ease. My new husband wasn't perfect, but despite that morning's confrontation, I was now appreciating the more positive aspects of his character. I told myself that marriage was about ups and downs, and no one was perfect, so perhaps I should concentrate on the good things?

Once everyone was introduced, David ordered more drinks for the men, and as Daisy and I had already ordered, asked the pale woman if she'd like a drink.

'She'll have water,' her husband said before she could speak. She looked a bit pissed off, but when David double checked with her that she didn't want 'a proper drink,' she shook her head. I thought to myself that even if marriage was about ups and downs, I couldn't be in a relationship like that.

We found out her name was Becky, and her husband was called Josh. They didn't look like husband and wife to me; they didn't fit together somehow. He was chatty and seemed full of nervous energy, while she just sat there like she was about to fall asleep.

'So, if the teacher isn't available, why don't you ladies have your own yoga class?' David suddenly said.

'Where?' Daisy asked, puzzled.

'Here, the mats are still out.' David gestured to the mats now piled up just a few metres away from where we were sitting.

'Oh yes, I'm sure you'd all love to see me and Sam with our bums in the air, wouldn't you?' She laughed.

'I can think of worse things,' David winked. I recoiled at

this, and as Daisy leaned over, slapping his bare leg flirtatiously, my stomach lurched. 'That's enough from you, David,' she said with a smile.

It was probably my insecurity, but there was something about the way they reacted to one another that made me feel jealous. David had remarked only the previous day that I was being a bit possessive, and he was right, I needed to let go. I was being silly, it was just an innocent exchange.

Still, I wasn't leaving anything to chance and decided to move and sit next to David when our drinks arrived. I'd never had an Aperol spritz before, and was surprised at the vibrant colour – a bright, beautiful distraction of neon orange with crushed ice. This was delivered by Paulo who seemed to be lurking around every corner in the hotel. He carefully placed a fresh coaster in front of Daisy and positioned her glass lovingly on top. All the time he was looking at her, making sure her glass fit perfectly onto the mat, that her straw was positioned in relation to her beautiful mouth, the mouth that he clearly wanted to kiss. But she didn't even look at him, just stared straight ahead. After all the nurturing of Daisy's drink, he plonked my glass down in front of me, and when I looked up at him to say thank you, he'd gone.

'Yum!' Daisy said, before sipping from the huge frosty glass and groaning with pleasure. Having virtually orgasmed, she gently pulled the straw from her perfect mouth and picked up the slice of blood orange that adorned the glass's rim. I had to look away briefly, before being drawn back to this spectacle, which all three men were also observing, their lips moist, foreheads speckled in sweat.

'Your drink matches your outfit and lipstick and... well, *everything*,' I pointed out.

'Oh, look at me sitting here like a big orange,' she said, looking from me to the glass and down to the cover-up like she hadn't noticed. It was then I noticed her nails, as bright and neon as the drink. Amid all the oranges and corals of her outfit, and that golden tan in the mid-morning sunshine, she positively glowed.

Her whole look was premeditated, right down to the Aperol accessory.

'Are you a model?' I asked, aware I probably sounded like a teenage girl.

She laughed at this. 'No, I wish. I was never tall enough. But I work with models, I'm an art director for a fashion magazine.'

'Oh wow! So I guess you're used to staying in luxury hotels like this?'

She nodded and emptied her glass, crunching on the last few crystals of ice, then carefully placed one of her neon-coral talons to her lips to wipe away a little escaped ice. She made it look so sexy. (I tried it later in our room with a mirror and ice from our refrigerator, but it just wasn't sexy on me.)

'The food here is amazing,' I enthused.

'Yeah, for the UK it's good, but we came for the views – island life in the middle of Devon,' she said with a sigh, lifting her face to the sun and closing her eyes.

'Have you been here before?' I asked.

She opened her eyes and looked ahead. 'No, we haven't been here before,' she said, and I felt there was something she wasn't telling me. I was used to conversations like this, where people hint at something and want you to pursue it. I had them with my clients all the time, and it felt to me like she had this sad secret she wanted to talk about, but couldn't.

'Are you celebrating something?' I pressed.

'Yeah, in a way.' Then she turned to me. 'What about you? Are you on your honeymoon?'

'Yes! How did you guess?' I gasped, aware my face was breaking into a smile.

'I guessed because of the way you look at him,' she

murmured, glancing over at David. 'I saw you last night, just watching him, drinking him in,' she added, still looking over at him as she said this.

I noted, rather painfully, that she hadn't remarked on the way he looked at me, but perhaps she just thought that was a given.

'So what are you celebrating?' I asked again, intrigued.

She shook her head. 'The end of something,' she said quietly. 'It's been a difficult year for us.' She lifted her face back to the sun, indicating the conversation was over. I sipped at my drink, not sure what to say next, but then she turned to me and said, 'I can't have children.'

'Oh, I'm sorry.'

'My therapist says I should talk about it, but every time I say it, I feel like I'm hearing the news myself for the first time.'

'That must be hard.'

'Yes. It's so hard, because we're admitting defeat, saying goodbye to the possibility, the idea of children, you know?'

I nodded.

'Thing is, you feel like a gambler, an addict, there's one voice telling you to stop, save yourself from more heartache, but the other one is saying, "one more time and we'll hit the jackpot."'

'It must take a lot to walk away from something you want so badly, even if you know there's no chance,' I said.

'That's it. And I blame myself, I left it too late, wanted a career and a life, and thought I could just put it on my to-do list and it would happen.'

'It's not your fault that it didn't happen for you,' I said. 'It's funny because I never expected to have kids. I wanted them, but didn't think I'd ever have them, it was the same with marriage. And now I just feel so lucky to have found the one – I daren't ask for anything else.' Life always felt to me like a fine balance, if it gave something then it was bound to take something away, and I was just grateful to have found someone to love. I know now that I didn't feel worthy and was amazed that someone loved me back; I wasn't going to be greedy and ask for children too.

'Yes, I know, but Tom would have loved children.' She paused and turned to me. 'He's younger than I am. He can have kids until he's old, he could meet someone tomorrow and start a family, it's so bloody unfair.'

'Yeah, it is.'

She sighed. 'How crazy is it that I exercise, I eat right, I massage oils into my skin – I've been taking folic acid since just after my first date with Tom, just in case. And everyone tells me what a great body I have, but it doesn't work, it doesn't *do* the one thing that it was put on this earth to do: have a baby. I'd always assumed I'd have kids, and when I met Tom, it was all I could think about. We had three rounds of IVF that just about broke my heart and my body, and when that didn't work, I still had this tiny little hope, like a chink of light somewhere inside that it might just happen. I mean, it happens for other people, why not us?'

'And that chink of hope?'

'It went away when, after the IVF, we were told I had a less than one per cent chance of carrying a baby to term. Tom said he couldn't see me go through it again and that I had to stop being a gambler, and accept that one more roll of the dice wouldn't make any difference. This holiday was about accepting that, and saying goodbye. We've stopped treatment, and we're closing the door on what we'd thought was our future. There is no gold at the end of our rainbow.'

'That's sad, and I'm so sorry it hasn't worked out, but there's still a rainbow.'

She turned to look at me. 'That's lovely, thank you.'

I patted her arm. 'Perhaps we should start a club?' I said.

She smiled and nodded. 'Perhaps we should. The non-mothers' club!'

She threw back her golden hair, drained the last dregs of Aperol into her mouth, swallowed hard and almost slammed the empty glass on the table. This caused Tom to look up. He seemed on edge around her, like he might have to jump in and stop her from doing something crazy any moment. She was, I guessed, quite a loose cannon. She struck me as a woman driven by urges and intuition rather than any kind of plan.

'Another drink?' she asked, and before I had a chance to respond, she ordered two more Aperol spritzes. I had barely drunk my first one, but when the next round arrived, she downed hers so quickly. I knew I wouldn't be able to keep up. I figured she was drinking to blot out her unhappiness, what she'd described as her *defeat*. The confident, beautiful woman I'd seen the previous evening was sad and desperate, and I hoped she'd be able to move forward. She simply had to find a way to accept, to adapt to a different life than the one she'd planned, but she needed time to come to terms with what she *couldn't* have, before she worked out what she *could*.

She picked up her phone and gazed into it. 'I've got no signal,' she said with a sigh. 'I need to check that the shoot's going okay in Australia.' She ran her hands through her hair anxiously, then put her floppy hat on.

'I love your hat.'

'Gucci,' she said absently. 'I love it too... Thing is, they're eight hours ahead in Perth so they'll be finishing soon. I need to check it's gone okay,' she added, getting up from her seat.

'Wow, such pressure.'

'Yeah.' She rolled her eyes. 'Everyone wants to work in fashion, and yes, there are glamorous times, but it's a slog, and the travel is gruelling. Sounds crazy, but I'd rather change nappies than change flights any day!' She began walking away.

I looked up at her, shielding my eyes from the sun. 'Where

are you going?' I asked, slightly disappointed. I was enjoying her company.

'There's a spot at the far end of the beach where you can get a signal, I'm going there.' As she said this, she glanced over at Tom, who glanced back, unsmiling. There was something in the exchange between them that I couldn't quite put my finger on, like she wanted him to follow her, but he didn't.

'See you in a bit,' she said to me, and wandered off towards the steps at the far end of the beach.

It was lovely sitting in the sun with a drink, and I hadn't even finished my first one, but I wanted to get a phone signal too. The men were talking and pale Becky had her eyes closed, so there wasn't much to keep me there. I liked talking to Daisy, she was interesting. So I put on my sunglasses, stood up and gestured to David where I was going. He smiled and lifted his thumb to say okay. For a moment I wondered if I should invite Pale Becky to join me, rather than abandon her by the pool with the men. I always hate leaving anyone out – I used to get left out at school, and it still hurts today. But Becky had her eyes closed and Daisy was nearly at the steps down to the beach, so I'd have to run to catch her up, and Becky didn't look like a runner to me.

I didn't want to go, I'd been quite happy sitting chatting with my new friend, and the far end of the beach beneath the treacherous cliffs made me feel uneasy. But I was compelled to follow her, so I did. I ran after her, calling her name and waving, but she didn't hear me and set off down the steps to the beach. I could have turned around and gone back, but I didn't. Sometimes I wonder if things would have been different if I'd gone back to the table with the football talk, the sleepy woman and my iced drink. But I didn't, I kept on walking towards Daisy and the beach, and I only had myself to blame for what happened next.

FIVE

DAISY

Daisy was desperate to check her phone. She was keen to know how the shoot had gone, but not like she used to be. The real reason she wanted to go down on the beach was because she found Paulo's presence really unnerving. Just like the previous night at dinner, when he'd stood so close serving her drink she could feel his breath on her bare shoulder. He was totally creeping her out. Surely it wasn't a coincidence that he seemed to be wherever she was? Daisy climbed down the rather rickety wooden steps to the beach, and once there pulled off her sandals, immediately soothed by the feeling of warm sand between her toes. For a few moments it calmed her, but then she thought about how she would have brought baby James to a beach like this. She stood at the bottom of the stairs and imagined him toddling along the sand with his little bucket and spade, her and Tom trailing behind him like an entourage.

She tried not to think of what might have been and counted her blessings as she stood quietly at the top of the wooden steps down to the beach, her art director's eye scanning the view for shots. Beneath her was the vast expanse of the hotel's private beach, with perfectly parallel lines of white parasols and sun loungers.

No one was around. The beach was always half-empty even when the hotel was full because it stretched all around the island so there was always more beach than guests. It was one of the reasons people honeymooned here: the privacy, the little inlets shielded from view where couples swam naked and alone.

Daisy looked around and saw a woman and a man wandering along the sea edge in the distance, and someone sitting on the cliffs, staring out to sea as the seagulls cawed above. She felt vulnerable and wished Tom had come with her, but he hadn't picked up on her anxiety and probably assumed she was fine. She took off her sunglasses, shielded her eyes and looked up at the cliffs. The lone person seemed to be looking back. It was a man, Paulo perhaps? The ends of her fingers tingled with fear. Suddenly a hand tapped her on the shoulder. She jumped, then spun round ready to fight.

'Sorry, did I startle you?' It was Sam.

'You scared me half to death!' she cried.

Sam smiled. 'I'm so sorry, I didn't mean to make you jump.'

'I was just thinking how here, alone on the beach, it wouldn't matter how loud you scream, no one would hear you.'

'But there's nothing to be afraid of, the beach belongs to the hotel, it's not like anyone can come in off the mainland without a boat.' Sam put her arm around Daisy. 'Are you okay? Perhaps we should go back?'

'No, no, I need to check my phone.'

'But there's an intermittent signal in the hotel, wouldn't you rather try there? It's hot down here and...'

'Ignore me, I'm being silly. I was a bit jumpy and you scared me, that's all.'

'You sure you're okay?' Sam was saying. 'You look terribly pale.'

To Sam, she probably looked like the picture of sophistication drinking Aperol in her chichi beachwear, but in truth she was just a scared and fragile woman.

Daisy assured Sam she was fine, composed herself, and the two women walked together along the beach seeking a signal.

'When did you and Tom meet?' Sam now asked, slightly breathless from keeping up.

'Me and Tom?' she asked. 'We met at a party, married soon after.'

'Did you know straight away that he was the one?'

Daisy smiled. 'Yeah, I think I probably did.'

'Any doubts?'

'Of course there were doubts, like do we have anything in common? He worked for a bank, I worked in fashion, we lived in different worlds. But I needn't have worried; we're similar people, we wanted the same things.' It stung her afresh to say that their early years together were spent longing for and working towards that same thing, a child. She took a moment, then said, 'What about you and David?'

'Like you, we married quickly. We've only been together about six months.' Sam looked up at Daisy, apparently waiting for her reaction.

'Wow! I thought we were quick marrying after eight months, but you were even quicker than us. But when you know, you know, don't you?'

Sam nodded. 'Yes you do. I'll never forget the first time I saw him. We were in a bar last February and he came over to chat. I thought he was gorgeous, but I was with my sister, and I thought he fancied her. She's so pretty and confident – nothing like me.' She rolled her eyes and Daisy felt a bit sorry for her.

'*You're* pretty!' she said.

Sam shrugged. 'Not like my sister, she's lovely – blonde hair, big blue eyes, just David's type.'

Daisy did a double take. Sam was blonde with blue eyes and she was pretty and funny. *How we see ourselves*, she thought, knowing whatever she said to this woman, she'd never believe she was good-looking. Women like Sam just felt unworthy of everything... compliments, friendship, love.

'So David was chatting to her,' Sam continued, 'and I just stood there like a wallflower, but then her boyfriend came to meet us. I thought David would leave after that, but he didn't – he stuck around, walked me home, and that was it, now we're married!' she said, sounding surprised that this had happened to her.

Daisy glanced over and smiled, wondering idly if he *had* in fact fancied the sister?

'And he took you to bed and that was it?' she suggested with a smile.

Sam laughed at this. 'Not quite,' she replied, 'I wasn't doing that again. I've been with some real losers who used me and dumped me. No, I waited until I was sure.'

'Ten, fifteen minutes later then?'

Sam laughed again. 'You are funny, and I'm sure David would have been delighted if I'd said yes after ten minutes. It was quite a bit of pressure for me and for him; he used to joke that I was going to be a nun and had no intention of sleeping with him. It was difficult, he was *very* keen. David has quite a high sex drive, it must have been torture for him, and there were times I almost gave in.'

'But you stuck to your guns?'

'Yes, in spite of David's seduction technique, which he applied daily!' Sam added with a giggle.

Daisy didn't quite know what to say to this oversharing, so she didn't respond. She just kept walking through the mid-morning sun beating down, the cool sea breeze offering only a little relief now and then.

'So when did he ask you to marry him?' Daisy finally asked.

'We'd been together about three months.' Sam raised her eyes to the horizon, reliving the moment. 'We were at his place, he'd made dinner and when I sat down I saw that on the table, next to my knife and fork, was a little box. I pretended not to notice and waited for him to point it out. Even then I wasn't sure if it was a ring, David is always teasing me.'

Daisy hoped he hadn't teased her about a proposal, no one should joke about something so important.

'Anyway, I opened it and inside was a gold diamond ring.' Sam was smiling at the memory.

'How romantic.'

'Yeah it was, and I was so happy. So of course I said yes, and he put the ring on my finger...' She paused. 'But a couple of hours later, I was in A&E having it sawn off.'

'What?'

'I'm allergic to gold.'

'Oh no, didn't David realise?'

'He didn't *know*, the subject hadn't come up. I let him put the ring on me because I didn't want to spoil the moment, but I nearly lost my finger!'

'Wow, what a start to married life.'

'Yeah, we spent hours in the waiting room, and all the romance had gone out of it by the time they came at me with a saw.'

'I can *imagine!*' Daisy gasped, wondering why on earth he didn't check with Sam first about the bloody metal. They really didn't know each other. Mind you, from what she'd seen of David, it seemed hard to get a word in. He'd probably spent the first few months talking about himself and never bothered to ask Sam anything.

'And after all that he said he stood by the proposal. I guess he *must* have loved me,' she added.

Daisy heard the hope and uncertainty in her voice, and felt another wave of pity for this almost stranger she was swapping stories with. 'And you've been married how long?'

'Five days, not even a week,' she replied with a beaming smile.

'And you're living happily ever after?' Daisy asked hopefully.

'Yeah great, it's just—'

'What?'

'Oh, I love him. It's that, oh, I dunno, I'm insecure. I get anxious, you know?'

'What about? David?'

'Yeah, I sometimes think I haven't spent long enough with him to know who he really is. I think I know him, then at times he feels like a stranger. It sounds stupid, I'm just being daft.'

They walked on in silence for a few minutes, then Daisy said, 'You're not being daft. Sometimes anxiety is there for a reason. I felt the same when Tom and I first married, but you soon get to know each other, you both have to ask questions,' she added pointedly.

'Oh, I'm just an anxious person,' Sam murmured, then grabbed Daisy's arm conspiratorially. 'It didn't help that my own mother told me to keep an eye on him at the wedding,' Sam said, smiling.

'Really?' Daisy gave a small gasp. 'Well, I guess mothers know best.'

'Mmm, not anymore. Mum has early-onset dementia, she's only in her sixties. She says weird things about everyone. She called her friend and told her that her husband was in Paris having a love affair with her cousin.'

'And was he in Paris with her cousin?' Daisy teased.

'No, he was in the kitchen. And her cousin had died ten years ago.'

Daisy couldn't help but giggle at this. 'Oh, that's funny. I don't mean about your mum being ill, I mean, the way you tell it...'

'Oh, we laugh about it all the time, me and my sister and

David. You have to laugh, it gets you through. David's never known her to be any different. He's so good with her though, very kind.'

'That's nice,' Daisy replied. She finally slowed down by the cliffs. 'Now, I think the signal was somewhere around here. That's it, we need to go towards those rocks,' she said, marching ahead while looking at her phone for a sign of activity. But as she negotiated the pale, giant rocks ahead, she could see what looked like a single Converse trainer, sticking out between the rocks. So she walked towards it and bent down to pick it up. As she grabbed it she was surprised at the weight, and in that instant realised it still had a foot inside it.

The blood froze in her veins. She looked away, couldn't move, just stood there holding the foot and trying not to see any more.

'Sam, Sam...' She heard her own voice, as Sam clambered over the rocks towards her. Daisy dropped the foot and then saw the rest of the body, and put her hand over her mouth in horror.

'What is it—' Sam didn't finish what she was about to say, she could see the look on Daisy's face. As Sam joined her, she saw it too.

'Is she... is she dead?' Sam asked, her face ashen. She started to cry – fear and panic seemed to have immediately engulfed her, whereas Daisy was still trying to work out whether the person was alive or dead. She stared down, unable to bring herself to touch the body, but it was plain to see that the head was bloody – both fresh red and older, blacker matted blood like jam. And the limbs were so perversely twisted, this person couldn't possibly be alive. The heat was beating down onto the pale-cream rocks as Daisy continued to stare down at the warped limbs, the sunshine-bright blood. Then suddenly, in the red, sticky mess, she saw a face.

'Oh, Sam,' she cried, her voice shuddering to a halt, her own eyes filling with tears now. 'Oh no.' Her heart was pumping so fast she thought she might die.

Sam, whose face was wet with tears and mucus, looked at Daisy in confusion. 'What?'

Unable to stand anymore, Daisy plonked down onto the rocks. 'It's Stella...'

SIX

BECKY AND JOSH

From the moment the girls return from the beach, everything changes. The sun is still blazing in the sky, the seagulls still cawing above, but nothing is the same.

'Where have you two been?' David asks, as they walk back to our group. We're sitting at the table by the bar. 'I thought you were going for a signal, but you've been ages.'

They're both pale and stiff and I just know something terrible has happened.

'What is it?' I ask gently.

Sam just bursts into tears. She's inconsolable, and it's left to Daisy to tell us what has happened.

'I think we just found Stella,' she says, 'the waitress, the girl who taught yoga?'

'She was lying at the bottom of the cliffs... she's dead,' Daisy adds in a shocked, broken voice, like she's hearing this for the first time herself.

'Shit! Have you called the police?' Tom asks.

'Yes, of course. We ran straight to reception, they called them for us. They're on their way.' Daisy stops talking for a moment then, as if to herself, she murmurs, 'Such a mess, so much blood.' Her voice is breaking, she's clearly trying not to cry.

'Oh God.' David stands up and guides Sam to a seat. He's hugging her and saying, 'That must have been so awful for you, please tell me you're okay.'

Meanwhile Tom makes room for Daisy on his seat and she joins him, resting her head on his shoulder, while everyone digests what she just said.

'I can't believe it,' I say, and put my hand over my mouth. 'Did someone *hurt* her, or did she throw herself off the cliffs?'

'Don't know,' Daisy replies. 'Once we knew she was dead, we just ran, we didn't hang around.'

'The police will probably come from Plymouth, I think that's the nearest station,' Josh says. But David, who I think always likes to be the one in the know, suggests it would be Cornwall and then Tom piles in with theories and the two men have a rather pointless gladiatorial stand-off about where the police will be coming from. Josh doesn't get caught up in it and ignores their almost-bickering, and typically he's more concerned about Daisy and Sam.

'That must have been terrible for you guys to find her like that,' he says.

Daisy nods. 'I was frozen to the spot. I'm just glad Sam was with me, she checked for a pulse and everything.'

'I'm the first aider at the salon where I work. I've been trained, so I knew what to do,' Sam confirms, shuddering at the memory. Her face is wet with tears. Both women are obviously traumatised.

'We have to go back to the lobby, we only came to let you know where we are. The police have asked us to wait for them so we can explain where she is and how we found her,' Daisy says, standing up to go.

'I'll come with you,' Tom says, and of course David now says he'll accompany Sam, who can't seem to stop crying, and off they all go, leaving me and Josh to just stare at each other in shock.

'She was so young,' I say. 'She seemed very popular with the guests, didn't she?'

'I guess so.' He shrugs, like he doesn't really recall her.

'Don't you remember, we were in the lobby on our first day, it had just started to get really hot and I felt faint – she helped me. It's her.'

'Yeah, I know, she brought you some water.'

'She did, and then sat with me while you were checking in,' I add. 'And then later that day, you'd gone for a run and she came and sat with me by the pool, asked if I was okay. I thought that was nice of her.'

I want to cry just thinking about the busy twenty-some-thing who'd taken the trouble to come and find me later that day. 'I was worried about you, Mrs...' she'd said, and I'd told her to call me Becky. We spent ages chatting, and when I told her I was a teacher, she said she was an art student, that she might like to teach some day. At twenty-two, she wasn't that much older than my Amy, and I remember thinking how lucky she was to be young and beautiful with her life laid out before her.

'It's okay, Becks, I know it's awful, but you mustn't get worked up,' Josh says, hugging me. 'I don't want you taking this on, getting all upset. It's not like you *knew* her...'

I pull away from his embrace. 'Josh, a young woman has *died*. We have a daughter who's only a few years younger than she was, I can't help but be upset. I don't have to *know* her to remember her, and what she did, and who she was. However small those things might seem now, she was a person and we mustn't just forget people when they die... or what's the point?' I start to cry and see the panic in his eyes. Josh can't handle me being upset, he sees it as his responsibility to make me feel better, to make me feel happy again.

'You're right, but I find this all a bit overwhelming, and worrying. Did she kill herself, or did someone hurt her?'

'I wonder,' I say, unable to imagine why someone so young, beautiful and apparently happy would want to end everything. But people hide their true selves, they present an image to the world and too often the world buys it. Perhaps she isn't what she seemed?

'I find the whole subject of death difficult,' he says.

'I know. I just wonder if I could have helped her in some way, but I never really *saw* her after that first day. I haven't ever ordered from the bar because you do that, and I haven't attended the yoga class because you didn't think I should,' I say pointedly.

'Oh, Becky, don't start all that again, you *know* why.'

'Yes, but it isn't *necessary*,' I say under my breath. I don't want to have an argument here, with people around, and he's now glaring at me, so I sit quietly for a few minutes. But all the time it's eating away at me, so I have to say something.

'She was down at the bar last night until late, something must have happened after that?' I suggest, looking into his face, but he shrugs again and turns away from me. I find Josh's response to what's happened rather odd. He'd usually be as fascinated and horrified as me, and keen to talk about it. But he seems to be avoiding the conversation, he's gazing ahead, suddenly interested in a guy doing laps of the pool.

'I could do that,' he says.

'I'm sure you could,' I reply with a sigh. I am disturbed by his lack of interest in Stella's death, and have to press him. I can't let this go. 'Did *you* see anything?' I ask. 'Last night... did Stella *say* anything to you?'

He turns back to me, his face a picture of surprise. '*Stella?*'

'Yes, when she was serving behind the bar last night, did she say anything that you remember?' I repeat.

'Why would she say anything to *me*?' His tone is defensive, irritated, then his face flushes. It's such a giveaway.

'It might not seem relevant, she may just have been talking about the weather, but whatever she said might now have some significance if she killed herself. You might be able to tell the police something that will help them piece together what happened.'

'I wasn't at the bar. I went for a run.'

'Oh right, yes of course, I just thought...'

'Well, you're wrong.'

'I know, but I thought you might have had a quick drink before... or after your run.'

'Yeah, I had a glass of water, then went for a quick run and came straight back to the room,' he said, but I knew he was lying.

'I wouldn't know, I wasn't awake when you came back, probably because you gave me two sleeping tablets. They really knocked me out.'

'You always have two.'

'I know, but last night I just felt the effects more.'

'Good, you need your sleep, which reminds me, it's almost lunchtime... Should we have a light lunch and then you can have your nap.'

'I don't need a nap,' I reply.

'I think you do, you're really on edge, Becky,' he says gently, which irritates me even more.

'Don't speak to me like I'm a child, Josh.'

'I'm not, I'm just trying to *help* you, I know how tired you get.'

'Yeah, and I'd be a lot less tired off the medication.'

'That isn't an option, so let's just leave it, shall we?' He stands up. 'Come on, let's go for lunch.'

I rise from my seat and immediately he grabs my elbow. 'I

can still walk!' I hiss. And he raises both hands in a surrendering gesture, and stands back for me to pass him.

'I'd like to sit outside on the terrace for lunch,' I say as he tries to march me in the direction of the dining room.

'Are you sure?' he's calling after me. 'It's very hot out there, you know what the heat does to you.'

I ignore him, continue to the sunny terrace where lunch is being served, and finding a table facing the ocean, I sit down. It's warm, *very* warm, but the sea breeze makes it bearable, and the view is stunning. He joins me wordlessly, and we order, then he leaves me to go to the bathroom, and I feel almost free for the first time in a long time. But my thoughts are whirring, and as hard as I try not to think about Stella being dead, I can't shake it from my head.

Josh is right, I *didn't* really know Stella, but I know my husband, and I know when he's lying to me. We both lie to each other, that's nothing new. I lied to Josh about being asleep when he returned last night. I *didn't* take my sleeping pills as he thought I had. I hid them under my tongue and pretended to swallow them. Then when he left our room supposedly for his run, I watched him in the dark from the balcony.

But he didn't go running straight away – he headed for the bar where he sat for quite some time having his drink. After a few minutes, he was joined by Stella, who was on duty. He went behind the bar and she followed him – but from the balcony, I couldn't see them, so don't know what happened behind the bar. But I waited and waited, and fifteen minutes later he emerged and then came back to the room. I pretended to be asleep, and he paced around for a few minutes then left again. I went back onto the balcony and saw him running. I assumed he was going for his run. But now I wonder if he was running away from something? I don't know, nor do I know why he isn't telling me about his encounter with Stella. I haven't told him what I saw... He'd be upset to think he'd hurt me. He's been through so much, why take any more joy from his life? We haven't had sex for a long time. But that was before Stella's body was found; now only one question machetes into my brain. Why would a man give his wife sleeping tablets then go and meet a beautiful young girl at a bar? And why is she now dead?

SEVEN

SAM AND DAVID

It was all so scary, there we were on our honeymoon, having a wonderful time, the next minute we're sitting in a back office of the hotel making statements to a police officer.

'Where would you like us to start?' Daisy said, all confident. She was far better at this than me. I've always been a bit intimidated by the police, and I was still in shock from seeing Stella's body on the rocks. God that was terrible. I can never get that vision out of my head, knowing all the blood, the mess, was once a person who lived and breathed and laughed.

'Do you think she might have killed herself, or did someone else do this?' Daisy asked.

'We have a forensic team down there now,' the officer in charge replied. But before he could say any more, Daisy jumped in. 'And will they be able to tell if someone murdered her?'

'We hope—'

'I mean, if someone *killed* her, then pushed her off the cliffs, could it *look* like suicide? Will you ever know if someone deliberately killed her?'

I saw an almost smile flicker across his face – she was being so specific, and not letting him get a word in. 'We can't answer any questions until we have more forensic information, and after we've conducted interviews. So thank you both so much for your statements.' He stood up, almost knocking over a box labelled 'wine glasses'. 'It won't be easy for you doing interviews in here,' I said.

'We're setting up a larger office elsewhere in the hotel,' he said, 'so we will probably be asking you to come back for more in-depth interviews once we've established a space, and what exactly has happened to cause the death of this young woman.'

'It's terrible,' Daisy said to me as we left. 'I can't think straight, shall we get a drink?'

There was no one in the cocktail bar, mostly because it was the middle of the day and the heat greeted us like a malevolent presence. The bar was built on the back of the hotel, like a huge orangery and pretty much made of glass, so heat clung to the windows and pounded down through the circular glass ceiling.

But after what we'd been through, Daisy and I didn't care about the heat, or anything really, because what just happened was bigger than anything. I couldn't get the vision from my head. Everywhere I looked seemed to be stained with blood. I had to focus or I might faint.

'I feel sick,' I said as we sat in the bar nursing two large gins.

'Yeah, me too,' Daisy replied, swilling her gin with ice and lemon around in the glass before taking a large glug.

'Stella seemed so carefree, so full of life, but looks like she was unhappy?' she offered.

'Yeah, who knows what struggles people have? She obviously threw herself from the cliffs.'

'Yeah, but what if she didn't take her own life, and someone else killed her?' she said. 'What if she had a stalker?'

'Why do you say that?' I didn't like where this was going, it worried me.

'Oh, because she was so pretty, and friendly and warm – apparently. And some weirdos see a pretty girl being nice as a come-on and before you know it, they think they're having a relationship with her.'

'Yeah, it *could* be, or it could just be an accident?' I said, raising my eyebrows questioningly.

'Nah.' Daisy shook her head and took another drink. 'What the hell was she doing late at night standing alone on the cliffs?'

'I don't know... contemplating suicide, I guess?'

'I just keep rewinding it, the shock of the weight of her foot in that trainer, the absolute horror of realising it wasn't just a trainer someone had left on the beach. It was a foot!' She recoiled at the memory.

'I know, and all the blood,' I whispered, like someone might hear, but the bar was empty except for us and the barman. Still, I felt like someone might be listening behind a pillar in the darkened doorway. The whole thing had made me feel paranoid, like someone was watching. 'I can't get the picture out of my head. I know it will be there in technicolour tonight just as I'm trying to get to sleep,' I murmured, still thinking of the twisted limbs, the beautiful dead face, the eyes open wide in surprise. 'As long as I live I will never forget it.'

'Nor me... I didn't know her at all,' Daisy said. 'In fact, I'd never spoken to her... I only know her name because Tom told me.'

'Did Tom know her?'

She shook her head. 'No, not really, I think he mentioned she was a student.' She looked troubled, and I wondered if she trusted Tom any more than I trusted David.

'Do you think any man is "one-woman"?' I asked, interested in her take on this as a woman who'd been married a few years.

'Oh I hope so, I really hope so,' she said with a sigh. I saw a sadness in her eyes and wondered if she was thinking about their struggle to have children. I never really had a great ambition to be a mother, and I was grateful for that – because at thirty-eight I had probably left it a bit late. Mum's illness had always taken up so much of my time, and one day, when she was gone, as sad as I would be, I hoped for a future where I could be free to travel and chase my dreams. I didn't want any more responsibility. But I could see this was very different for Daisy. It had been her dream, this had broken her, and I felt her pain, the unbearable torture of wanting something so badly and not being able to have it.

'I'm sure your Tom is a one-woman man,' I offered, to make her feel better. 'You two look so good together, and it's obvious you're both madly in love. Don't lose the wonderful thing you have by wishing for something even better, sometimes what you're looking for is right under your nose.'

Daisy smiled. 'You're so sweet, but...' I saw a flicker of doubt in her eyes, and she was about to say something, but before she could, Tom and David appeared.

'Are you both okay?' David said. 'We were worried about you. Have you spoken to the police?'

I nodded as he sat down next to me. I rested my hand on his knee, grateful to have someone concerned for me.

'What did the police *say*?' David asked.

'Nothing really,' I replied. 'They asked us how we found the body, why we were there, but they don't know yet if it's suicide or murder.'

David snorted. 'It's not murder, not at Fitzgerald's.'

'Why not here?' Daisy asked.

'Because everyone is decent, they're on holiday.'

'Oh, so *decent* people don't kill then?' Daisy asked sarcastically, fire burning in her eyes.

'More like because it's an island, and no murderer worth their salt would kill someone on an island where you can't get on or off until the boat arrives,' Tom pointed out, presumably attempting to diffuse Daisy's anger at David's remark.

'Well, I'm saying suicide,' I offered.

'What about that Paulo, the manager guy? At dinner the

other night you told me that he was standing really close to her, you said it was sexual harassment,' Tom said to Daisy, ignoring my verdict of suicide.

She rolled her eyes. 'I didn't say it was sexual harassment. I said I hoped he wasn't *sexually harassing* her. I just find him creepy. Even if he didn't do it, there's the possibility that him, or someone *like* him, was giving her a hard time and so she ended it.'

'Or *he* ended it because she wouldn't do what he wanted?' Tom suggested.

'Something like that *could* have happened,' I offered, knowing Paulo would be a likely suspect. 'I guess she lives... *lived* in the staff house, and presumably so does he?'

'I don't know where she lived, but think we're all getting a bit carried away,' David said, stepping in like the adult. 'I'm sure, for whatever tragic, terrible reason, the poor girl took her own life and we might never know why, but let's hope she's finally free of whatever torment she endured on this earth.'

'Amen, vicar,' Tom murmured, and David shot him a look. I pretended not to notice, but I thought it was mean of Tom to make fun of someone for saying something kind.

'I agree with David,' Daisy said. 'It's easy for us to speculate and let our imaginations run away with us, so let's just order another drink and hope that poor girl can rest in peace.'

David gave Daisy a little smile, a discreet thank you for saying she agreed with him in the face of her husband's meanness.

David called the barman over to take our order, and when the barman asked for our room number, Tom called his number over David.

'No really, I'll buy the drinks,' David said, furious at Tom, who seemed to be constantly baiting him.

'Oh, boys, stop fighting,' Daisy chastised jokily. 'You can both buy the drinks if you like, make *two* orders.'

'Okay, let's do what the lady tells us,' David said to the barman. 'I always do what a lady tells me.' He winked at her for the second time that day and stared a little too long at her. I felt a shiver run through me. I'd seen him give that same admiring gaze to Stella only the previous day, and I suddenly felt very uneasy, but told myself there was nothing to worry about. I had to stop trying to second-guess everything, and imagine things that didn't exist. David was a friendly guy who was comfortable around women, that didn't mean he wanted to sleep with them all. Just as I was pondering this, and reprimanding myself for being paranoid, Josh arrived in the bar.

While the others greeted him, I looked around for Becky. I felt like I'd ignored her earlier when we'd been sitting at the pool bar.

'Where's your wife?' I asked.

'She doesn't drink,' he replied.

'Yes, I heard her asking for water earlier, but she doesn't *have* to drink to come into the bar,' I said. I realised I might sound abrupt, so softened it with a smile.

'Yeah, she could have a fruit juice or some non-alcoholic gin?' Daisy chimed in.

'Well, it isn't just that she doesn't drink. She's gone for a nap, she likes to nap in the afternoon,' he added, then turned away from us and started a conversation with Tom about the beer, which I thought was a bit rude.

I wasn't letting him just fob us off with 'she likes to nap'. What the hell was going on between those two? What kind of marriage was it when the husband spent all his holiday in the bar and his wife 'napped' upstairs every afternoon?

'Until we know what happened to Stella, I wouldn't want to be alone in *our* bedroom... I hope she's locked the bedroom door,' I said, determined to make a point.

'Yes, I've locked her in,' he said, clearly a bit irritated by this conversation.

'You've locked her *in*?' Daisy gasped. 'You mean she can't get out.'

'God no, no, I mean she's locked in.' He smiled at Daisy. 'She just needs to sleep in this heat,' he said kindly. It seemed Daisy commenting on his wife's afternoon nap wasn't half as annoying as me remarking on it. I remember thinking how pretty girls really did have an easier time of everything, and I thought of Stella, always smiling, always happy. I tried not to dwell on it, but I wondered what her last thoughts were when she fell from that cliff and landed on the jagged rocks below. I shuddered and, looking around at my fellow guests, wondered if any of them had *any* idea what happened to her.

EIGHT

DAISY AND TOM

Fitzgerald's was still beautiful, still glamorous, and despite being more than one hundred years old, she was still standing. But it's true to say it was a different place after Stella's death, and happiness and hedonism were now fused with dread and suspicion. Pent-up heat and tension shimmered through the building, snaking out through the garden to swirl around the pool, putting everyone on edge. After dinner, some of the guests congregated in the library for coffee and liqueurs. Daisy loved the library; it was so classy in an old-fashioned way, and the smell of leather and old books hit her as soon as she walked in. It was cosy, but large enough for about ten people to sit comfortably, with a mismatch of armchairs, a couple of sofas and a chaise longue. Everyone immediately settled onto velvet armchairs and creaky leather Chesterfields, while Daisy took a seat next to Sam, who was gazing out of the large window that looked out onto the sea. Because of what happened that morning, she felt close to Sam. The horror of finding Stella had bonded them. Both women gravitated towards each other, seeking some form of comfort, an opportunity to go over what had happened. And when Becky joined them, they welcomed her, soon realising what a good, solid sounding board she was. Becky provided the fresh eyes on their story, the calm perspective they both needed. As a teacher she was used to being handed problems to solve and she leaned in to their thoughts, discussing and theorising, then handing them back like marked homework.

'You are both probably suffering from mild traumatic stress,' she told them. 'And I'm no therapist, but my advice would be to keep talking to each other. You have shared something horrific, and you can probably help each other through this. We once had a stabbing at the school, and I made sure my students all talked about it with me and each other; I know it helped them move on. So talk to your partners too. They have to be there for you.'

It occurred to Daisy that Tom hadn't really been there for her on this; perhaps he felt he'd done his time?

'There's a rumour going around the hotel that though she was found at the bottom of the cliffs, the forensic people are saying her arms were covered in bruises *before* she fell,' Tom was saying quite animatedly. His enthusiasm for the rumour annoyed Daisy because when she tried to tell him what she'd seen on the beach, he'd told her to stop because it made him feel sick. And there he was, discussing the finer details of pre-mortem bruises and broken limbs like a bloody forensic examiner.

'Well, whatever it was, I won't sleep tonight,' Sam said. 'I've told David we have to put a chair up against the door as well as lock it, just in case.'

'Tom and I are checking if we can leave first thing,' Daisy said. 'We can't bear to be here a minute longer. This isn't a holiday, it's starting to feel like a prison.' In truth it was Tom who'd demanded they leave, and at first Daisy had disagreed; it was their holiday, and they needed to heal. But as he pointed out, the whole atmosphere in the hotel had changed since they'd found Stella's body. 'Suicide or murder, Daisy, I don't want to be hanging around the hotel being questioned by police and scrutinised, I just want to relax.'

She looked out through the library window, recalling how only yesterday she'd taken such joy in the fact that being on a small island, every window looked out to sea. Now she just felt trapped, and there seemed to be no escape. Wherever she looked was the vast ocean, and instead of it being a beautiful view, it was preventing her from leaving.

'Look at that sky,' Becky said, trying to ignore the men's rather lurid discussion about how Stella might have died. 'I reckon there's going to be a storm.'

And right on cue, the rain began to pat on the windows.

Daisy gazed around the library, which was designed to be a nod to country piles by the sea. It made her think of a family all gathered round the open fire as the storm began to lash outside, and for a nanosecond she forgot she'd never have a family. Then she remembered again; it flooded back like the sea, unfettered, unable to hold back the tide that washed her away and turned her to nothing. She'd never *had* a family, and she would never *have* one.

As the skies started to flash and rumble outside, the guests inside were bound together by their primal fear of the storm and the aftermath of the day's events. The lights were dimmer, inside was quiet and cosy, while outside was loud and thrashing, angry waves leaping and swirling, the spitting rain now heavier against the windows.

'I think I might be psychic,' Sam said, and Daisy smiled. She'd wondered how long it would be before they all returned to their childhoods and ghost stories told in a circle. 'I had this really weird feeling when we first arrived,' she continued. 'It's hard to explain... a sense of foreboding. Have *you* ever felt that?' she asked Becky.

Becky screwed up her eyes, contemplating the question.

'Not exactly, I'm not sure I believe in being psychic, but I do think we all have instincts, and we should trust them. If you feel threatened or in danger, there might be a reason for that.'

'I agree,' Daisy said, 'I had a difficult childhood, and I sometimes get those same feelings of fear.' She shivered slightly. 'It might be nothing, but I feel it now, that there's something close that might be dangerous.' Her words hung in the air a few moments. The other women stared at her, but Daisy couldn't offer anything else.

'Well, I knew something was off as soon as I walked through those doors into the lobby,' Sam said. 'It's really beautiful, but this place has a scary history and I think stuff like that hangs around, an evil force.'

'What's the history?' Becky asked.

'An actress was pushed off the cliffs...' Sam lifted her hand to her mouth. 'Oh God, I hadn't thought about it until now, but it was just like Stella.'

'Oh, this is giving me the creeps,' Daisy said, wrapping both her arms around herself. She didn't like to listen to this. She'd had a difficult enough day and didn't want to ride Sam's ghost train right now, but like a car crash, found herself macabrely drawn to listen.

'Oh and about fifteen years ago... a young couple were found dead in their hotel room.' She leaned forward and whispered quietly, 'Room 24 – the honeymoon suite... mine and David's room.'

Just as she said this, a loud clap of thunder smacked just above, making everyone gasp as the lights dimmed.

'Oh God, I can't take any more,' Daisy said.

'It's only weather,' Becky said calmly. Daisy couldn't work her out. She gave nothing away, just seemed quiet, sensible, and intelligent. But then why did she allow her husband to control every move she made? It didn't add up.

'Do you have children?' Daisy asked. This was usually one of her first questions to strangers, it was her compass.

'Yes I do, I have two,' she beamed. 'Amy's sixteen and Ben's fourteen, growing up too fast. I wish they were here with us now, but Josh thought it would be more relaxing without them – which of course it is,' she said with a regretful smile. Mentioning her kids was the most animated Daisy had seen her, and she tried not to think too much about it. If she did it would lead her down a path she didn't want to go down.

'You can tell you're a mum,' Sam said. 'You seem very wise and sensible and...'

'And that sounds very boring!' Becky said with a chuckle, and she started to talk about how she could do mad things even as a mum and how her children were always telling her off if she swore or did anything crazy. Despite being the one who brought up the subject of children, Daisy couldn't quite handle hearing this. So she tried to take her mind somewhere else, and focused on a pile of board games on the lower shelves of the library. She was suddenly nostalgic for a seaside holiday she'd once taken as a child with her mother. The women's hostel they were staying in had arranged the holiday. It was her happiest memory, the only time she'd felt safe enough to fall asleep and stay asleep until morning, something she didn't take for granted even now. But as a grown-up she had Tom to hold in the night. It was usually the middle of the night when everything flooded back: a door opening, light seeping in. Then the terrifying sound of the door closing quietly, creaking floorboards, the weight beside her in the bed, the smell of alcohol, and a rasping whisper. She was ten years old, and Mummy had just married her new boyfriend.

'You have a daddy now,' she said. Just a few nights later, he silently pushed his way inside her, and never left.

And now, alone on a beach, at home in the garden, at night as she tried to sleep, he was always there. She could be awak-

ened by a memory, a moment, and there it was, like yesterday –
'Daddy' and the darkness.

And now, tonight, in this beautiful hotel, lightyears away
from her tormented childhood, Daisy felt the fear: a familiar
feeling that danger was lurking, and she might not live until
morning.

'I'm glad we're inside, and not out there,' Sam was saying.
Daisy followed her gaze to the darkened window, a sliver of
moon high in the sky, rain still lashing down.

Suddenly, another clap of thunder, and all three women
flinched and looked at each other. 'I was always scared of
thunder until Mum told me it was God's tummy rumbling,' Sam
said with a smile, and it seemed to Daisy that Sam needed to be
liked, and tried to cheer the others up, whatever was happening.
'This storm will cool everything down. I couldn't sleep last
night it was so hot.'

Becky nodded and took a sip of her sparkling water.

Then Sam leaned closer to both women and said conspiratorially, 'David and I were both naked with no bed covers and
the window open.' She giggled at the memory, making the other
two giggle with her.

'Outrageous,' Daisy said, in mock indignation.

'I remember the novelty of being newly married, that
feeling of thinking it will never end. Feels like it was yesterday,
even if it was a lifetime ago,' Becky said with a sigh. 'We've been
married twenty years, and when it's hot we don't get naked. I
take a shower and Josh just goes running.' She gave a little
chuckle.

'What? Josh goes *running*? In this heat? Phew!' Sam started
dabbing her face with a hankie.

'Yeah, since we got here he's gone running every night. He
likes to go late, says it's cooler then.'

'No, it isn't. It's been just as hot late in the evening,' Daisy
agreed, 'and the air conditioning here in the hotel is rubbish!'

'He goes on the beach? How late, after midnight?'

Becky shrugged. 'Yeah, it's always late.'

Sam looked around quickly then pulled her chair closer to the others and said, 'Was he out last night? Did he see anything...?'

Sam seemed keen to pursue this, and Daisy wished she'd stop going on about Josh and his running. He talked about it enough, she didn't need to hear Sam going on about it.

'No, he didn't see anything,' Becky replied. Daisy felt her bristle; what was Sam trying to say?

'Oh, it's just... being out there late, around the time she died, I thought he might have seen something?' Sam pressed. She clearly never gave up. Daisy could feel the tension from Becky, like she wished she'd never said anything about her husband's late-night runs. 'No, he didn't. He didn't see *anything*,' she stressed, clearly trying to put a stop to whatever Sam might be trying to ask or even insinuate.

'You wouldn't catch *me* jogging in that heat,' Sam was saying. 'Day or night.' Daisy wondered why Sam seemed so keen to keep on clumsily talking about Josh.

'Yeah, it's *so* hot,' Daisy said in an attempt to change the subject. Sam's comments were so loaded it was creating an atmosphere.

'It's like a *tropical* heat, isn't it?' Sam wafted her hand in front of her face in an attempt to cool down.

'Relentless,' Becky said, and Daisy wondered if she was referring to the heat or Sam.

'Yeah, so David and I were tossing and turning so much last night, we called for room service.'

Sam was clearly still determined to overshare the previous evening's bedroom activities, but probably glad of some light relief from the intense questioning, Becky smiled. Sam was amusing, even if she didn't mean to be, but Daisy wondered if her insecurities about her own husband were being projected onto Josh. Then again, Josh seemed odd too. He was always watching Becky, telling her what to drink and eat. Earlier that evening, when Josh was about to order drinks, Daisy heard Becky say, 'I'd love a proper drink,' but he shook his head, and ordered her a glass of water. It seemed rather cruel to Daisy; she didn't understand how any woman could be so submissive, especially someone as bright and intelligent as Becky.

Meanwhile, Sam was still regaling them with the story of the previous evening's 'honeymoon fun!'

'So it was two o'clock in the morning and David's on the phone ordering three ice buckets, but he didn't order *drinks*... just ice!' She was smiling and shaking her head at the memory. Sam clearly thought her new husband was hilarious, innovative and amazing, as no doubt did he.

'*Room service*? How did you call room service, you can't get a signal on your mobile in your room, can you?' Becky asked.

'No, no one can get a signal in their rooms,' Sam confirmed. 'We used the landline of course.'

Daisy couldn't help but notice that Becky had stopped smiling.

'But Josh told me...' Becky paused. 'He said we weren't *allowed* landline telephones in our rooms – it's so we can relax.'

Frowning, Sam looked from Becky to Daisy, obviously thinking the same thing: *why would Josh say that?*

'Yeah, there *are* telephones in the rooms, *especially* as there's no mobile phone signal. What if there was an emergency? How would anyone get room service?'

All three women fell quiet, and they sat in silence for the first time that evening.

Then Becky looked at Daisy. 'Do *you* have a landline in your bedroom too?'

She nodded, feeling almost guilty, and wondering again what the hell was going on between Becky and Josh. Daisy widened her eyes discreetly at Sam, who responded with a look of barely concealed horror.

Becky glanced over at Josh, and Daisy wondered how to open up the conversation again, to find out if this was as messed up as it sounded. But before anyone could return to the subject of bedroom telephones, David was back from the bar, followed by two waiters each carrying bottles of champagne and glasses.

'For you,' he said, leaning over his wife and handing the first, dripping glass to Daisy, who smiled awkwardly. She found David rather overbearing, and this ostentatious display was a bit cringey for her tastes.

'What about me?' joked Sam. 'Shouldn't I be first? I'm the bride, after all.'

Still standing, David looked down at her but addressed everyone. It seemed to Daisy that everything David did had to be announced. His money, his business, his largesse was all out there within minutes of meeting him.

'I'm learning about my new wife every day,' he was saying, holding his glass high, taking the floor. 'Today's lesson is that she's very impatient, and has to be served her champagne first...' He paused, and his rather stern expression softened. 'But she is my wife, so I must obey!' Everyone smiled, and Sam giggled as he handed her a glass, then took her other hand and kissed it in a rather elaborate romantic gesture. Daisy felt rather awkward. Why *didn't* he give the first glass to Sam first instead of leaning over and making a point of giving the first one to her? It was embarrassing and even though she was joking about it, it clearly pissed Sam off that he was making a fuss of Daisy.

He then pushed a glass at Becky. 'Go on, girl, get it down you. It might put a smile on your face for this poor sod.' He gestured at Josh, who seemed to wince at the man's remark.

Fury rose up inside Daisy and she exploded, just like the champagne. 'Wow! So you'd like Becky to drink alcohol, to put a smile on her face, to make her *husband* happy?' she said sarcastically. 'So her *smile* belongs to him?' She couldn't help herself. Josh was obviously a controlling pig, and David was an arrogant sod who'd just revealed himself to also be a borderline misogynist.

David frowned, his face turning purple-red with anger. 'Ah there you are! I knew you were too good to be true. You're one of those feminist activists in your spare time, are you?' he asked, revealing yet more misogyny and even more ignorance.

'I don't *have* any spare time, I'm too busy ironing my husband's shirts and making his dinner,' she spat.

'David?' was all Sam could mutter. She looked mortified, and though Daisy had a lot more to say, she didn't want to embarrass her. But David seemed to view Daisy's backing off as an opportunity to go right back in.

'Take no notice of Miss Misery Guts here, go on, have a drink, love,' he said again to Becky, who was clearly revolted by this man, but remained polite – if somewhat tight-lipped.

'Thank you, but I'm not *your* love, and I don't want a drink.'

'Don't want a *drink?*' He turned to face the others, who had to listen because they were now drinking the champagne he'd paid for. In effect he'd just purchased five people to be his audience.

'I've never heard of anyone who didn't want a *drink*,' he continued. 'You must be mad.'

'Come on now, David,' Sam said, applying a fake smile, in a valiant but futile attempt to smooth things over.

'Don't tell me what to do, darling,' he said in a faux-friendly tone, but Daisy heard the vitriol rolling around in his voice. Everyone sipped their champagne in silence. The tension in the air was punctuated only by claps of thunder, while everyone desperately tried to think of something to say to relieve the pressure.

But they didn't need to, because seconds later, the hotel loudspeaker cut into the thunder and lightning, inviting everyone up into the ballroom, where they were promised 'an update from the police.'

That started everyone talking again and there was quite a buzz. Everyone walked to the ballroom as directed. Once there, staff guided guests to tables, and on a long table in front of the smaller ones sat several police officers, and a man and woman in civilian clothes who looked like detectives. It reminded Daisy of the top table at a wedding, but this occasion was anything but celebratory, despite the grand ballroom being a homage to the 1920s complete with crystal chandelier. It didn't feel to Daisy like the most appropriate space to be updated on the death of a young woman, but as Tom said, they were in a hotel so had to work with what they had.

The six new 'friends' all sat at the same table, their acquaintance now cemented among the other tables where strangers sat. Bizarrely, staff began taking orders for coffee and tea. Daisy noticed Paulo with his notepad taking beverage orders from 'the top table.' Typically, he was standing far too close to the woman who, after a few minutes, stood up and introduced herself as DCI Granger.

'For those who may not know, Stella Foster, a much-loved member of staff here at Fitzgerald's, died today,' she said, getting right down to the matter in hand. 'Her body was found on the private beach by two guests, who quickly alerted us. What initially seemed like a tragic but straightforward cause of death has, on further examination, become more complex than first considered. Consequently, this is now a murder investigation and we will be continuing forensic examination of the crime area.' She paused, looked around the room. 'I have asked you here this evening to inform you of the current state of play, and also to let you know we will, over the next couple of days, be conducting interviews with both guests and staff here at the hotel.' There was a mumble of voices, which meant she had to raise hers. 'Therefore,' she said loudly, 'we would request all guests to stay on the island until initial interviews have taken place, then wait to hear from us regarding any plans to depart.'

'So, you're telling us we can't leave?' Tom asked loudly.

DCI Granger frowned. 'If you have a medical reason or an urgent reason to leave the island, then please let one of our officers know so we can assist you. However, we are hoping everyone here will remain at Fitzgerald's and assist us with our enquiries,' she snapped. 'Meanwhile, be vigilant. If anything or anyone seems suspicious, report it to one of the officers on duty. There will be a twenty-four-hour police presence in the hotel and around the island. Your safety is our priority, along with catching the perpetrator. And until we do, might I suggest you take your personal safety very seriously and lock all bedroom and balcony doors.'

Daisy felt the implication here was, 'If you don't do what we say, you're going to look very guilty and we're watching.' She shifted uneasily in her seat as everyone began whispering and grumbling, trying to work out what this meant for them.

'I hope they don't keep us any longer than we planned, I need to get back to my business,' David was saying in that self-important way.

'Me too, I've got clients booked in for the day after we get back, they will go mad if I'm delayed,' Sam replied.

Meanwhile, poor Becky was devastated. 'But the children, I want to get home for the children?' She was looking at Josh with pleading eyes, and he just shrugged, defeated.

Daisy looked at them all and suddenly felt very trapped. She looked across at Sam, who, in a terrified voice said, 'I'm scared.'

David put an arm around her shoulder and addressed the rest of the group. 'The police obviously think that whoever killed Stella is still here, and I for one am not sitting around waiting for them to strike again.' Daisy shivered. As irritating and pompous as he was, he had a point; until the police found out who killed Stella, they were all sitting ducks. 'Tonight we must double lock our door and the balcony door,' she said to Tom. 'But I know I won't sleep, because whoever killed Stella is still here.' She looked around the room, and everyone was looking back at her, thinking the same and wondering *who?*

NINE

BECKY

Tonight's our twentieth wedding anniversary, and I'm alone. An hour ago, two dozen roses arrived in our room, along with lemonade made to look like champagne in an ice bucket and a tray of chocolate-dipped strawberries. The lemonade's now warm, the chocolate's melting as is my make-up, and Josh still hasn't come back from his run. After last night's police update, I feel so isolated and sad. We were supposed to leave at the end of the week, and I couldn't wait to see the kids, but now, who knows when we'll get home? Josh tried to talk to the detective, but she said, 'Legally, we can't force anyone to stay here *yet*. *But* I have to tell you that anyone leaving will still be interviewed, and before they leave there may be a delay while we obtain a warrant for access to their hotel room.' He said she was very cold, very businesslike, and dismissed him before he could ask any more questions.

I'm devastated. I really don't want to be interviewed by detectives, I just want to get back home. I miss the kids terribly, and being able to at least talk to them on the phone would help, so last night when we got back to the room, I asked Josh about the landline and he repeated what he'd already told me: that it was hotel policy not to have phones in the room.

'Well, everyone else has one,' I said.

'They might have made a special request. I promise you they don't offer landlines in rooms for the very reason I told you, it's about rest and relaxation.'

But now we're stuck here I'm going to make a special request for a phone in our room. I have to talk to the kids and my mum, if this gets in the news they'll be so worried.

Some might say I'm lucky being locked down in luxury with my husband. He always said this holiday was supposed to be about the two of us spending time together and having pure relaxation. Looks like Josh will get his wish after all. Not only will we be here together, we're not really allowed to leave. I thought he'd be pleased to have me locked down on an island where he can check on me every moment, but he seems more anxious than ever. Today he's been edgy, unable to speak to me without snapping. I was glad when he went off on his run, and started to get dressed for the evening, but then a waitress arrived with the lemonade and strawberries. And instead of that making me happy, it's just made me feel even more alone to watch the contents on the celebratory tray become warmer and soggier by the minute, while I lie on the bed in my best dress waiting for my husband.

A sudden rustling at the door alarms me. Is it the police? Do they have a warrant to search our room because Josh asked the detective if we could leave? Are we now under suspicion? Or is it someone else? I hold my breath as whoever it is tries the door handle. The police wouldn't do that.

'Hello?' I call weakly, aware I have no access to a phone if this person is in any way dangerous, and when there's no response I decide not to answer the door.

In the tense silence, my head's suddenly filled with an image of Stella. I imagine her lying on the rocks, her head crushed from the fall. Bruised arms, twisted limbs. Daisy and Sam described it all in some detail last night. I wish they hadn't. I try to release the breath I'm holding but it catches in my throat and I start to cough, big racking coughs that make me wonder what's happening inside me. As I finally get my breath, the door bursts open, and Josh is standing over me, 'Becky, oh God, are you okay?' He looks scared.

'Was it you at the door?' I wheeze, pointing at him.

'Yes, sorry did I scare you?'

I nod, and cough again.

'Have you taken your tablets?' he asks.

'Yeah, of *course*.' I lie back. I'm on the edge of tears.

He moves across the room, relieved I've taken my medication.

'I was talking to one of the officers in the lobby just now, and he said it could be two or three days before they get the forensics back.'

'I want to leave now,' I say, getting off the bed, my voice cracking with panic and tears.

'Calm down,' he says, walking towards me, helping me gently into the armchair by the bed. 'There's no need for that, you mustn't upset yourself, we're safe enough here.'

'If someone *did* push Stella, would it show up in the forensics? I wonder if she killed herself and the police are just taking a chance, just to see if someone confesses?' I ask, my voice still croaky from my coughing fit.

'They can't do that,' he says. 'They must have some evidence that suggests she was killed. Perhaps she was pushed?'

'But how would they *know*?'

He shrugged. 'I've no idea, I'm an accountant, not a detective,' he replies. 'It's stuffy in here. Shall I open the window?' He's clearly not interested in continuing the conversation, and without waiting for my response, he leans over to open the window. I wait for a breeze, some movement of air, but there's nothing. In spite of the storm last night, the heat hasn't gone away. In fact it's even more intense than before, and the air is still and thick. I feel quite breathless.

'Oh good, the fake champagne arrived?' he says, plucking it from the bucket. I'd have preferred champagne, but I don't want to seem too ungrateful, it's the thought that counts I guess. It's now dripping everywhere and after waiting for my applause or thanks and receiving neither, he plonks it back.

'The chocolate's melted too,' I mutter, glancing over, unsmiling.

'Look, I'm sorry. I was running, you know how I forget time when I'm running,' he says.

'You seem to forget a lot when you're running,' I respond, thinking about him with Stella at the pool bar the night she died. There must be a reasonable explanation why he was there, but I won't ask yet. I don't want him to *know* I was watching. I want to keep my secrets too, they're all I have left, the only thing he can't control.

He's kneeling down now and putting his head on the arm of the chair like a child. 'Tell me I haven't ruined our special night, I tried so hard to make it perfect.'

I touch his head and stroke his hair.

'You look lovely,' he says staring up at me, taking in my new dress, hair washed, made-up face. I'm reminded of Ben, who has his father's big, brown eyes, and it occurs to me that whatever happens, I always end up caring for Josh.

'That blue suits you,' he says.

'It's too big.' I pull at the loose folds of material. He drops his head back onto the arm of the chair, and despite being annoyed with him, I'm now compelled to make him feel better.

'I *do* appreciate it,' I say, gesturing towards the lemonade and strawberries. 'But I wish you'd been here, *with* me, I've been ready for ages, just sitting here on my own.'

'I only went for a run,' he mumbles into my arm, where his head is currently resting.

'Love, you don't "only" go for a run anymore, you run for miles, to the exclusion of everything and everyone else. You said yourself you lose track of time, and now, with a killer prowling the hotel, I'd like you to stay with me more please.'

'I will, I promise,' he says like a chastised child.

'I know you're under pressure,' I say gently, 'and I also know that stress makes you weird.'

'What do you mean?' He lifts his head to look at me.

'You know, you obsess about stuff – and everything else, including me, falls by the wayside.'

'You and the kids always come first, you know that.'

'I know you love us, but you abandon us too, it's happened before, with the church, then the tennis, and it's happening again now, with the running, and the money.'

'I just find running therapeutic, and also it could be a way out of this, I *can't* give up, because if I get enough sponsors then the money...'

'Enough, enough, Josh.' I can see the pain in his eyes. 'It's more important that you're here with me, I'd rather have *you* than the money. It's like last night, even after the police suggested we lock our doors and be vigilant, you just went out and left me here, and didn't get back until after 1am! You were gone for more than *two* hours, Josh,' I add, remembering him creeping into the room, thinking I was asleep.

'I'm sorry.'

'Don't apologise, just be aware of the safety aspect, for both of us – we don't know if this person is targeting women or men, staff or guests. But also, think about what this running obsession is doing to you, and me,' I add, attempting to wipe my eyes without him seeing, but he's hugging me again now and I realise he's unreachable. And I'm tired. I'm tired of life, and of Josh and all the promises he doesn't keep, and there's no point in talking because there's too much to say.

'We're late for dinner, why don't you get showered and dressed?' I say, feigning brightness and pulling away.

He gets up and marches across the room, throwing off his top and shorts and leaving them in a pile in the middle of the bedroom.

'Sorry you were worried,' he says. 'I lost track of time.'

'What makes it worse is that there's no phone signal, I couldn't even call you.'

'I told you, it's the healing process,' he says, fastening his shirt and wandering back over to the chair and kissing me.

'Well, I'm going to ask for a landline in here tomorrow, whatever you say.'

'Fine, fine,' he murmurs. 'So, can I now please take my shower so I can take my beautiful wife down to dinner on our twentieth anniversary?' He wanders to the bathroom and leaving the door open, he shouts over the noise of the shower. 'Twenty years. Can you believe it?'

'Seems like yesterday,' I sigh, wishing it was, remembering the young man I married, and how we'd thought we had all the answers to life. I'm so tired I drift off for a few minutes and I'm woken by him coming back into the room.

'I need to get my sponsorship forms printed out before dinner,' he says, walking from the bathroom drying his hair.

'Josh, that'll make us late,' I say, rousing myself and bending to fasten my shoes.

'It won't take a minute,' he says, getting down on his knees, starting to fasten my shoes for me. 'I thought I'd leave some leaflets in reception, and I want to tag some of the guests on Facebook, get them over to our page. I've made Facebook friends with almost everyone I've met so far this holiday,' he says proudly.

'Why? So you can chase them for sponsorship?' My heart

sinks. 'Given what's happened, I don't think it's really appropriate, Josh. It's bad enough you asking people for money at the best of times, but everyone's concerned about Stella's death, they won't be interested in your running.'

'Oh my *God*, Beck.' He finishes my shoes and stands up, holding his arms in the air. 'It's not about my running! And I don't just *ask people for money*, they're *sponsoring* me; you're making me sound like some kind of conman!' He drops his arms and moves away, hurt. 'David and Tom have already offered me £100 each,' he says.

I don't have the energy to fight him, I know after all these years, that there's no stopping him when he's like this, so I don't even try.

'Tom's a bit quiet but...'

'His wife is lovely, I wonder what they do?' I mused.

'She's an art director, whatever that is, and I think he works in money, which is why he'd be a good sponsor.'

'Not necessarily,' I say to myself really, because he's not listening.

'She's got about two hundred thousand followers on Instagram,' he continues. 'If she could post something about sponsoring me and the crowdfunding that would be great.'

'Oh, how do you know she's got two hundred thousand followers? We only met them yesterday.' Though it feels like so much longer after everything that's happened. I guess the two girls finding Stella and the tragedy itself has really bonded us all far more quickly than a usual holiday friendship.

'I checked out her Instagram. Haven't you?' Josh says honestly.

'No, I can't because I can't get a signal in the hotel, and I barely leave here,' I replied, making my point. 'What's on there?'

'Oh, just Daisy in her little shorts with models and photographers in different countries.'

'I don't want to hear any more. I find beautiful people in beautiful places depressing these days.'

He nods. 'Yeah, sickening.'

'Little shorts?' I say, suddenly realising what he just said. 'No wonder you were checking out her Instagram,' I tease.

'I wasn't looking on there for pictures of *her*. You don't need to see Daisy's Instagram to see what she's got under her clothes. I mean, that bikini she had on yesterday, you could see her bum!' He sounds about twelve years old. 'And last night, she had that low-cut dress on that left nothing to the imagination.'

'You didn't have to look,' I say with an indulgent smile. Our sex life has been pretty non-existent for some time. I wouldn't blame him for looking.

'I didn't know where to put my eyes,' he's saying. 'The material of her dress was so thin you could see her underwear, and... and the blatant breasts were embarrassing.'

'*Blatant breasts?*' I repeat with a giggle. 'Oh, Josh, you sound like a Victorian father. It's hot, she was wearing a low-cut dress made of thin material to stay cool. And there's nothing wrong with a woman wandering around in a bikini on holiday,' I said. 'Look at you, you're blushing now as you remember it.' I'm smiling at his embarrassment.

'I know, I'm just glad she's not *my* wife. I wouldn't be comfortable if you were sitting there with everything on show.'

'Jesus, you sound like David,' I say.

'Oh no, that's the worst insult ever,' he groans.

I watch him as he dries himself off and begins dressing for dinner. Josh has such high standards, the world often surprises and disappoints him.

'Perhaps Daisy could get her magazine to feature something?' he murmurs. 'They might do something on *us*, our story, they might even pay us. We've got flights to pay for at the end of August remember,' he adds.

'But I thought we had £24k in the bank already from donations and your sponsored runs?'

'We do,' he says, instinctively turning away from me, 'but we can always use more.'

After dinner, we go for drinks in the cocktail bar with the others. I'm tired but like everyone else I want to know what's happening with the investigation. Sam says the lady who cleans her room has a nephew in the police, and she's going to try and get updates. 'She calls me Miss Marple,' Sam says, 'and she told me they might be able to find matching fingerprints from the killer.' A shiver runs through me, but I try to remain composed, detached, like I'm not in any way affected by this news. But I am petrified.

'Well, I was chatting to one of the receptionists,' Daisy starts, 'and she told me something very interesting.' She pauses, like she isn't sure whether or not to say. Every one of us has stopped talking, and in the taut silence we all wait, desperate to know, and I wonder who's the most interested – and why?

'*Tell* us then!' I say, dying to know this fresh titbit she's brought to the table.

'Well, the woman on reception knew Stella well, and she said that recently she'd been freaked out by some guest who came to the bar every night,' Daisy says. 'Was this guest a man?' Sam immediately asks.

'Yeah. Apparently he was always staring, and making comments.' We all seem to glance at our husbands to see their reactions to this. They don't flinch.

'And you believe this woman?' David asks.

'Why wouldn't I? She was a friend of Stella's.' She glares at David. 'And apparently, Stella hated him looking at her and she told him, and they argued, the night she died.'

'No?' Sam gasped.

'Rubbish!' David snorts.

'Did this woman say who it *was*?' Tom asks, clearly annoyed, either at what she's said, or the fact she didn't tell him first. He's wiping sweat from his upper lip with the back of his hand and suddenly no one's smiling. The atmosphere in the room has gone from nought to zero, as we sit together in the unbearable stillness. Josh doesn't say a word.

'No she didn't. I don't think she knows. But *I* have my theories.' She licks her lips. I wonder if she's just teasing them.

'Who do *you* think it is?' Sam asks, breathless with anticipation.

She shakes her head. 'I'm not saying.'

'But you'll tell the police, I hope?' Josh says.

'Of course, in fact I have a meeting with DCI Granger booked for tomorrow.'

'Do you?' Tom looks surprised. 'You didn't say. Why are *you* speaking to the police, shouldn't the woman from reception be the one to talk to them?'

'She works here and doesn't want to get involved.' I reckon Daisy's definitely playing games now, trying to smoke the guilty one out. 'Besides, we're all going to have to be interviewed. Hopefully I can get mine over with, I have to be at work next week, I have a shoot in the Seychelles.'

'Good luck with that,' David says. 'I have a million-pound business and they won't let me go back early, I doubt they'll let you off to go to some photo session.'

'Well, let's wait until next week, be interesting to see who's still on the island and who's in a prison cell, won't it?' She's now glaring at him. She looks like she wants to kill him. Anyone with a modicum of social intelligence would step back from this now, but not David.

'I'm sure you have your theories, and I'm sure the police will love your story, might even get an arrest out of it. But it won't stick,' he responds. 'I bet there are plenty of male guests in this hotel who sat at the pool bar staring and making comments to young Stella,' he adds.

'Yes, and we all know who they are,' she spits.

'Absolutely, so tomorrow, when you go for your little tête-à-tête with the police, might I suggest that you tell them to arrest every red-blooded male in this hotel?' Then he laughs at his own, sick joke.

'David!' Sam says, reprimanding him.

Daisy shoots him a look and murmurs, 'Wow.'

'Sorry, sorry, ladies,' he says patronisingly, 'but it's true.' He raises both hands in a surrendering gesture, but with mischief in his eyes.

Josh is shifting in his seat next to me and as soon as Daisy has finished telling us what she knows, he whispers to me that it's late and we should go back to our room. I really wanted to find out more, but he might make a scene if I refuse, and I'm tired, so agree to leave. He puts his arm through mine, and we say goodnight. Back in our room, he says he's tired and goes straight to bed – *after* making sure I take my sleeping tablets. I wonder if he's planning any more nocturnal runs once I'm drugged to sleep? But I'm becoming an expert at hiding the tablets under my tongue, and I stay wide awake, and wait. Once I hear his deep, steady breathing, I check to make sure he's completely asleep, then climb carefully out of bed. Using the torch on my redundant, signal-less mobile, I do what no wife should do: I go searching in my husband's stuff. I don't know why I'm doing this, I know it's not fair, but I just have this feeling he's hiding something from me.

I open the first drawer, and feel around the folded T-shirts, the underwear – all pretty innocent, until I reach further back into the drawer and feel something under the soft fabric. I shine the torch into the back of the drawer and claw at the cloth to uncover what's there. On unwrapping his black hoodie, I realise it's been hiding the hotel room telephone.

TEN

SAM

It was the morning after Daisy had told us all that Stella had a stalker, and two days after Stella's body had been found. David and I had argued because he was still saying we should leave, but I thought it made us look like we were hiding something, and I didn't want the police giving us special attention. But I was learning that David was a law unto himself and had little respect for anyone, even the police. I told him that he was going to make himself look guilty because of the way he was behaving. He was so determined to leave.

'It's like you're running away,' I said. Anyway, that set him off; he started shouting, and I yelled back and I ended up just storming out of our room and slamming the door.

I decided to cool off and go and have breakfast, and was walking through the foyer when I saw Tom and Daisy sitting there. I couldn't believe what I was seeing. She was wearing a ripped silk nightdress; it was covered in dirt, and what looked like blood. Her face and hair were also covered in mud and there were clumps of dirt and blood in her white-blonde hair. As I approached, I saw red wheals and bruising around her neck.

'What happened to you?' I gasped, horrified.

She slowly looked up. She had a blanket around her shoulders, and pulled it tight.

Her eyes were bloodshot, with dark circles beneath them, her face was expressionless, and her arms were wrapped tightly around herself.

'She was assaulted last night,' Tom said. 'She's been giving a statement to the police. We're just waiting for the police's permission for her to get dressed; they need her clothes to check for DNA. Then we're going to the mainland. She has to be checked out at the hospital.'

'Oh no, Daisy?' I asked, sitting down next to her.

She looked up at me, and her chin started wobbling. Her eyes were puffy, her face stained with mud and blood and tears.

'She went for a walk,' Tom said. He could barely get a sentence out he seemed so angry. 'Near the cliffs, someone leapt out at her.'

I had my hand over my mouth; I couldn't speak.

Daisy just sat very still.

'She shouldn't have gone out there, bloody stupid. I told her not to go, but she stomped off in a mood as usual.'

'Oh piss off, Tom,' she hissed under her breath. 'If you'd bothered to come and find me it wouldn't have happened.'

'I'm done with playing your attention-seeking little games,' he responded. A vein stood out on the side of his head as he spoke.

I was shocked to hear them talking to each other like this. I thought they were as blissfully happy as they were beautiful, and their anger surprised me. I could see Tom might have a bit of a temper, he was the kind of person who didn't say much but probably bottled it all up then let rip, but not Daisy. She'd seemed so sweet and kind. It was shocking to see her sitting in the foyer covered in mud and blood and bruises in a ripped silk nightdress. Equally shocking was the hate in her eyes as she glanced at Tom, the tight, nasty mouth when she'd told him to piss off... The transformation was unbelievable. I admit for a moment it crossed my mind that she might be possessed, that someone who'd been a victim of the dark history of the hotel had come back for revenge. I was really creeped out, it was like I was seeing another side to her. Possession and evil spirits aside, unfortunately it looked like they might both have anger issues.

As uncomfortable as it was sitting with them in the frosty silence, I didn't like to just get up and go. So after a few minutes, I turned to Daisy and said, 'Do you have any idea who it was that assaulted you?'

She shook her head.

'So stupid to be out there,' Tom was muttering.

'Shut *up*, Tom!' she hissed.

I was desperate to know and probably a little insensitive in my questioning. 'Do the police think it might be the same guy who... killed Stella?'

'Don't know.'

'She couldn't identify him to the police, if she had they might have caught him by now and we'd all be able to go home,' Tom snapped.

Daisy started to cry.

I put my arm around her. I was glad I'd bumped into them. She needed some support – she was so shaken up and Tom wasn't being at all sympathetic. But just then, a police officer came out of the spa area and said that the boat had arrived, she could change once she'd boarded and the police doctor was waiting in Plymouth. Daisy and Tom stood up, said goodbye to me, then walked with two police officers through the lobby. I stood and watched as they went out to the small docking area where the boat waited to take them.

I started to walk to the dining room, when I saw Becky sitting in the far end of the lobby, around the corner from where I'd been with Daisy and Tom.

'Becky, something terrible has happened,' I said, walking over and sitting next to her on the chaise longue.

She looked so thin – I was glad the storm of the previous evening had left us or I reckoned she'd be in serious danger of being blown away.

'It's Daisy, she's been attacked, looks like whoever killed Stella has tried again!' I said.

'Is that what the police think?'

'Probably, I mean let's face it, a girl gets killed and another one is attacked in the same area within two days, it has to be.'

'Oh God!' She groaned, and put her hand to her mouth. Becky was so delicate I suddenly wasn't sure I should have told her.

But she groaned again, then put her arm around me. I hadn't expected that. She'd seemed slightly stand-offish until then, but I'd misread Becky.

'What happened?' she asked finally.

'All I know is she rowed with Tom and stormed off into the night, on her own and was attacked. She put herself in a very vulnerable position wandering outside in the dark after a few drinks. We have to be careful, Becky.'

'Yes, we mustn't take any chances, somebody here is dangerous,' she said.

'I just keep thinking about Stella, and now this,' I murmured.

'Thank God Daisy's okay...' she said.

'I feel bad because I was having a go at David for flirting with her last night. Come to think of it, he flirted with Stella too. They were speaking in French, I don't speak French, so I couldn't join in.'

'Didn't David translate for you, or bring you into the conversation?' she asked.

'No, they were only talking for a few minutes, he speaks French to one of the waiters too. And to be honest, David has this thing about me being jealous, he says I'm too much. And with Stella, I didn't want to come over as the jealous wife, you know?'

She raised her eyebrows. 'Still sounds a bit rude, to exclude you like that.'

I wished I'd never said anything. I felt like she was judging David, or perhaps me for not speaking bloody French. The resort was lovely, but sometimes I felt so small there, like every single guest spoke another language, and had a yacht moored somewhere hot. I was so out of my depth, but Becky seemed nice, not snobby or rich. I felt comfortable with her.

'David wasn't being rude,' I insisted. 'He just seems to have this effect on women, in any language,' I said with a sigh.

'He's catnip,' she murmured, but I could see she wasn't convinced.

'I sometimes wonder if Daisy likes him. I know she's got Tom and he's gorgeous, but Daisy always seems to be trying to start an argument with David, which makes me think she wants his attention.'

'I don't think so,' Becky said. 'I got the impression they irritate each other.'

'Yeah, probably,' I said, relieved, glad of Becky's second opinion. In truth I doubted Daisy had a secret crush on my husband, I was more worried about David having the hots for her, but didn't want to introduce that into the conversation. It would be painful and embarrassing if Becky had noticed it too and said so. David had commented to me the previous night when we were in bed that he found her 'challenging', and she needed to be 'tamed'. I found this a bit disturbing, like there was a sexual undercurrent, but I hadn't said anything, because it would only start another row about me being possessive. But I couldn't sleep. I kept thinking about what he'd said, and the way he said it.

'So what time did this happen to Daisy?' Becky asked, keen to return to the attack.

'I'm not sure, she's gone to have a medical examination, so I didn't get a chance to ask everything. But it must have happened after we left, which would be about eleven?'

'Yeah, Josh and I had gone by then, we left early.'

'David and I went to bed, leaving her and Tom in the library,' I said. 'Presumably, they went back to their room and had the row because she was dressed for bed.'

'I wonder what they rowed about?' Becky said.

'Who knows? What does any married couple row about? We had a row too last night, and I'm sure it shouldn't keep happening on a honeymoon.'

'It might be a way of clearing the air before you start real married life back home?' she suggested. 'What did you argue about?'

'I was pissed off with David to tell you the truth, and had a bit of a go at him about ignoring me all night.' I was aware I was oversharing, but felt I could talk to Becky and she did ask. '"Oh don't be so stupid, Sam," he said, "you're starting to sound like Marie, I hate possessive women." Well that just wound me up, I mean I might have jealousy issues, but how *dare* he say I'm like Marie.'

'Marie?' she said, confused.

'Yeah, oh sorry, that's his ex, "mad Marie", I call her – she virtually stalked him even after the marriage was over. Anyway, we both said some things we shouldn't, which ended up with me storming out and *him* sleeping on the balcony.'

'This was last night?'

'Yeah.'

'So he was on the balcony, in a storm?'

'There's an awning on the balcony that keeps you pretty dry. I assume he was under that. I was so furious with him I just ignored him. So then this morning he's still insisting we leave, and I said I'm not going and it all started up again.'

'Oh God. Well, hopefully after we've been interviewed they'll let us go?' Becky said.

'Yeah.'

My mind began to wander. David said royalty and celebrities often holidayed here, he said they kept themselves to themselves and we wouldn't even know they were staying. I was freaking out just imagining the prospect of someone famous being involved in the death of two women. I thought about the guests I knew, like Tom and Josh – even David? Was he really asleep on the balcony, or had he slipped over the wall and bumped into Daisy wandering the cliffs drunk? At my side, the palm plant shuddered, like a breeze had wafted through, but there was no breeze, just hot, heavy air that never moved. I wiped my wet brow with a tissue and tried to put David's flirtatious behaviour into context. It was just who he was, and he liked women. It didn't mean he attacked Daisy. I was being obsessive and possessive again. I had to check myself, I could get so carried away, and it drove David mad.

'I can't believe it,' Becky was saying, as I now dragged myself from a horrible vision of David 'taming' Daisy with his hands around her neck; I told myself not to be so stupid. This wasn't an Alfred Hitchcock film, it was real life, and beautiful blonde women didn't get killed just for being beautiful and blonde. Still it wasn't adding up, I was scared, and the very fact that I even considered David to be in any way involved made me realise, I didn't *really* know my new husband. And that was the scariest bit of all.

ELEVEN

DAISY

It was horrible. All Daisy could remember was getting on the boat with Tom and the police officers, and she suddenly felt woozy. She thought it might be travel sickness and she turned to Tom to ask for her water bottle, and next thing she knew she was waking up in a hospital bed. She could barely open her eyes, and when she did, she wished she hadn't. Tubes were coming OUT from her arm, a machine whirred next to her and some weird guy was standing above in a white coat, looking down into her face.

'We don't expect there to be any long-term damage,' he was saying. Disorientated, Daisy was back in Goa where she'd spent her 21st year smoking too much weed and dancing on the beach. She could hear the sound of a drumbeat in the distance, then realised it wasn't a drum but the sound of her heart. She was scared; where was she and why was she here? She opened her mouth to ask, but everything seemed so far away, and the drumbeat in her chest and head drowned out any other sound. She slowly, carefully, lifted her head to ask what happened. She gathered breath, opened her lips, but every time she tried to speak, nothing came out. She recalled a gloved hand clamping down on her mouth. She couldn't even scream, and now she tried. Very hard. Her eyes were screaming, her lips were stretched so taut they were white. But no sound came from her mouth.

The previous night, Daisy and Tom had had a terrible row – a vicious, blood-curdling thing that seemed to have been building up between them for years. All the disappointments, the terrible loss, had weighed down on both of them, but just kept bubbling away until it was ready to erupt. It was a long overdue stream of consciousness from both of them, wrapped up in hurt and suppressed rage at the injustice of their lot. Their feelings were so raw, their words so visceral, that Daisy felt now that even if they'd both walked away, the row would continue.

'You have to stop mourning for something you've never had,' he'd cried. But that was the problem, her grief wasn't something she could take off, like a coat. Daisy's loss was part of her, it was seared into her flesh, it filled her mind, and she mourned for what she'd lost in the past and what she'd never have in the future. How could she say goodbye to all that?

The fact that a murderer was at large wasn't even a consideration, and in that moment the prospect of real danger didn't scare her. In truth, if she'd been given a choice, she'd have chosen death over this terrible limbo she'd been living in since she and Tom had lost their son. So, unable to take any more pain, she'd simply run away. She hurled herself into a raging storm, wearing only a thin summer nightdress, her feet bare. She was so desperate to be anywhere but with him, in that hot airless room with all the hurt and blame and guilt crowding in on them.

Daisy ran, and ran, and ran. She ran through the hotel lobby, out into the gardens and up through scrubland onto the cliffs. She didn't know where she was going or what she'd do when she got there. She just remembered a coastal path she and

Tom had walked, on their first day on the island. The rain lashed, thunder clapped and the lightning bounced around the sky like fireworks on the fifth of November. But, as she slowed down to catch her breath, even in the noise and chaos of a storm at night, Daisy had this feeling she wasn't alone. It was a primal thing; at first, she felt it in her gut, then she realised the splashing sounds had a regular beat to them. *Someone was running after her.* Was it Tom? She hoped it was, and stopped and turned around, but in the rainy blackness she couldn't see anyone. She told herself the sound must be wind whipping through the tree branches, or even the beat of the tide. She could see from the path that the waves were high – the ocean had been caught up in the drama of the storm. So she carried on running, but again, she heard what sounded like heavy, splashy footsteps in a rhythm behind her. Now she could feel the presence; someone *was* behind her, and they were getting closer, and closer. So she tried to run faster, but was aware even in the dark that she was running towards the edge of the cliffs. All she kept thinking was, *this is what happened to Stella, and now it's going to happen to me.* But she was trapped, and had no choice because if she changed direction she'd just be running into whoever was pursuing her.

She quickly turned her head. Someone was definitely running towards her, and she was shocked at how close they were; within seconds, her pursuer was right on her heels. As she turned, she saw their arms outstretched like they were reaching for her. But they were faster than she was and grabbed at her hair, pulling her to the ground. It was muddy and she slipped, falling easily and landing heavily. Then they jumped on her. Strong hands now clamped around her neck. She was vaguely aware they were gloved hands. She lay there thinking, *this is it, I'm going to die tonight.* And for a few seconds, she almost let it happen. Daisy almost gave in and slipped away. And why not escape the agony she'd lived with for the past few years, and leave behind a future that held nothing but emptiness? But just as she felt herself going, something surged through her, and she wanted to stay, she wanted to know how her story ended. She looked up into her attacker's face. They were wearing a hoodie and a mask, it was impossible to see who they were. And somehow she found the strength to bring her knee up hard into her attacker's groin. She heard a roar of pain. It was a man; she hadn't been sure before but the noise was a male voice. He rolled off her, groaning, as she clambered to her feet, flailing around in the mud and the rain. She started screaming and running back in the direction of the hotel. She didn't stop screaming or look back or slow down until she reached the lobby. And now she was in a white room. Tom was there too, she could hear his voice.

Tom was saying a prayer to whoever was listening, promising that if Daisy came through this, he would live a better life and take care of her better. He hadn't left Daisy's side since she was brought into the hospital earlier that day, and now he was just talking to her on a loop. He'd been doing this since they arrived, and later told her the doctor had suggested it might help, as Daisy wasn't in a coma but may need to be 'ushered back in.'

So Tom kept talking to her, apologising for arguing the previous night, and for saying some of the things he'd said. Then sometime in the afternoon, he started talking, really talking in a way he never had before. 'I know you think I don't care, that I don't feel your pain, but I feel it as much as you do. I wanted to be a dad as much as you wanted to be a mum. It kills me that we lost James, and I think about him every day. I'll never take him to school, to football, never read his bedtime story, and it's always there that "never" word, but we can't tear each other or ourselves apart over it. We'll never forget him, he'll always be a part of us, of our lives, but I think it's time to accept there won't be another James. That's what this holiday was for, to adjust and accept what the future is going to be without him, or any other James or Emilys or mini Toms and Daisys. Why don't we just make this a great life together, the two of us? It might not be the shape we'd planned, but it can still be a *good* life. We can still fill it with love and happiness, and we can laugh again, like we used to. I can live without children, but I can't live without you, Daisy.'

And suddenly she felt her left eye twitch and she seemed to move and groan, and then her eyes opened wide, like she was still in shock. Scared of what she might do, he stepped back a little.

'Daisy, Daisy...' He kept calling her name while pressing the buzzer to bring in one of the medical team. Two nurses appeared within seconds and started to rub her legs and arms and talk to her. Soon Daisy was sitting up in bed, a little dazed, with a cup of tea.

The nurses had alerted the doctor, who introduced himself as Dr Krishnan. Along with Tom, he was clearly delighted at this development.

* * *

Later that day Daisy was discharged from hospital and at the request of the police, she and Tom returned to the island. She was now lying in the oversized bath back in their room, while Tom dropped rose petals onto the water. He looked at her through the steam. Their eyes met, and she felt like she was falling in love all over again.

'Thanks for being there,' she said contentedly.

'I hate that someone did this to you,' he said, his anger bubbling under. 'If I ever find out who it was, I promise you I'll kill him with my bare hands. Don't worry, I'm staying right by your side from now on.'

'Thanks. I just wish I could remember something about him, anything to help the police, but I can't.'

She touched the thick, white dressing on her head, stained pink with blood, and Tom winced. She could see how he hurt for her, and she started to realise how much they had to lose if they didn't fight for what they had.

'I'm scared, I feel so weak and vulnerable, I hate it,' she cried. Tears were beginning to stream down her cheeks.

'I feel like the answer's in my head, I just need to find it.' She said this like a big, long sigh, the warmth of the steam prickling the pores in her skin. She felt exhausted and her head was showing her things she couldn't comprehend. The steamy warmth mingled with the pungent smell of roses, took her off to a street market in Marrakesh, myriad sounds and smells moving her as she strolled through her own crazy, head.

'The mind is a beautiful and terrible thing,' she murmured, repeating the doctor's comment earlier. She was still confused and wasn't sure where she'd heard it – perhaps among the rose petals in Marrakesh? She tried to close her eyes, but every time she did, she heard thunder, saw flashes of lightning and felt the gloved hands around her neck.

'Tom, what if whoever hurt me meant to kill me? What if they come back and try again? I feel like I can't trust anyone?'

When he didn't answer, she slowly opened her eyes and through the steam she saw him just watching her.

TWELVE

BECKY

After the storm, the heat returned like a bad friend. The hotel has been taken over by the police who've still had no break-through in finding Stella's killer, *or* Daisy's attacker. I wonder if they ever will. Meanwhile, everyone's scared, and both guests and staff want to leave the island, including me and Josh. Even the hotel's old-world glamour seems shabbier than when we arrived; the crystal chandelier doesn't glitter, and the opulent colour palette has faded into muted shades. The cocktail bar's ornate glass ceiling and huge windows are still beautiful, but instead of inviting in light, the sun on the glass is turning it into an oven. The heat throughout the hotel is even more intense. You can't escape it. Like a stalker it follows us, creeps around and settles wherever we are, making us tired, tense and argu-mentative. And in this hot, claustrophobic setting, friends are questioning friends, wives are looking differently at husbands, no one trusts *anyone*.

There are rumours too, of course; they slide under our table, squirm around the bars and the pool, surprising, frightening, sometimes amusing. They keep us going through the long, enclosed days, where we can't go outside unless in groups, and stop us sleeping on the long hot nights. This doesn't feel like a holiday anymore, it feels like a prison sentence. We can't even go to the beach alone because it isn't deemed safe. Plus, the police are down there searching and we can only walk in certain areas, and quite frankly it would seem inappropriate anyway to be frolicking just yards from where someone lost their life. So when we aren't congregating in the bar or the library or sitting by the pool, we are confined to our bedrooms. And they are unbearably warm, but no one is comfortable opening any windows in case *he* tries to break in.

So essentially, this means we're all stuck in a hot room with our spouses – it's like lockdown all over again, and the tension is real. As David has said rather ungallantly on the matter, 'I can't spend all day with Sam, it's supposed to be a holiday not a punishment.' But the theories are fascinating, and as everyone's bored and looking for some kind of entertainment, their imaginations have gone wild. It started with Paulo – of course it did. He apparently pushes women off the cliffs, then feasts on their remains, been doing it for years apparently.

Along with other lurid and outlandish tales about pretty much every member of staff, the guests are also centre stage. I only hear about everyone *else's* husband, because one rarely hears rumours about their own – *the wife is always the last to know*. There have also been rumours involving the supernatural, mostly that the actress who threw herself off the cliffs years ago is back to wreak revenge, along with the couple who killed themselves. But the one doing the rounds today, is that Daisy *didn't* really get attacked, and just made it all up for attention. Who knows the truth? The police can't seem to find anyone, she can't seem to remember anything about him, and – again rumours – the police can find no physical evidence the attack took place. I reckon she was attacked, but the torrential rain that night washed everything away. After all, the bruising around her neck is pretty physical – but no one wants to squash a good story, and the idea she made it all up seems to be the favoured one. I hope she's okay; she and Tom didn't come down to dinner last night, which isn't like them.

In the middle of all the fear and tension, and silly story-telling, the focus is fear. People are scared. I'm terrified. At the same time, like when so many bad things happen, there's often an unforeseen flip side as something good emerges. I welcome the sense of community this terror has created. Sam and David walked an older lady to her room after dinner last night and checked inside her room before she went in. Josh has started a daily walk for anyone who feels they need exercise and doesn't want to be stuck in the hotel all day. At night everyone gathers together in little groups after dinner there's lots of mutual support and camaraderie, and no one leaves anyone on their own in a public area. I feel guilty that I'm enjoying this, but we take our pleasures where we can at times like these. The main thing is, we're all together and aware that as long as we *stay* together, we are safe.

But on the downside, I think being trapped here is making me paranoid about everyone, even Josh. He's been so tense, and I'm sure I'm not imagining this, but it started when Stella died. I keep wondering if he *saw* something, if he *knows* something? But then I remind myself that there are other things playing on his mind, like work and money, and me. The pressure on him isn't helped by the fact the police are being really vague about when we can leave the island. They don't seem to realise that people have lives to return to. I'm *desperate* to see my children, and Josh is worried about his job. I know his boss has been giving him a hard time recently about having so much time off, and I think he's concerned this could be the final straw. That's why we were so keen to leave, but yesterday, in spite of the police's request we all stay, a group of guests were packed and ready for the boat – it never came. I hope they find the killer soon, because people can't be stuck here indefinitely. Added to which, it's the hottest summer on record in the UK, and the throbbing, relentless heat is making everything intolerable. When it isn't boiling hot, there's a storm on the way and even stepping outside, it feels like hot air is being pumped into the atmosphere. The air-con in the hotel is old and doesn't work properly, so there's no relief, not even in our rooms, so no one's sleeping either.

'I just feel permanently exhausted,' I say to Josh when he finally turns up from his run and we head for a coffee by the pool. I was hoping to see Daisy and Tom here, but she's probably still shaken up from yesterday.

I fan myself with the coffee menu and fill Josh in on all the news about the police, and the rumours and what everyone was saying this morning in the lobby.

'Honestly, with this hotel as a backdrop it feels like we're in an Agatha Christie crime thriller on the TV,' I say.

He stares at me with this really weird look on his face.

'What?' I ask.

But he just shakes his head.

'What's wrong with *you*?' I ask again. It's not like him to sulk.

'Nothing, I just wish you wouldn't keep going on about it. A woman died and another woman's been attacked. The police are everywhere, it's tense, horrible – this isn't a crime thriller, Becks, it's real life.'

'Calm down Josh,' I say under my breath. 'Just because I'm talking about it doesn't mean I don't care about the people involved.'

'I'd just rather you didn't *keep* talking about it.'

He doesn't wait for my response. Instead, he calls Paulo over and orders some coffee for himself and the dreaded green tea for me.

I'd rather have met with Sam instead. At least she doesn't judge me for taking an interest, for God's sake there's been a murder and an assault now and it seems only the women want to talk about it. We both sit in silence for a few minutes watching other people on their holiday, rubbing in sun cream, jumping into the pool complaining of the incessant heat. They're desperately trying to enjoy themselves, but the holiday is over for all of us. We just want to go home and know we're safe and won't be murdered in our beds at night.

'Okay?' Paulo says, suddenly at our table, placing the drinks carefully down, looking at me in a way no one has looked at me for a long time. I blush slightly. I know his type, he's a flirt, but he goes too far.

'Thank you,' I say, looking at him. He gives me a wink.

'How are you guys today?' he asks. 'Is this weather warm enough for you?' He does a mime of wiping his forehead and we both laugh politely.

'We're hot but good,' Josh says with a smile.

Then Paulo unexpectedly leans in, one hand on the table between us. 'I'm not supposed to talk to the guests about this,' he says. 'But have you been interviewed by the police yet?'

We both shake our heads. 'Have you?' I ask.

'No, not yet. I don't know the ladies,' he adds.

'You probably know Stella better than we do, you worked with her?' I say.

'I don't mix with my work colleagues,' he replies, shaking his head vigorously. I realise then he thinks I'm trying to accuse him of something.

'I didn't mean—'

'I didn't know Stella, I *worked* with her but I didn't know her,' he's saying as he walks away, leaving me open-mouthed.

'That was odd,' I say.

Josh rolls his eyes. 'I *told* you not everyone wants to talk about it, Becks.'

I take a breath. 'It was *him* who brought it up not me. What is it with you at the moment, Josh? You've been in a really bad mood the past couple of days.'

'I haven't.' He takes a sip of coffee. 'I'm fine,' he adds with feigned lightness.

'You just seem really irritated by the slightest things, and if I so much as mention anything to do with the... the... suspected *crimes* or whatever they might be, you get really angry.'

'I'm not angry, I'm *not*,' he snaps, slamming his cup in his saucer and splashing coffee onto the table. 'It's just that too many people want to get involved, everyone has an opinion, but no one *knows* anything.'

'Oh, I think you're being really cynical, Josh. People are concerned, they're upset and scared. Even I'm a bit scared I might be attacked or drowned or—'

'That's why when I'm not around you need to stay in the room, don't go wandering off.'

My heart sinks at this. I don't want him using this as an excuse to treat me like a bloody prisoner even more than he usually does.

'I have no intention of staying in my room night and day,' I say, feeling like one of the kids when they're told to go to bed.

'I only say that because I worry about you.'

'I'm here to enjoy myself, that's what you said, and sitting in a hot hotel room waiting for you to come back from a run is *not* enjoying myself.'

'I'm not surprised you're fed up. After dinner, all you seem to do is talk to Sam and Daisy about who killed Stella and who attacked Daisy. It's not healthy, Becks.'

We finish our drinks without speaking and wander back to the lobby where people are waiting to be interviewed by the police.

We sit down in silence. I glance over at Josh and wonder what he's thinking. Guests and staff are milling around, no one can settle and I feel like everyone seems to be pretending like they have nothing to hide – but everyone has something to hide, don't they?

'Josh... why don't we have a landline in our room?'

He looks at me, and after being married for so long, I know when he's about to tell a lie. Before he can speak, I carry on.

'Everyone else has a landline, it isn't part of the hotel's "holistic approach" not to have a landline, is it?'

He looks surprised at my anger. I've tried not to be angry about anything recently, but I can't help it. He's lied to me before, and I hate how it makes me feel.

'Did you move the telephone?'

'No.' He tries to look puzzled, but Josh is a rubbish liar.

'So why is it wrapped up in your sweatshirt in a drawer in our room?' I ask coolly.

He takes a breath, or perhaps it's a gasp. Before he can answer, the door to the spa opens and a police officer appears in a cloud of jasmine and bergamot. He appears to have a list of names. He apologises for taking up our holiday time, and promises to get through the interviews as quickly as possible.

'I... I feel sick,' Josh mumbles. His face is ashen.

'Is it the heat?' I ask, but he just shakes his head, and to my horror I see real fear on his face. 'Becks...?' he starts, but before he can say anything else, his name is being called.

'Josh Andrews?' says the police officer. 'DCI Granger is ready for you now.'

Josh reluctantly follows the officer down the corridor, not looking back. I feel really strange, what was he about to tell me?

THIRTEEN

SAM

I was in *bits*. What had happened to Daisy freaked me out on so many levels, and I could barely sleep just thinking, *who's next?* In the end, David gave me one of his sleeping tablets, and eventually I fell asleep, but the following day I felt like shit. At breakfast I'd had to wear sunglasses, because my eyes were all puffy from crying, and I couldn't face a full fry-up, which isn't like me – I just sipped on a black coffee. Meanwhile, David was on a full fry-up with two eggs.

I was becoming aware of how self-absorbed David was. It was four days since we'd found Stella's body, and only the day before yesterday Daisy had been assaulted – yet here he was tucking into breakfast and behaving like nothing had happened. His only reaction to Daisy's assault was to try and leave the island 'because I have a business!' I was torn between being angry at his apparent lack of caring about Daisy, and relieved because it showed that he wasn't planning a fling with her, after all. The trouble was, my husband liked women and didn't even try to hide it. I'd seen the way he looked at Stella, and how he couldn't take his eyes off Daisy in her neon bikini. I'd also watched her challenging David, flirting with Josh, ruffling his hair and teasing him about his running. And all the time, I'd watched David watching her, and wondered if he wished he was married to someone like Daisy instead of me.

Before we'd arrived on honeymoon, I'd been so sure of David, but from the moment we stepped into the lobby of Fitzgerald's, I'd let my mind run away with me. I'd imagine I'd seen him looking at every woman in his midst; the previous day, he'd been looking over at some woman by the pool, and when she went inside, he said he needed the bathroom and headed in after her. He was gone so long I thought he might be meeting her in secret, but eventually I found him in the bar. I'd been cheated on so many times I just didn't feel able to trust a man again. I thought I'd feel different being married, but I was as insecure as ever. I reminded myself that he was adjusting too. Because Marie had been so clingy, he just assumed I was the same. But I didn't want to spend my honeymoon trying to second-guess my husband, so it was best not to ask too many questions, or he'd accuse me of being possessive again.

Still, my jealousy aside, I didn't feel completely sure of David as a person. He obviously had a soft spot for Stella and then Daisy, and now I was questioning whether he really was on the balcony all night when Daisy was assaulted. He could so easily have slipped down over the balcony, or even walked across to the next one and down onto the lawn. These thoughts had been plaguing me. I didn't need bloody sleeping tablets, I needed to know the truth.

'David, can we talk?' I said later that morning as we lay by the pool.

'Of course,' he said with a smile, turning from his book to look at me.

'It's just that – I feel you've been a bit distant these past couple of days.'

He took a moment to register this, and seemed genuinely

surprised. 'Oh, Sam, I'm sorry, have I been neglecting you?' he said, touching my upper arm, beginning a slow caress.

'Do you want me to make love to you more, is that what you're saying?'

'No, everything in that department is fine,' I said. It bothered me that he seemed to think sex was the cure for everything. He leaned towards me for a kiss, and as our lips met I felt that rush I always felt with David. We had a connection, but I was beginning to wonder if it was simply lust, not love... He *told* me he loved me several times a day, but usually when we were making love. And how could I resist him? He was incredibly handsome, seductive, confident and I'd fallen quickly. But what if I'd fallen *too* quickly? After the whirlwind, the romance, the attention, the apparent caring, a different man seemed to be emerging.

I just hoped that if I shared my fears with him, he could reassure me and we'd be fine again, and live happily ever after.

'So what is it you're so keen to talk about?' he asked, folding the corner of the page and putting down his book, like he was indulging a child.

'It's just that the last couple of nights I've been lying awake...' I paused. 'I was thinking about Stella and now Daisy too...'

He looked right into my eyes so deeply I felt exposed, but it was good, it's what I wanted – I had his attention.

There you are, I thought. I hadn't lost him after all, he'd just been away a while. His hand left my arm to touch my face, while his eyes danced on my breasts.

'Come on, talk to me,' he murmured in his bedroom voice, the intimacy now thick between us. I hoped he wasn't going to try and derail this with sex. He seemed to do that a lot, never took anything seriously, apart from sex. I sat up on my sun lounger and he watched as I swung my legs to the side and put my arms around myself.

'I still have this vision of Stella lying on that beach,' I said, staring ahead, remembering the beautiful blonde hair crusty with sand, her body twisted in death. 'I can't get it out of my head.'

'I know it's not easy, and so horrible for you, because you found her.'

'Yeah, it's changed me, this whole experience has made me question everything. I've started to see people differently, and no one is who they seem,' I said. 'My mind is constantly racing, thinking, "Did he do it? Did *he* do it?"'

He nodded.

'I mean, Josh was out running on the night Stella died, he was on the beach when Daisy was assaulted – who goes jogging in a storm?'

He raised his eyebrows. 'Certainly not the obvious thing to do.'

'And Tom, he let Daisy go off into the night after a row?' I leaned forwards. 'I heard someone say they didn't believe she was attacked. What if it was Tom who attacked her, and that's why she isn't offering any identification, because she's covering for him. If so, he might have killed Stella. I saw him talking to Stella a few times while he was sitting alone at the pool bar.'

'Yeah, yeah, and Tom's quiet but he can be quite confrontational, he has a temper. I can see why he might be a likely suspect.'

'But that's the problem, if you look around us, *everyone* is a suspect – everyone has a motive. Daisy said the receptionist told her Stella was bothered by a creepy guest hanging around, you said yourself that could be any one of the men in the hotel.'

He shifted uneasily at this and lifted his hand, his body language subconsciously rejecting this. 'When I said that, I *was* joking.'

'Many a true word spoken in jest,' I replied. 'And the truth is, any of the male guests could have said or done something inappropriate or propositioned Stella.' I paused. 'And perhaps she threatened to tell his wife?' I allowed this to sit for a moment, watching his face for clues.

He shrugged dismissively and looked into the distance. 'Who knows?'

'So, what I'm trying to say is, I've been imagining all these scenarios. And... and then you've been so distant since... well, since Stella's death... and I hate to say this, but I even wondered about *you*.'

I saw a shadow cross his face, it was almost anger, but then it was gone.

He looked absolutely horrified. '*Me?*'

'I know, it's mad,' I said, 'but you weren't paying me much attention, apart from when we were in bed, I felt like you'd changed towards me. And I kept thinking about the night Stella died. I woke up and you weren't in bed...' And there it was, it landed splat right in between us. I was playing a game with him, and he hadn't a clue. I liked being in control for once.

He looked so hurt. He flinched, and instinctively moved away, taking his hand from my shoulder where it had been resting.

We both looked at each other. I felt like the world had stopped turning and everyone around us seemed to be in slow motion with their sun cream and splashes.

'I'm sorry, I just had to let you know what I'm feeling, that's what being married is about, isn't it?'

'What are you saying?' he said, trying but failing to hide his anger now.

I took a deep breath and told him: 'That I saw you outside, on the night she died. I saw you talking to Stella in the garden.'

He moved slightly then slowly stood up. I held my breath, thinking he was going to get up and walk away, that I'd just ended my marriage on my honeymoon.

But then he completely blindsided me and said, 'I'm

honestly glad you shared that with me, Sam.' He pushed his sun lounger right next to mine and sat back down, his knees touching my knees. We sat facing each other and he didn't speak for a long time, then looked at me and smiled.

'I really appreciate your honesty – it's one of the things I love about you.' He paused and took a breath. 'Yes, I probably *was* chatting in the garden with Stella, I don't *remember* it clearly, but I talk to all the staff.'

'Have you told the police you talked to her on the night she died?' I asked.

'No, why *would* I?' He couldn't hide the irritation in his voice.

'Because Granger said we should mention anything and everything, it could be the difference between stopping this and letting it drag on.'

'But it isn't relevant, we didn't talk about anything *relevant*.'

'How do you know it wasn't relevant?'

'I know it was innocent, we only chatted for about ten minutes.'

'I saw you talking to her for longer than ten minutes.'

'You spied on me?'

I wasn't surprised. This was turning into a pattern: I'd accuse him of something and he'd flip it over so I was the one in the wrong.

I shook my head. 'I saw you from the balcony. I was looking out at the stars.'

'I can assure you it was an innocent career chat, she wanted some advice and then I left her to go and have a nightcap in the bar. The barman can vouch for me if the police ever find out I was chatting with her, but they won't, will they? Because it *wasn't* relevant.'

'All I know is you came in around 2am,' I said, which was true.

'I'm sure I was back earlier than two o'clock, you were probably asleep. And I probably slept on the balcony so I wouldn't wake you.'

'What were you were doing until 2am?'

'I was *having* a few drinks,' he said, exasperated, and throwing the focus back on my behaviour added, 'so you're still having trust issues?'

'Yes, I am having trust issues, because you were out doing God knows what until 2am. I checked the clock.'

'Wow, you checked the clock? You check up on me all the time, don't you?' he sniped.

'On the night Daisy was attacked you weren't with me in the room either,' I continued, aware I was goading him, but it was true.

'I was on the *balcony*, just a few feet away. You *know* why I've slept there a few nights – because it's been so unbearably hot, you *know* that.' He was trying to sound reasonable, like he was in control, but his face was flushed.

'I couldn't *see* you on the balcony though,' I said, catching my breath.

'I was under the awning, the storm was amazing, you should have come outside and watched it with me.'

'It doesn't make any difference what you *say* you were doing. If the police ask me about the night Stella died, I'd have to say I saw you talking to her, and if they were to ask about the night Daisy was assaulted, I couldn't swear you were with me all night, because you weren't. I won't lie for you, David.'

'I'm not asking you to lie for me, I'm asking that you just don't mention these things. You're giving them far more credence than they deserve and you'll open up a hornets' nest. Why say I was talking to Stella, when I don't even remember what was said? And why say I wasn't asleep on the balcony when I was!'

I assumed he was about to storm off; it was his default position to walk away when he'd lost an argument, or he was angry.

But again, he surprised me – something made him stay. Something made him feel like he needed to get me back on side, and giving me full eye contact, he suddenly reached down and put his hands either side of my legs.

'Look, I don't want all this to come between us. What we've got is so special, and none of this matters. We aren't involved in any of it, so let's just enjoy what time we have left of our honeymoon – and no more silly talk, eh?'

'It's not silly talk, it's worrying. I feel like I don't know you, David.'

He held up both palms. 'Well, that's where you're going to have to trust me,' he snapped, then seemed to think better of it and leaned in again, placing his palms on my outer thighs. 'You're driving yourself mad imagining me being distant, coming up with all kinds of horrific scenarios involving other women,' he said. Then he moved even closer, and his voice softened. 'It's *you* who's been distant, your head's been so full of what's been going on you haven't had time for me.'

I thought about it for a little while, as he gazed into my eyes and gently stroked my legs. *Had* I been so obsessed with the murder and what happened to Daisy that I'd been in my own world and neglected my husband?

I looked at him, trying to fathom the truth from his face, but it was impossible. He could tell I was wavering.

'I'm not blaming you, darling,' he said gently, giving me his full attention. It felt good to have him close like this, and the way he looked at me was like sunshine on my face; I'd never been loved like this before. 'Someone died, and your friend has been hurt, it's frightening,' he was saying, 'and totally understandable that you'd be preoccupied, and feel out of sorts.' He kissed me on the forehead. And I felt this wave of love, far deeper than any sexual longing. I thought: *I've just told him I thought he might be a killer, and he still loves me.*

I leaned in towards him, kissing him full on the lips, my hand sliding up his bare leg, his doing the same on mine.

'I love you, Mrs Harrison,' he said.

'I love you too, Mr Harrison,' I replied. We both sat back on our loungers, holding hands, gazing at each other.

'Thanks for understanding me,' I murmured.

He squeezed my hand. 'You're bound to feel insecure sometimes, our relationship happened so quickly and we need to take our time. Unfortunately, due to no fault of our own, this isn't exactly the relaxing honeymoon we'd planned, with people dropping down dead.'

'*Daisy* isn't dead,' I reminded him.

'No, no of course she isn't, but you know what I mean?'

I nodded. 'Yes, it's been bittersweet, our honeymoon, hasn't it?'

'Exactly. But we're good, aren't we?' he asked, and again my heart filled up.

'We're better than good,' I said, reaching out and touching his chest, my fingers caressing the smooth skin, shimmering with sweat all the way down to his six pack.

'I can't sit here with you doing that, I may lose control and leap on you here, in front of everyone,' he said, his voice thick with desire.

'Do you really want me that much?' I asked, always flattered by his passionate feelings towards me.

'Yes I do, is that so strange?'

'I don't know, I sometimes wonder what you see in me when there are women like Daisy around,' I said.

'Don't start thinking I fancy Daisy,' he said with a smile. 'She's not my type, far too feisty, and she loves herself.'

'Well, I'd be lying if I said it hadn't crossed my mind, but she's really nice, she doesn't love herself.'

'She does, her Instagram is full of selfies and half-naked photos.'

'But you don't have Instagram.' I was immediately on the alert.

'Oh, Sam, you sound like a stalker again,' he said in a sing-song voice. 'Nothing untoward, m'lud,' he said, holding up his hands in a surrendering gesture. 'She showed me herself.'

'Did she?' I asked doubtfully.

'Yes, on that first day when your yoga class was cancelled and we all sat around the pool, she was showing me where she'd travelled to with work.'

I had no recollection of that at all. In fact, I was with Daisy throughout, I even left with her to find the signal. And not once did she show him her phone.

He leaned in and kissed me on my neck. It was just as thrilling as always, but I was anxious. Nothing seemed to be adding up with David, and now he wanted me to lie to the police about where he was on both nights, which made me wonder again just who I was married to.

FOURTEEN

DAISY

Daisy stood on the balcony of their hotel room and looked out, way beyond the island, into the infinity of the ocean. It was a beautiful day, the sea was glistening turquoise, the sun was beating down. And she was terrified.

There was crime scene tape on the beach where Stella's body had been discovered, and now it was also on the cliffs where Daisy almost lost her life. Whoever killed Stella, and whoever attacked her, still hadn't been found. She scanned the beach from her vantage point anxiously hoping to see something, *someone*. But Daisy had nothing. She couldn't identify her attacker, nor could she give the police anything useful. All she knew for certain was that her attacker was a man: he seemed to have a manly strength, and when she kicked him, the groan was definitely a male voice.

The police had set up an incident room in the spa, and Daisy had just returned from giving a statement to DCI Granger and her sidekick. Granger had been very sympathetic and sensitive when asking difficult questions around the attack, particularly when trying to ascertain if there was a sexual motive.

Daisy wasn't even sure of that. 'It was all one big struggle, and he may have *tried* to touch me in a sexual way, and if I'd not fought back, who knows? He might have intended to rape me. But he was also trying to strangle me, while I kicked out, and to some men that *is* sex,' she said with a sigh.

A full medical examination had shown bruises around her neck and a head injury from being pulled to the ground by her hair. Not only had he torn out some hair, but she had landed heavily and cut her head on the rocky path, which explained the bloodstains and the initial memory loss. When Granger asked her for an estimate of her attacker's height and weight, Daisy couldn't even make a guess. The most she saw was when he was trying to strangle her and even that was limited. The storm was raging, he was wearing dark clothes, and she remembered his face was shielded by a mask. Detective Granger had shaken her head at this and remarked, 'Face masks were Covid's gift to the crime fraternity. Nightmare – you can't identify anyone when they're wearing a mask, and CCTV ID? Forget it.' She shook her head in frustration and shuffled her notes, then looked up again at Daisy.

'So, you're now the second woman to be attacked, and given the first was definitely murder, we're looking at this being attempted murder.'

Daisy gasped in fear. 'That's what I was scared of. So it *is* the same man and he *did* want me dead like Stella?'

'I have to stress, we have no concrete evidence about your attacker or their motive at this stage. Nor do we have enough evidence to work out who killed Stella, but we have some theories, and there's a good chance it's the same person.' She leaned forward on the desk, and looked right at Daisy. 'I don't want to scare you, but it might be that he has a type; you and Stella are similar build, same blonde hair.'

'Christ!' Daisy groaned. 'So, he may be some nutter who

was once dumped by a slim blonde and he now hates slim blondes everywhere?'

Granger took a breath. 'Interesting theory, but we're about facts and evidence, not conjecture. All I *will* say is that there's every reason to believe whoever they are, they are still here on the island, in the hotel even, and like I said to all the guests, be vigilant. Lock your door. The officer presence has been increased, and they are aware of your status in this.'

'So I can't leave?'

Granger shook her head. 'We'd rather you didn't. You might be able to help us find who did this, you might just remember something, and of course we can't yet rule you out.'

'Me?'

Granger smiled. 'I work by the book, and I believe you were attacked, but until we have proof of that, which we don't – you could just be providing a smokescreen.'

'No, no I...'

'I'm not in any way saying that, I'm just pointing out that from our perspective, this investigation has to be watertight.' She smiled at Daisy. 'And one advantage is that here on the island everything is contained, we have reason to believe he's still here. And he could be anyone. So don't let your guard down for a moment, and stay in touch. If there's anything at all bothering you, or something you think we should know, then tell us. We'll be increasing our police patrols around the hotel, the cliffs and beach, but I have to tell you, Mrs Brown, my team are limited. Resources are at an all-time low, and there's only so much we can do to protect you, so please don't do anything to compromise your own safety.'

'You mean like wander out to the edge of the cliffs in a storm?' Daisy replied, feeling foolish.

DCI Granger just raised her eyebrows in confirmation.

'So Stella's murder and my attack are linked?' Daisy murmured.

Granger nodded. 'Very similar MO. There's just one difference – it looks like Stella's attacker strangled her with bare hands before pushing her off the cliff, whereas you say your attacker wore gloves?' she looked down to check her notes.

'Yeah, he did. So in theory it *could* be the same guy, and he's realised that he might be identified by his fingerprints on the body, or in her bruises?'

Granger had taken a breath at this. 'He might *think* that, but it's a long shot to be honest. If his nails scratched the deceased's skin, or there was some DNA from sweat that might, *might* lead us to someone. But it's complex, DNA isn't as easy as they make out in books and films – reality is a bitch.' She smiled.

'But he may *think* you can get fingerprints from bruises, so he's wearing gloves now?'

'Perhaps.' Granger conceded. 'It might be he's just being more careful. He thinks he got away with it the first time, so doesn't want to risk being caught a second. But anything's possible, and we're ruling nothing out at this stage. Be assured we have our best people on this, so you just leave all the theories to us and concentrate on staying safe.'

Daisy nodded. She was thinking about standing up to leave, but there was something about the way Granger was staring at her that made her stay seated.

The detective was now resting her head in her hands and gazing at Daisy.

'Just one last thing.' Daisy began to feel slightly uncomfortable, then Granger spoke again: 'Tell me, apart from the similarities, the blonde hair, the build – and the fact that you found her body, can *you* think of any link between you and Stella Foster?'

Daisy shook her head. Granger was making her feel uncomfortable now.

'Did you *know* Stella Foster?'

'No, not at all. I knew who she was, but I never *spoke* to her. We'd only been here a few days when she died, and in that time I think she may have served our table, but other than that I never came across her. My husband knew her better than I did.'

'Really?'

'Yes, only in passing – he talked to her at the bar when he was being served.'

'Did your husband ever say anything to you about Stella?'

'Not really. When I said he knew her better than me, that's because I didn't know her at all, and he'd just been at the pool bar a few times.'

Granger nodded, while Daisy's heart sank. She could have kicked herself, but she had to be honest. Tom had talked to Stella. He'd hung around the pool bar with her when Daisy was in the spa or the gym, or late at night he'd go 'for a last drink,' when Daisy turned in and presumably Stella was there working. But now the police might run with it, and even if he *had* spent time with Stella and talked to her at the bar, it didn't mean he *killed* her. Had she just unwittingly put her husband in the frame for murder?

'Can you think of anything? *Anything*, however insignificant it might seem?' Granger asked, like she'd seen hesitation on Daisy's face and thought she was keeping something from her, which made Daisy feel irrationally guilty.

'No... no, I can't think of anything else.'

Granger sighed and leaned back in her chair. 'Well, it's certainly a mystery. I'm convinced there is a link, however convoluted it might be. I'm just trying to think of everything. Whatever his twisted reasoning, I just hope we get him before he hurts anyone else.' She started piling up her papers and stood, a sign that the interview was over. Daisy picked up her bag and walked out of the spa, into the lobby where Tom was waiting.

He immediately embraced her and for a moment she was relieved, felt safe, until he pulled away and started firing questions at her. 'What did she say? Do they have any idea who attacked you? Did she say if they have any idea who killed Stella yet?'

'Wow. So many questions, and no to all of them,' she said spikily as she pushed passed him, but he stayed close on her heels, his face eagerly waiting for information.

'One thing Granger did confirm is that he might be targeting me, so I need to stay safe.'

Just at that moment, Paulo appeared, walked quickly through the lobby past them, and Daisy flinched.

'You okay?' Tom murmured, watching him disappear.

'Yeah, I'm just a bit jumpy, that's all,' she replied as they walked into the lift to go up to their room.

'I feel really weird,' she said once in their room. 'I feel like everyone's the potential murderer and out to get me.'

'It might be the head injury?' he suggested.

'It hasn't affected my thought processes, Tom, I'm not going mad. I think it's a perfectly normal reaction to having been assaulted,' she said, unlocking the balcony doors and heading outside. She felt claustrophobic after that interview. She wondered if Granger had been testing her when she said there was no actual proof she'd been assaulted.

'I'm not sure Granger believes I was assaulted,' she murmured, as Tom joined her on the balcony. She was still scrutinising the horizon for a shadowy figure in a face mask.

He shrugged. 'Well, they have no proof because they can't find him. You might have felt better if you'd been able to give the police some information, if you'd remembered something.'

'I might,' she responded, feeling prickly again. 'It's not my fault I can't remember. How much proof does she need, I didn't inflict those injuries on myself!'

Tom didn't respond, just leaned on the balcony rail next to her, looking out at the sea.

'She asked me if there was any link I could think of between me and Stella,' Daisy said.

'Is there one?' He turned to look at her.

'Not an obvious link, it's not like I knew her or anything.'

'No, no you didn't,' he murmured.

'But you did?'

He seemed puzzled, but at the same time she could tell he knew exactly what she meant. 'We weren't friends or anything.' He looked at her. 'Daisy, what are you saying?'

'Nothing.' She couldn't meet his eyes. She felt horribly guilty she may have dropped him in it with the police.

'I hope it is nothing,' he replied, 'because that is messed up. I *didn't* know her. I *talked* to her, she served me at the bar, said this was her second summer here and she was thinking of going back to college in September to do her master's degree, that was pretty much all she said.'

'Have you told the police you had a conversation with her?'

'No Daisy I *didn't*,' he said through gritted teeth, 'because it was *just* a conversation.'

She saw the vein standing out on the side of his head, the vein that appeared when he was angry or under pressure, and hoped to God he was telling the truth. Granger had told her not to be alone, but with his interest in what the police thought, she suddenly felt uneasy in his presence.

'I need to get out of this room,' she said. 'The balcony feels like it's getting smaller, and hotter. It gets all the heat in the afternoon, it's unbearable.'

'I'm coming with you. We've been told no one should be on their own.'

'No, I'm fine.'

'Don't be stupid, you nearly got yourself killed last time you went out on your own.'

She knew from his tone he was hurt and angry, but the idea of sitting in that sticky room with him for the rest of the day was making her feel claustrophobic.

'I am fine, I just need a break,' she insisted, and put on her sandals, and without even saying goodbye, headed down in the lift to the lobby.

The lift doors opened and warm air hit her like heavy breath in her face. Fitzgerald's felt like a different place – no hushed tones, and gentle music. Now forensic staff and police officers tramped roughly through the pastel décor, shouting orders and filling the air with crackly radio noise. Suddenly, in this petri dish of wealth and privilege where no one was ever inconvenienced or told what to do, people were being inconvenienced and told what to do.

The reception desk was crowded with guests wanting to leave, wanting information, wanting compensation; you name it, they were demanding it. Most were just desperate to leave on the next boat, but apparently the boat hadn't come that day, and probably wouldn't come the next day either. Daisy wondered if they'd ever escape from this bloody place. She wandered into the bar looking for a friendly face, but only came across David.

'We aren't prisoners. Legally, they can't *keep* us here!' he boomed from his bar stool, pint glass in hand.

'Well unless you fancy *swimming* back to the mainland, it looks like they *are* keeping us here – legally or not,' Daisy said, before going back to the lobby. She sat a while; at least she wasn't holed up in a bedroom with Tom.

'Are you waiting for someone?' a gruff voice barked. 'Because we need to clear this area.' It was a police officer. He was doing his job and obviously had a lot to do, but the tone of his voice made Daisy want to burst into tears. She realised then that they'd been so cocooned in that bubble of luxury with warm, willing staff and happy holiday people that real life felt sharp and abrupt in comparison. So with nowhere to go, and no one to talk to, Daisy decided to go back to her room.

She was too shaky to take the stairs, so took the lift she'd walked out of just minutes earlier, and pressed the button to take her to the second floor. It was a slow, old-fashioned lift which fit in with the rest of the décor. It was more ornamental than practical. The hexagonal mirrors, typical of the art deco style, were all over the walls of the little box she now stood in. She held her breath as it slowly approached the first floor, then noticed that the button was flashing – someone had called the lift from that floor. Whoever it was, would now be waiting to get into the lift and once the doors opened they could just walk in. She would be completely shut in with them; once the lift set off the doors were closed. There'd be no way out, they could do anything to her. 'Shit,' she murmured under her breath, trying to stay calm as it trundled to a jolting stop on the first floor. Her heart began beating to the tune of the machinery taking her slowly, jerkily upwards, to who knew what? Her heart beating fast, she remembered DCI Granger's words: *Whoever it was that attacked you, he's still here, and he could be anyone.* She held her breath, every limb, every sinew stretched and taut, readying herself to run. She stared at the closed doors, dreading them opening, recalling the clap of thunder and him standing there, dark clothes, a mask, a flash of lightning. And as the door slowly revealed who was on the other side, she gasped in terror, and quickly ran through the doors and down the corridor. It was only when she was far enough away did she turn around.

'What's the rush, lady?' It was Paulo. He was holding a tray, a disgruntled and confused look on his face.

'Hey, are you okay?' he called after her, but she wasn't taking any chances and set off running down the corridor again to the staircase, which in her blind panic she couldn't find. For a few minutes she darted up and down the hallway, now crying.

She could hear his voice, she had to get away. Eventually, she found the stairs and ran up them two at a time until she reached the second floor, when she did a final dash to their room and banged on the door, yelling for Tom. When he opened the door, she fell into his arms, sobbing. Eventually, she was able to tell him, and he put his arms around her.

'Babe, it's fine, you're okay, you're safe now,' he said, holding her tight. 'I told you I would come with you, and from now on I will.'

'Thank you,' she said through her tears. Any fears she may have had about her husband disappeared as he hugged her. They lay together on the bed, where she fell asleep in his arms.

When Daisy awoke, the evening sun had melted on the horizon, and Tom wasn't with her. Her immediate reaction was fear, then anger that he'd gone without a word. He'd promised to stay and look after her after what had happened. She assumed he'd gone down to dinner on his own, or was drinking in the bar and not giving her a second thought.

By the time he did turn up, she was furious.

'I've been with the police,' he said, looking exhausted. 'One of them came to collect me. He knocked on the door, and I decided not to wake you, thought I'd be back in a few minutes. But they kept me there for more than an hour.' He sat on the bed, put his head in his hands, and Daisy immediately felt bad. Was this a result of her saying he knew Stella?

'Granger was a total bitch,' he said, lifting his head.

'Oh God, was she?' Daisy felt terrible. It was probably all her fault.

'Yeah, and she kept asking me what time you'd left and why I didn't go after you, like she wanted to catch me out, like she didn't get that couples argue and one might leave.'

'I guess to her it doesn't make any sense, but it was simple, I'd had a drink, and was upset,' Daisy said. 'Did she mention Stella?'

'Asked if I knew her, I said no.'

Daisy felt sick; either Granger was testing him, or was happy with his reply. But Daisy couldn't face talking about it and Tom realising she might have dropped him in it, so she distracted him with food.

'Shall we order room service tonight?' she asked. This did the trick, and they pored over the menu, which made her feel slightly better. And after a dinner of fresh crab salad, a chilled white Sauvignon and a tart raspberry mousse, Tom stood up, held out his hand, and they walked to the bed together.

'I really don't feel like...'

'It's fine,' he said, 'neither do I. I'm just glad you're okay. It's been horrible, from the moment you found the body, to last night when... I can't bear to think about it. And then the horrible encounter with that bitch of a detective...'

'Let's just turn off the lights and lie in the dark together,' she suggested, not keen to go down that road.

'Shall I open the French windows, get some air in?' he asked.

She shook her head. 'No way, I'd never sleep. We'll have to make do with the noisy air conditioner on its own tonight.'

'Yeah, I think that is definitely the original one they installed when they built this place. What are you doing?' he asked.

Daisy was lifting their pillows, running her hands under the duvet. 'My nightdress, the pink one. I left it under the pillow, it isn't here.'

'Sleep naked, it's warm enough,' he said, climbing into bed.

'No, it's not that, it's just – why isn't it there? Have you moved it?'

'No, why on earth would I move your nightdress?'

'That's a mystery,' she murmured, climbing off the bed, checking around the room. But there was no sign of her nightdress, so she checked in the drawers. Perhaps the maid who tidied their room had put it away? But it wasn't there either. She thought about Paulo loitering in people's rooms, and the waiter from that evening with the cheeky wink who'd brought their dinner. The nightdress was under her pillow on the bed; had someone been in their room? But who would do that?

Now she was really, really scared. Turning to her husband, she heard her voice crack with fear. 'Tom, it's definitely been taken, someone's been in here.'

'What are you talking about? No one's going to come in here to steal your bloody nightdress, Daisy, what's wrong with you?'

'Tom, it could be him, the killer?'

'It could also be your head injury is making you paranoid. You're behaving really oddly, babe.'

'And so would you if you'd been assaulted and had to fight for your life!'

Tom rolled his eyes; he always implied she was dramatic, overplayed everything, but she didn't. In fact, she was under-playing the fact that she'd faced death head on. And then she realised why he wasn't taking her seriously.

'You don't believe me, do you? Even *you* don't believe I was attacked.'

He looked slightly sheepish, guilty almost. 'Yeah, I do, it's just that so far there's no real evidence.'

'So you think I tried to strangle *myself*?' she screamed at the top of her voice. Before he could answer there was an abrupt knock at the door.

'Shit, that's probably a guest complaining about the noise,' he hissed, but on opening the door, Tom stood back in surprise. In the doorway, were two police officers.

'Is Mrs Daisy Brown here?' one of them said, as Daisy stepped forwards, her mouth open in shock.

'Yes, that's me. Why?'

'Daisy Alice Brown,' the officer started. 'We are arresting you in connection with the murder of Stella Foster. You do not have to say anything but it may harm your defence if you do not mention when questioned something which you later rely on in court. Anything you do say may be given in evidence.'

FIFTEEN

BECKY

When Josh returns from the police interview, he doesn't say much. Of course I ask him, several times, what questions they've asked and if they've told him anything, but he says they haven't.

'It was just routine,' he says, but I know something is bothering him.

'Just before you went to the interview, you started to say something, like you wanted to tell me something, get it off your chest, you know?'

He flushed. Josh tends to flush when he's caught out, or shown up in some way. It's unusual in a man, and I've always found it quite appealing that even if he tries to hide the truth, his face always gives him away. Ben, our son, is the same; I always know when he's lying.

He doesn't answer me at first, just tries to look puzzled at my question, but I know him so well, and I'm not fooled by his confused expression. He knows exactly what I'm talking about.

'Josh,' I press him, 'what were you going to *say* to me?'

'Oh, I was... I... I just wanted to say that I love you.'

I'm not convinced. 'Are you okay, is it stress? I just feel like you're behaving out of character, like you're hiding things from me – and not just the telephone?' I add, making my point that I haven't forgotten that he lied to me about the landline.

He glances over at the phone, which has now been reinstated on our bedside table.

'That's what I was going to tell you,' he says awkwardly. 'I hid the phone because I wanted this holiday to be just about *us*.'

I almost laugh at this. He's never with me, always out running, but I don't say anything, just wait for further explanation.

'I knew if I suggested we disconnect it, you'd refuse, so I lied and said it was the hotel's rule. It was only so you could relax and we could have more alone time.'

I roll my eyes. 'But we don't have much alone time because you've been disappearing for hours on end.'

'Look, I've been running to clear my head, it's the only thing that keeps me sane.'

I understand this. Josh has suffered a lot from stress and anxiety over the years, and in the past twelve months this has become a lot worse. 'I know that it's an outlet,' I say, 'and it's okay but do you have to go several times a day and night too? And if so, why not at least leave me with a working phone so I can *talk* to someone.'

'I should have, but you know what it's like – the kids would be calling all the time to ask where their socks were or how to make a pancake. Then your sister and friends and your mum would be on the phone wanting to know if we're having a lovely time and wanting a blow-by-blow account. I just wanted this to be a proper escape,' he says.

I believe him; he's always complaining about me being on the phone when I'm at home, so this makes sense. And I know he's only doing it for me. 'Everything I do is for you,' he says daily, and it's true. Ever since we met on our first day in Year 12, both sixteen, both shy and quiet, we just clicked. I love him, but without the light relief of the kids, and a lifeline to my family and friends, I've found the holiday to be quite draining if I'm honest.

I'm just waiting for Josh to come out of the bathroom so we can go down to lunch, when the landline rings. When I pick up, it's DCI Granger.

'Could I speak to Josh Andrews please?' she says in a haughty voice.

I call Josh and he emerges from the bathroom wiping his face with a wet towel. 'I'm trying to cool down,' he says, by way of explanation as he picks up the receiver.

'Who is it?'

'Granger,' I whisper, and the blood drains from his face.

He says hello, then says 'yes' a couple of times, then ends with, 'Okay, I'll be down in a minute.'

I feel uneasy at this. As he puts the receiver down, I'm waiting for him to tell me.

'I take it she wasn't inviting you to lunch?' I ask.

He shakes his head. 'No, she wants me to go back down to the office, they have some new information, whatever that is.'

My heart starts pounding. I want to hug him, tell him it will all be fine. But I'm not sure it will.

'I'll come down with you,' I say. 'I'd rather sit down there on my own than up here.' For once, he doesn't argue with me and insist I stay. He just shrugs and we go down to the lobby in silence. I watch him disappear down the hallway to the spa. He passes two police officers standing in the hallway who don't acknowledge him, but I swear they look at each other after he's gone past. I'm upset and bordering on tears, when I see Sam walking towards me, I'm overcome with relief to see a friendly face.

'You okay, love?' she says. Her easy smile and open nature is refreshing in this place where everyone suspects everyone else. Just seeing her lovely warm smile makes me cry, and she immediately hugs me. I've known her a matter of days, but she feels like an old friend, and I tell her about Josh being asked to see the police again. She tries to reassure me.

'I feel sick,' I say, knowing I might be.

'Come on, let's get you outside.' She bundles me out to the sun terrace facing the sea. The sky is big and blue and despite the heat there's a fresh tang of salt in the air. She orders mint tea and cucumber sandwiches served on china plates. The tea is served Moroccan style in tall glasses with fresh mint, and though I'm worried about Josh, just being out in the open air makes me feel so much better.

'Thanks for rescuing me,' I say.

She smiles. 'It was just an excuse for *me* to eat posh sandwiches and feel like a lady. I don't often feel like a lady!' She's sitting across from me, her hair golden in the sun, her round face smiling; she's prettier than she thinks she is.

'You do realise that you have to put your pinkie finger out when you drink posh tea or it doesn't taste right?' I say.

She laughs. 'Like this?' She holds out her little finger exaggeratedly and sips on the tea, then pulls a face like she's just sucked a lemon. I smile at this.

'Do you feel better now?' she asks, genuinely concerned.

'I do, thanks to you. You're not a nurse, are you?' I joke.

'No, but a hairdresser isn't that far removed.' She smiles. 'I'm used to medical emergencies, births, tears, divorces, proposals, you name it we've had it in our salon.'

'Gosh, you could write a book.'

'Yeah, I could. We listen to everyone's problems, and you just get a sixth sense about people.' She bites into a sandwich. 'You know if they're happy or sad, or if something's bothering them?' I feel like she's waiting for me to tell her my problems.

'I can imagine. I used to love going to the hairdresser's, haven't been for a while.'

'Why?'

I waft my hand away. 'I don't have time.'

'You should *make* time,' she says. 'Does Josh not like you going to the hairdressers or something?'

'No, it's nothing to do with Josh, I'm just too busy.'

'Becky, I hope you don't mind me saying this—' she starts, but I cut in.

'Okay yes, it's a wig, I'm wearing a wig.'

She looks genuinely shocked. 'Bloody hell, that's a good wig, I didn't realise,' she says, scrutinising it from across the table. I think she's being kind, it's actually not a very good wig. 'You know, like I said, you pick up on things when you're a hairdresser?' she says.

'Yes.'

'Well, you're very quiet, and you don't drink, do you?'

'I don't drink at the moment,' I say. Why do people see someone who doesn't drink as a problem, shouldn't it be the other way round?

She doesn't say anything, just finishes her sandwich and takes a sip of her tea.

'Tell me to mind my own business...' she starts. 'But it's just that...' She looks up from her cup and saucer now. 'You said Josh told you there were no phones in the hotel bedrooms.'

I roll my eyes. 'Yeah that was a bit of a misunderstanding. He didn't want me on the phone constantly calling my mum and my sister about the kids. Or the kids calling me about everything,' I say with a smile. 'He wants us to enjoy our anniversary without interruptions.'

'Oh? It's just that he's often out running, down in the bar in the afternoons and when we ask where you are, he says you're tired and having a nap. David joked to him the other day that he locks you up in there.'

I prickle slightly at the thought of David discussing me and Josh.

She's looking at me now, checking my reaction. I just shrug – what is there to say?

'I hope you don't mind me asking, but is everything okay with you and Josh? It just seems a bit odd that you're in your room and you don't drink and he seems to be in control.'

'He isn't... well, he is I guess.' I sigh.

'I'm only asking because the other day, when we were all together at the bar, someone asked if you were okay and he said he'd locked you in the bedroom for safety. And then I heard him ask if you'd taken your pills. Is he *giving* you medication? Is *that* what makes you tired in the afternoons and he locks you in your room?'

'Yes and no,' I say, unsure if I want or need to explain my life to someone else.

'It happened to a friend of mine, her boyfriend put ground up sleeping pills in her drinks when she wasn't looking. She was like you, tired all the time, you know?'

I just listen, horrified.

'When she got to the hospital the doctor said a few more pills and he could have *killed her*,' she whispers the last two words, like she can't bear to say them. She touches one of her sandwiches, then thinks better of it and wipes her hands on the linen napkin. 'What we can't work out, is that Josh seems like a really sweet guy, and we can't imagine him being like that. David says I have a vivid imagination, he told me not to say anything to you, to mind my own business, but I feel like we're friends and if you want to talk, or you need help...'

'I had no idea we were so interesting,' I say. Perhaps I do need to have the conversation after all? She pours us both more tea, and we sit in silence sipping it.

'I feel bad now, I shouldn't have said anything,' she says.

'No, it's fine, you're just concerned for me, and when you list everything, the drugs, the early nights, Josh apparently stop-ping me from doing stuff, I can see why you might think I'm being controlled. But it's not like that... I don't really like to talk about it.'

'Oh? Only tell me if you feel comfortable,' she says. 'I want to help you and if you need to get away from him...'

I shake my head. 'I don't need that kind of help. Our marriage is good, we have two beautiful kids, and we're happy, most of the time. And when he goes for a run, I do have a nap and he locks the bedroom door from the outside, but it's for my own safety. I have a key.'

'Oh, it just doesn't make sense...' she starts.

'It makes perfect sense, because he loves me, because he's scared. Because I'm dying.'

'What?' Sam looks at me, confused, like she's waiting for a punchline.

'I have cancer, I've been told I have a matter of months.'

She drops the sandwich she's about to eat. She looks like she's going to be sick, as her face turns white.

'Oh, Becky, I don't know what to say.'

'No one ever does, it's one of the reasons I don't tell anyone, and once people do know, they treat you differently.'

'It's... I'll try not to treat you differently, Becky, I just need to process it. Is there nothing they can do for you?'

I shake my head. 'No, by the time I was diagnosed it was too late, it had already spread.'

'I'm so, so sorry.'

'Please don't – look, I want you to think of me the way you did two minutes ago. Let's pretend there's nothing wrong with me, that I'm just like you. If I hadn't told you I could still pretend.'

'Would you prefer we didn't talk about it?'

'No, not now I've told you because you'll be looking at me thinking *where is it? How does it feel? What's her story?*'

She smiles a smile of recognition. 'You're right. But this isn't about what I want, it's about you. If you want to tell me your story then do, if you don't – let's go back a few minutes and pretend you never said anything.'

'I feel like I need to explain, if only to help you understand me and Josh. It clearly looks like a really weird relationship,' I say with a smile. 'So, about two years ago, I found a lump. I was a bit concerned, but was so busy, working full-time, picking up and dropping off kids, that one month turned to two and before I knew it six months had gone by. Then Josh had some mental health issues, was stressed at work, then he lost his driving licence – he got caught speeding. So I was now the sole driver in the family and the kids needed lifts and I took Josh to work and picked him up, and there was just so much to do that I didn't have time to worry about a little lump. I came last, I guess, and by the time I took my little lump to the doctor, it was stage four breast cancer.'

Sam stares at me, her mouth open in horror. 'Oh, Becky.'

I sip my tea, recalling the mild panic in the hospital room as the doctor held my scan results in one hand and my breast in the other, he asked one of the nurses to call the consultant. That's when I knew I was in trouble. When the consultant arrived, all I remember is how much I liked her shirt, thin red stripes that reminded me of candy canes. I closed my eyes while she examined me, and looked more closely at the scan while I wondered *will I make it to Christmas?* How we fall into the familiar when everything's strange, we cling to what we know, the places in our head where we feel safe, and it seems Christmas candy canes were my go-to. The consultant was kind, but she couldn't hide the pity in her eyes as she joined the other doctor in breaking it to me that there may be 'something to be concerned about,' in the scan. After a biopsy and several days of tortuous waiting, I returned to the hospital for the verdict. Back in the examination room I felt like I was watching the climactic ending to a film – I could hardly breathe waiting for the outcome. Would I die, or would there be a happy ending?

Throughout this new examination, the two doctors continued to talk to each other in their own language over my body, as if I was already a corpse. Perhaps that's what I was to them? They knew how my story ended before I did.

'So, that's why Josh has to be with me, has to make sure I take my meds, hides the phone and stops me from doing too much,' I said. 'I hate it. I used to be so fit, so full of energy, but now I'm trapped in this useless body. I panic, and long to get out, but the only way out of this is death, and I don't *want* to die. And Josh and I don't tell people, because I don't want to be treated differently, I don't want to be "the dying woman."'

'Now you've told me it all makes sense, your lack of energy, the tiredness, the medication and the way Josh stops you from doing things. But he isn't *controlling* you, he's *caring* for you.'

'Absolutely, he's the most caring, considerate man, but he finds it hard to handle. He's never been good with reality or responsibility, that's always been my department. But he's really stepped up for me, and it takes every ounce of courage and strength for him to do that. So he runs, he *literally* runs away. Running is the only way he can cope with what's happening to me.'

'It all makes sense now. Thank you... for telling me. I realise you'd probably hoped to have this holiday without addressing all this, and I step in with my clumsy questions.'

'No. I'd rather you know the truth than think badly of Josh, he loves me so much I know it's killing him too.' I feel my eyes filling with tears, and try to blink them back. 'I remember the day I told him, it was as though I was saying *he* was the one who was going to die, he relies on me for so much. But the kids... telling the kids was the worst thing I've ever had to do, it was worse than when I first heard the prognosis.'

'I can't imagine, that must have been terrible?'

I wipe my eyes with a tissue – I always have them to hand. 'That's one of the things you do when you become a mum,' I say, holding the tissue, and trying to smile. 'You always have tissues with you, even when they are grown up. Just in case.'

'So, how did the kids take it?' she asks.

'Brilliantly as I'd expected. I know they're hurting too, but they try not to let me see. They're so protective of mine and Josh's feelings – they're like the adults really.'

'That's wonderful, I'm sure your kids are like you. Calm and wise.'

'Thank you, but I'm as flawed as everyone else and sometimes I just scream at everyone and sob and...' I wipe my eyes again, remembering how I yelled at the kids for arguing just before we came away. 'I'm desperate to see them, hug them... My time with them is so precious.'

We sit in silence and I'm aware the dynamic between us will shift slightly. There's always a bridge between revealing my status and moving forwards – it happens with new friends and old. Everyone's the same, the awkwardness, and the way they subconsciously distance themselves like I'm already gone.

'But Josh is trying to save you... at least I'm assuming that's what he's trying to do. I completely got that wrong too, I thought the running thing was just ego or something. But the charity he's running for, is that to do with you?'

I nod. 'Yes, that's a *whole* other story. Josh wants to fight for me, he won't have it that I'm a lost cause. I've had some treatment, but it almost killed me. Josh wants me to try everything, but I know it would only extend my life from weeks to months, and I don't *want* to spend those months in and out of hospital, attached to tubes. I want to *live*.'

I see her shudder at this; people find it hard to face death, even when it isn't their own.

'So, I go along with Josh's pointless dreams of finding a cure in America, because I can't bear to see *him* upset. Our time together is precious, but he just disappears for hours on end preparing for the next sponsored run, and in trying to save my life, he's *missing* it.'

'I can see that,' she almost whispers, looking at me with new eyes. But for once I don't see pity, I see understanding.

She sighs. 'I can see why you feel so frustrated, but at the same time he's just trying to save you. That's what love is.'

I feel my chin wobbling, but swallow down the tears. Sam is a good listener, I can talk to her in a way I can't to anyone else, even my sister or mum.

'I know you guys have been together a long time, haven't you?'

'Yeah, and I don't know how he'll cope without me. Sometimes I feel like there are two versions of him: the one that's helpless and inconsolable, and the other one, who wants to jump on a plane to America and find a cure. I love him, but I don't understand him.'

'Do we ever really fully understand our partners?' she asks.

'Probably not,' I reply.

'I know I don't understand David.' She sighs. 'My sister said I should wait and not marry him so quickly, but I was worried someone else would get him.' She sits back, gazing around, until her eyes alight on a glamorous young woman sitting close by.

She leans forwards, beckoning me in with her eyes. 'Becky, do you think...' she starts, and I brace myself, anticipating another difficult question about my illness in hushed tones. But she takes me by complete surprise. 'See her over there, do you reckon that's a real Hermes bag?' she asks, directing me to the bag with her eyes.

This makes me smile, and lifts my heart. I'm still Sam's new friend, and our relationship, as new as it is, isn't going to be bogged down by my illness – Sam won't let it. Sam is going to keep talking handbags and husbands and let me live until I die.

'I've no idea if it's Hermes or not.' I giggle.

'I reckon it is, but there are so many good fakes around these days you just can't tell at a distance.'

'And I wouldn't recommend going over to her and inspecting it,' I said.

She laughed. 'Who cares? I think the sun's over the yardarm, don't you?' She calls over a waitress and despite my objections, orders two large G&Ts.

'Josh will go mad. He says alcohol's poison to me.'

'Oh, if you'd rather not I understand.'

'No, let's go for it,' I say, feeling a rush I haven't felt for a long time.

'Becky, would you ever lie for Josh?' she suddenly says.

I feel a prickle of unease. Does she know something about Josh, has she heard something?

'It depends, why?'

'It's just that... I keep thinking about something David said.' She looks away from me then back again; she clearly has something difficult to tell me.

'What?' I blurt, then hold my breath. What now?

'Well, David has asked me to say I was with him the night Stella died, and then when Daisy was attacked.' I'm shocked at this... What's he up to?

'And was he?'

'Not really.'

'Then you can't lie to the police,' I say.

But before she can answer me, one of the managers appears at my elbow to tell me it's time for my interview with the detective. I look across at Sam. 'I have to go, but let's talk about this later?'

She nods, and I walk to the interview with a million thoughts in my head. David definitely has an eye for the ladies. He was always at the pool bar where Stella worked, he said himself in that horribly disrespectful way – that every red-blooded male at the hotel liked to look at her. And perhaps the tension between him and Daisy is sexual on his part? He's constantly trying to engage her in battle, seems to want her attention and may have watched her leaving the hotel and followed her and ran out after her. I don't want to break Sam's confidence, but it would be in everyone's interests if the police know about this. I'm still trying to work all this out when I see Josh on the other side of the lobby. He's sitting with his head in his hands, and when I call him, he doesn't seem to notice me. I turn away and follow the waiting police officer through to where the interviews are being held. I'm worried about Josh, but I need to be present for this interview. Once inside the spa, I become *very* present as the acidic hit of bergamot and the sweet stench of sandalwood whacks me in the face. Stacked shelves of miracle skin cream line the walls and sitting beneath a poster of a woman lying face down with stones on her bare back, is DCI Granger.

'Good afternoon, Mrs Andrews, please take a seat.' She doesn't smile. 'As you know, we're speaking to all the hotel residents regarding the death of Stella Foster and the subsequent assault on Daisy Brown. And now we'd like to ask *you* some questions about anything you may have seen on the dates these unfortunate events occurred. Please remember that this is now a murder investigation, so anything, however small, could be significant. But let's start on the evening of Stella Foster's murder,' she says, taking out her pen. 'Where were you and what do you remember?'

My finger ends tingle, and the sickly scent of sandalwood stalks me down the wood-panelled corridor. I just told Sam she mustn't lie to the police for her husband, but there's lying and there's hiding the truth. Are the two things different, and would I be lying to the police if I fail to tell them that my husband was out running on the nights both women were attacked?

SIXTEEN

SAM

I was disappointed not to see Daisy and Tom at dinner again. I'd called her on their room phone, but there was no answer, which was odd.

'I wonder if Daisy's remembered any details about her attacker?' I said to David as we ate our starters.

'I don't know, but when I just went to the bathroom, she was being escorted out of the building by two policemen. She was in tears.'

'Oh God, David, and you didn't think to mention it?'

'I've only been back at the table two minutes, and to be honest, it does seem to be one long drama with that one. First she's the one to find the body, then she's the one to be assaulted... a lot of what's going on around here seems to keep coming back to her,' he said.

'When you put it like that, she has got a bit tangled up in everything, hasn't she? Poor Daisy, she's really been through it these past few days, but I don't think she's *involved* in any way, do you?'

As I waited for a response, a waitress brought a jug of water to our table. She was young, her uniform tight, and David watched her as she bent over to place the water before us. Her breasts seem to brush his arm; it wasn't my imagination, he noticed it too because I saw a look pass between them. It was a moment, blink and you might miss it, but she flushed and we both watched her as she left our table.

'Have you ever had a threesome?' he asked casually, his eyes still lingering on her as she walked away.

I almost choked on my wine. 'No, I haven't.'

'Are you shocked at me asking?' he said, his eyes now dancing.

I looked into his face, trying to fathom out whether he was teasing me again. 'I am shocked, yes, it's not something I'd ever want to do,' I said, which was a lie. I had thought about it, and the very idea of watching the man I adored with another woman was my idea of torture.

'Oh, Sam, you're so bourgeois,' he said affectionately.

'One of my clients has regular threesomes,' I said, so he'd think I was worldly and not being a bore.

'Oh, you must invite her over sometime,' he replied, with a smile. He was teasing me, but the way he said it made me wonder if he meant it on some level. I wanted to ask him if *he'd* ever had a threesome, but I could guess what his answer would be, and I didn't want to hear it. I knew what he'd say and it would make me feel inadequate and jealous. I wondered if he used to make Marie feel like that.

He was still watching the young waitress, and I wanted him to think I was sophisticated enough to be okay with it.

'She's pretty,' I said. In response, I saw his jaw twitch. Was it anger at me, or just the embarrassment of getting caught looking at a pretty girl?

To my surprise, he moved his chair round the table to be closer to me, his place settings now too far away. He was always doing stuff like that; just when I thought he might be angry, or I'd upset him, he'd behave in the opposite way I expected. And other times, when I thought we were happy and he was feeling affectionate, he'd say something I hadn't anticipated, like, 'You've put weight on,' or 'Darling, you look really old tonight.'

But now he was being lovely, sitting right next to me, his arm around my waist, kissing my neck.

'You can't do that.' I giggled. 'Not here, in the dining room.'

'I can do anything I want to,' he whispered in my ear, his hand moving around my waist. And then it began, the gentle touch of his fingertips circling my body. Even though I was fully clothed, I felt this jolt of lust like electricity. I was suddenly weak, shaking as flames began inside me. Now he was caressing my bare back, his fingers soft and warm playing with the shoulder straps, then continuing the smooth, gentle, circular touching, before reaching for my hand, and looking into my eyes. Just until I was his again.

'I wouldn't want to do a threesome, but it's not because I'd be jealous,' I lied.

He didn't answer me.

'It's just that I sometimes think you just assume that all women are the same. That I'm the same as Marie, jealous and...'

'Shh, it's over now, we're safe from her. We're safe,' he murmured into my neck, where his lips now kissed me, and I let out a discreet groan. My insides unfurled, desire creeping through me like a sleepy cat waking and stretching.

I'd never had this kind of passion with anyone else. He knew just what to do to possess me. And looking back, I can see now how the sex obliterated any doubts I may have had about David and me. Sex with him was like a big eraser; it wiped everything clean.

I'd thought we could do the same with Marie, just wipe her away. I'd have moved to another country to escape her if he'd wanted to. He'd told me all about her crazy jealousy, how if he was working late, she'd be on the phone every five minutes, accusing him of having sex in the office with one of his colleagues. She once even FaceTimed him in a hotel bedroom when he was working away. She was so convinced he was with another woman, she demanded he show her every nook and cranny of the bedroom. Understandably, those events had scarred him and he had become intolerant of any kind of jealousy or possessiveness. I did wonder if there was more to it and perhaps David had played around while they were married. But I hadn't truly understood what he'd been through until we'd been together just a few weeks and she started calling me, leaving threatening messages, telling me they were still together. David said she was crazy. He told me he was taking out an injunction against her and suggested I put my social media on high privacy settings. 'She might be knocking on your door if she has any idea of where you live,' he'd said. Apparently, she'd once turned up on one of his female friend's doorstep with a kitchen knife in her pocket saying 'something was going on.'

'And don't walk home alone,' he'd warned, 'take a taxi.'

Later on, during a particularly manic phase, she'd followed me to work, calling after me and peering through the window of the salon. I'd been so scared, all my colleagues were on high alert and locked the doors if they saw her hanging around. Once they even called the police and she went crazy. David said that might teach her a lesson, make her realise how serious it all was, but it didn't stop her.

She'd call me late at night. God knows where she got my number, but I'd pick up to silence, then after a few seconds hear her draw breath. Then it would start: 'He's not the man you think he is... He can't help himself... He's a cheater, always will be... He hates women, he uses them... He only wants women for sex.' The worst ones were when she'd call and say, 'He was with me tonight, slept in my bed, sorry but he's hard to say no to, isn't he?'

I tried to rub her words away, but when I was on my own

and David was out or working away, everything she said was like a wound, and each wound left a scar. I swear I heard her voice even on my wedding day, during the vows. But the scars she'd left were reminders, doubts, nuances, moments when he'd glanced at a waitress, held another woman's hand a little too long, or whispered to them in French. And in those moments, I heard Marie drawing breath and whispering in my ear: *See? I told you.*

'You're very pale, darling, are you okay?' David said. 'Here, have some more wine.' He was pouring a second large glass of red for me and I was immediately whisked back into the present.

'Sorry, I was just thinking about Marie. Poor Marie,' I said.

He stiffened but touched my chin with his finger and gently lifted my face. I felt like he could see Marie loitering in my eyes. Pushing her away, I took a large glug of wine. I still would have preferred white, but David always chose red. So I drank red.

'Sorry, I don't know why I mentioned her, I just think of her sometimes.'

'It's our honeymoon, Sam,' he said with a sigh. 'It would be good if you could *stop* thinking about my ex-wife... God knows I have.'

'Can you *blame* me after what happened, David?' I asked incredulously.

My affection for him was often quickly replaced by anger, an anger that bloomed in my chest and caused me as much pain as it did rage.

'I'm still getting over it, that night at her flat changed me... I will *never* forget...' I murmured.

'Sshh. Don't upset yourself, I told you, you're safe now.' He was stroking my hair like I was a child about to have a tantrum. 'I know, I know, it must have been terrible, I'm so sorry, darling.'

'I shouldn't have even gone there, it was all part of her plan obviously,' I said, pushing his hand away, aware a tear was snaking down my cheek. 'I just wish she'd left me alone.'

'You need to stop torturing yourself,' he said, his demeanour suddenly changing again. 'I sometimes think you want to talk about her, it's like you're obsessed, you want to know everything about her, about us.'

I prickled again at this. 'David, I'm not some love-struck teen, jealous of the girl before me. I just find it hard to understand why you don't share my guilt, when it was *you* who left her.'

His face flushed with anger. 'Sorry, I can't listen to this. I'm tired of your... *obsessions*,' he spat, throwing his napkin onto the table. I expected him to storm out on me, but he didn't. He did the opposite of what I expected, and stayed where he was in his seat glaring ahead, refusing to even look at me.

I took another glug of wine, and then grabbed at the bottle, pouring more into my glass. I was already feeling tipsy, but I didn't care. I just wished we had the marriage I'd thought we had when we arrived here. I didn't want another night of arguing, not speaking to each other, so I held out the olive branch.

'David, let's not argue again, let's just have dinner and—'

'Let's just have *dinner*?' His voice was raised. A couple of diners glanced over, but he carried on. 'This afternoon, you accuse me of wandering the beach at midnight when Daisy was *supposedly* assaulted. You've been quizzing me about bloody Stella Foster for days... and now you're back on the Marie bandwagon. We're on our *honeymoon*! What's *wrong* with you? You're bloody *paranoid*!' he hissed, his face a fury in red.

And there it was again, the whispering, Marie's voice in my ear: 'He's the psycho, but he'll convince you *you're* the one who's mad!'

The waitress arrived with our starters and I tried to concentrate on the food in an attempt to blow away the spectre of Marie.

I replaced my horror with a smile as the waitress plonked down my plate then carefully laid David's before him with another lingering look. Then along with the rest of the guests, we silently devoured the tiny bodies of sea urchins hiding under a wispy veil of parmesan tuile, finished with a truffle purée and an acidic squeeze of lemon. I swallowed the food, all the time trying to push her away, but she was as insistent as ever; she lived in my head. Only now it wasn't the screeching madwoman, or the sinister late-night whisperer that I saw, but staring eyes in an eerie silence. I shivered at the memory and even though it was sweltering, I felt the need to pull my pashmina around my shoulders.

I emptied my glass, aware David was looking at me, I really couldn't work out whether he was going to tell me he loved me, or get up and walk away. He'd abandoned me at parties and restaurants however his mood took him, and just as I was waiting for him to leave, he said, 'Let's order more wine, shall we?'

I shrugged. Our relationship had gone from being the most secure and happy I'd ever been in, to the most uncertain and insecure. Being with him had changed me for the worse, and I realised that night how much I now hated myself.

He suddenly called the waitress over and asked her about the main course. 'I enjoy my lamb pink,' he said. And the way he looked at her when he said this, the way the flat of her palm caressed her own neck as he spoke, told me that another conversation was going on beneath the one I could hear.

'I know what you're doing. Don't try and make out I'm the crazy one,' I said too loudly.

He stared at me, frowning. 'What on earth are you talking about?'

If I'd been sober, I wouldn't have raised my voice, or said any of the things I did. But the red wine was thrumming through my veins and I had to speak the truth. 'You know exactly what I'm talking about. Marie was right, you're a cheater, you aren't capable of love.'

'Please don't make a scene,' he muttered as the waitress discreetly walked away. David shifted uncomfortably in his seat and smiled wanly at the next table who were staring.

'Just calm down,' he murmured, looking around the dining room to see if anyone had heard me.

'No, *you* calm down,' I snapped back again, just as loudly.

We sat in silence until the waiter arrived with more wine and made a huge performance, offering us both a taste. I shook my head vigorously when he proffered the bottle over my glass. 'No, let *him* do it,' I said, like I was bored. But David ignored me, and went along with the charade, as the waiter poured with a flourish, twirling the bottle around as he did. Then the interminable wait while David swilled it round in his mouth and gave his approval for the waiter to pour for us.

'Perfect!' he said, then muttered something in French and the men both laughed heartily while I sat there like an idiot.

'Such a performance,' I hissed as the waiter left. 'I mean we can pour our own bloody wine. And you can speak bloody English!'

'Just because you only speak one language and don't know anything about wine? And as for the waiter pouring me a taster,' he continued, now in full force, enjoying every word, savouring every morsel of insult. 'They might not do it at the kebab shop where you used to dine on the pavements before you met me, but in a decent restaurant, *that's* what waiters do.'

'Oh fuck off, David.'

'*There* she is, you can take the girl out of the slum but you can't take the slum out of the girl.'

Was that how he saw me? Did he view our union as an act of charity, some Pygmalion fantasy where he 'educated' the peasant in the ways of the middle classes? I wanted to cry, but wouldn't give him the satisfaction.

Inside I screamed and raged, while he turned around to see if anyone had spotted his red-faced, angry wife. It was then it dawned on me: he actually got off on making me feel bad, causing me emotional distress. It made him feel like he was better than me, because in his eyes it kept me down, made me feel bad about myself. He was happy as long as I was grateful and behaved myself, but the minute I questioned him, he turned on me.

Meanwhile, my own anger was rising by the second. I slammed down my glass, red wine spattering on the white table-cloth and hitting his white shirt. I sat and waited for the rage, for him to say something vicious and spiteful that would cut into my flesh and leave a gaping wound. But no, he sipped his wine and took his time gazing through the window at the now dark-ened sea. I sat in silence opposite, as the moon trickled an eerie light through the windows. I knew then this wasn't right, and my whirlwind romance hadn't been a fairy tale after all. I began to ask myself the question I really didn't want the answer to. What really happened between David and his first wife?

SEVENTEEN

DAISY

Daisy was terrified. Being in a police cell was a horrific climax to everything else she'd been through. The officers had taken her on the boat back to the mainland and delivered her to Newton Abbot Police Station, where apparently senior detectives now wanted to ask her some questions regarding the murder. No one was really telling her anything. She'd been locked down on an island, and now she was locked in a prison cell, and she couldn't stop crying. Panic and fear were filling her chest, and despite telling them that she might have a panic attack any minute, no one cared enough to find her a paper bag to breathe into.

Throughout the boat and car journey, she'd cried, shouted, protested her innocence, and asked for a solicitor, who was apparently on her way. She was at a complete loss as to how things had escalated so quickly, and how the police could possibly believe she'd murdered Stella Foster. How had she become implicated in the girl's murder? She didn't have to wait too long to find out, because soon she heard the rattling of keys and a bolt being moved, then an officer opened her cell door to take her to the interview room to meet her solicitor.

DC Jody Cotton looked very young, but in her neat blouse and skirt and short hair, seemed organised if nothing else. She asked Daisy some basic questions, wrote stuff down and explained the process.

Daisy was tired, her head hurt and she was finding it very hard not to cry. But every time she thought about the look on Tom's face when she left their bedroom with the officers, she burst into tears. He'd looked horrified, not at the injustice of what was happening, but at Daisy herself. 'No. Oh, Daisy. No,' he'd murmured, as she was being ushered out of the room. She'd tried to tell him that it was all a big mistake, but he didn't seem to want to listen, just closed the door quietly before she was even gone from the hallway. That had hurt more than any of this.

She sat with her solicitor, wondering how to convince them she wasn't lying, when the door opened and in came DCI Granger. She'd brought along another detective, an older man who was introduced as DI Firth.

'So, welcome to the bright lights of Newton Abbot,' Granger said, without smiling. She took a seat at the table opposite Daisy, as did DI Firth, and they both looked at her for a few seconds. Daisy wasn't sure if they were trying to work her out, or smoke her out, but either way, it was very uncomfortable.

'So...' Granger eventually came to life and started going through notes and turning the tape on to record the interview. 'Now, we have some questions for you, Mrs Brown.'

'Daisy, call me Daisy please.' The formality was killing her, making her feel even more alone and alienated. She cleared her throat. 'I just want to say, I'm happy to answer any questions, I want to help you, trust me we're on the same side.'

'Mmm, trust is a funny old thing, isn't it?' Granger looked at her, and Daisy felt like the woman could see inside her head, and every bad thought she'd ever had. 'Because when we last spoke, I felt like you were on the level, Daisy. And as hard as it is for a woman in my profession, I felt like I could perhaps even *trust* you.'

'You can...' she heard herself reply weakly.

'Apart from the obvious – that you've been arrested on the suspicion of murder, did you know that giving false information to the police is an offence?'

'False information? I didn't give—'

'Oh but you did, and that could lead to a fine, a conviction for wasting police time or even a prison sentence – on top of anything received for murder – for the more serious offence of perverting the course of justice.'

'I haven't murdered anyone and I *was* assaulted, I didn't lie about that. I know people are saying I did, but why would I?'

'Why indeed? But it's all getting a bit muddy and I now need you to tell me what really happened with you and Stella. And of course, the "assault"?'

Daisy's solicitor was about to step in, because it seemed like Granger was throwing everything at her client, but before she could, Granger moved on from the appetiser to the main.

'In fact, the assault isn't why you've been arrested and brought here for questioning today,' Granger announced.

Daisy didn't know whether to be relieved or worried.

'Though I have to warn you, we are still investigating your attack, and if there is anything you'd like to tell us, something you may have previously *forgotten* about, now would be the time to share.'

Daisy understood now what Tom went through during his interview. The woman was a sarcastic bitch who seemed to be enjoying this torture.

'What I *told* you was all true, I just hope you can find him so he can't hurt anyone else.' Daisy touched the bruises on her neck to make her point.

'So, as I said we're still investigating the assault, and as yet we haven't found anything that would implicate or identify another person on the cliff path that night.'

'Well you wouldn't, it was pitch black in a storm,' Daisy shot back, knowing she wasn't helping herself, but feeling angry at the sheer injustice of this.

Granger didn't respond to her minor outburst, just gave her a look that said, 'you'll regret that,' and moved on. 'So, you may recall at our last meeting, I asked if you knew Stella Foster.'

Daisy nodded. 'Yes and I said I knew who she was, but didn't *know* her.'

Granger looked down at her notes. 'What you actually said when I asked if you knew Stella Foster, was, "No, not at all. I knew who she was, but I never *spoke* to her. We'd only been here a few days when she died, and in that time I think she may have served our table, but other than that, I never came across her. My husband knew her better than I did."

'Tell me something, Daisy, were you trying to throw your husband under the bus? Trying to point us in another direction?'

'No, I have no idea what...' Daisy looked appalled. 'I'd *never* do that, not to *Tom*.'

'So, you're *still* saying you didn't know Stella Foster?'

'I *didn't* know her.'

'So why were you messaging each other on Instagram?'

'What?' She looked at her solicitor and back at Granger. 'We *weren't*.'

'You followed her, she followed you, and you messaged each other eleven times.'

'No! I have a lot of followers, it's my job, I work in fashion – but I'd have realised if I was following Stella. And I'd certainly know if I was messaging her.'

'Would you like to *read* those messages?'

'Yes, but they don't exist. I didn't *know* her.'

Granger pushed the transcript of the direct messages across

the table at Daisy, who picked them up eagerly, desperate to find out what was going on.

'But these aren't messages to Stella, these are to Pink Girl... oh no.' Daisy dropped her head into her hands.

Granger looked around the table, then back to Daisy, who emerged slowly from her hands, pulling them back through her hair as she did. 'Pink Girl was Stella's online name?'

'You didn't know that?' Granger asked, like she didn't believe her.

'No, if I did I would have said, I would have told you at our first meeting. Pink Girl wanted work experience, or a job – anything, on the magazine I work for. You can see that by the messages, they're clearly business.'

'And you didn't think to mention this?'

'No, of course not. I didn't know it was her, so there's no obvious link, is there?'

'But she knew who you were?'

'Yes, because I post under my *real name* – she didn't. How could I possibly know that was the same person working in the hotel. There probably aren't even any selfies on her page, because she was a photography student; she took pictures of places and other people, not selfies, so she wasn't identifiable.'

'You say your husband talked to her?'

Daisy felt Granger's devastation. Her face had dropped, no more perky, sarcastic remarks.

'Yes, Tom chatted to her, and come to think of it, she told him she was a student.' Then Daisy remembered. 'He described her as an art student, which she probably was – she must have specialised in photography. It's semantics, but that's why I didn't even think about her being the same person. There was nothing to say she was.'

'Okay.' Granger almost seemed resigned to losing this one. 'Just one more thing?'

Daisy's heart hit the ground.

'You and your husband have a happy marriage, do you?'

Daisy looked uncomfortable; she wasn't even sure Granger was allowed to ask this, but as Daisy's solicitor wasn't objecting, presumably she could.

'Yeah, yeah, we've had our issues.'

'Issues?'

'Well, we lost a baby, and it's not been easy for either of us.'

'I'm sorry about that, I really am,' Granger said.

Daisy shrugged.

'A troubled marriage, as I'm sure you'll appreciate, can lead to people doing silly things, acting out of character.'

Daisy groaned inwardly. You couldn't say *anything* to this woman without her turning it into a motive for bloody murder? 'It's not a troubled marriage, I never said that.'

'It's just that you ran out of the hotel into a storm the other night, so desperate to get away from your husband you didn't even get dressed. And then tonight when my officers came to your room to arrest you, apparently there was a lot of shouting and screaming.'

'It was a stupid argument, we're trying to work on our marriage, that's why we're here, to deal with our problems.'

'Do you worry that Tom might talk to other people about your problems?'

'No... do you mean other women?'

'Someone like Stella?' Granger suggested.

Daisy immediately reacted. 'Did he talk to Stella about things like that?'

'I don't know, I just wondered if that's what had upset you?'

'Look, nothing *upset* me. I'm not the jealous kind, but if my husband was telling *any* other woman intimate stuff about our marriage, I'd be upset.'

'You would?' Granger wrote something down.

'Yeah, wouldn't you?'

Granger didn't answer. She kept writing for a little while, then suddenly looked up.

'You're now free to go Daisy. If you stop at the desk on your way out the sergeant will discharge you.'

'And that's it?' she asked, shocked and relieved that this had all come to an end.

'Yep, that's it, but we're still asking for people to stay on the island until further notice.'

'Okay,' Daisy said. She stood up, thanked her solicitor then walked to the door.

'Oh, and Mrs Brown?' Granger said.

Daisy turned round.

'Remember we're still investigating the assault you reported, so we may need to invite you back,' she added, with a warning look. It chilled Daisy to the bone.

EIGHTEEN

BECKY

Josh has gone for a post-breakfast run, and rather than stay in the room, I'm sitting by the pool reading my book. Suddenly, a shadow comes over the sun. I look up, and there's Sam. She's standing above me in a bright peach kaftan, with matching neon lips.

'Daisy was arrested.'

'What?'

I pull myself up from my recumbent position on the sun lounger.

'Daisy. I saw Tom just now, he's in bits. Apparently the police came to their room and took her to the mainland for questioning.'

'Oh my God!'

'She spent the night in the cells, and now they're letting her go. She's on her way back from the mainland.'

'Do we know why?' I say, as she clambers over me to take the sun lounger to my left, moving Josh's T-shirt and book.

'No, Tom doesn't know either.' She raises her eyebrows and settles herself down.

'I don't believe it.'

'I know it can't be true, but they must have something on her?' She gives me a look of concern.

I am stunned. 'This has been such a weird experience, I didn't think it could get any weirder, but it just did.' I turn to Sam. 'I don't believe Daisy has done anything, do you?'

Sam gives a long sigh. 'I don't think she's actually *done* anything. But there's been talk about the assault, that it might not be quite how she told it.'

I shrug. I'd heard that rumour swirling around the hotel, but didn't want to believe it.

'She said herself she can't give the police any information about him,' Sam continues, raising her eyebrows. 'I like Daisy, and I don't think she would lie. But I haven't known her a week, how well do any of us know each other?'

'True, but why would Daisy make up something like *that*?' I ask.

'Perhaps she wanted Tom's attention? They rowed, she stormed off, he obviously hadn't run after her and she wanted to make him feel guilty?'

'Mmm, I could see that, I suppose.'

'Me too. And I know we look at them both and think what a gorgeous couple they are and assume they're happy, but the other day, before they went to the hospital, they seemed really angry with each other. She told him to piss off.'

'I can't imagine that.'

'No, I was surprised too, but it made me think, perhaps they aren't who we think they are? Perhaps their marriage is in trouble?'

'Who knows what goes on in other people's marriages?' I say, not willing to speculate. 'But if someone did attack her, it's got to be the same person who killed Stella, so let's hope they find him soon.' I glance at other guests around the pool. 'It could be anyone.'

'Even our husbands,' Sam replies. She obviously wants to tell me something.

'Yes, you told me yesterday that David had asked you to lie to the police for him?' I say. She pauses as if she's trying to work out what to say. 'If you'd rather not say what it is he doesn't want you to tell them then it's fine,' I offer. After all I wasn't sharing my doubts about Josh, so why should she?

She looks uncomfortable. This isn't easy for her. 'No, I do, because I'm worried about it. You said yesterday I should tell the police, but it's really quite incriminating.'

'Isn't that even more reason to tell the police?' I say gently.

'I suppose so, but I don't want to get him into trouble if he's innocent.'

'So what is it that he wants you to lie about?'

'He wants me to say I was with him all night when Stella was killed and when Daisy was hurt.' She turned to me. 'But what really bothers me is that on the night she died, I saw him chatting to Stella in the hotel gardens.'

'Have you told him this?'

'Yeah, and he says she asked him some career advice, which I find hard to believe. I know it doesn't *mean* anything, but he's also saying he was drinking in the bar until after 1am, but he can't prove it because the bar shuts at twelve, so the barman would have left.'

'He could still have been there though, it becomes an honesty bar after midnight and the staff leave.'

'Yeah, he could, but Elizabeth who cleans our room has a nephew on the police force, and she tells me all sorts – she calls me Miss Marple, reckons I'm trying to solve the murder myself. Anyway I asked her if the police knew what Stella's time of death was. She said it was after midnight.'

'And he wants you to lie to the police about where he was and not mention that he was talking to Stella?'

'Pretty much.' She nods slowly.

'Perhaps you should tell the police?' I suggest. 'Granger said *anything* and *everything*, however insignificant.'

'I can't tell the police I think my husband's a murderer. What if he isn't?'

'But what if he *is*?' I say. 'If he's innocent, why is he asking you to lie?'

'That's what's worrying me.'

'You told me yourself that you feel like you hardly know him. It *can't* do any harm just to speak to that detective. Imagine how you'd feel if someone else is murdered and they discovered it *was* him?' I point out, knowing that I'm a hypocrite because who knows where Josh was on those two nights?

I can see by her face she's sorry she told me. 'I'm probably overthinking it,' she says, clearly trying to back pedal. I decide to back off. I've said all I can, it's up to her now.

Just then I see Josh walking along the edge of the pool towards us, and I'm about to wave, but something in his demeanour stops me. His head's down, his hands are in his shorts' pockets and he looks like he did the day I was diagnosed – like he's carrying the weight of the world on his shoulders.

'Hi, are you okay?' I ask as he joins us, sitting awkwardly at the bottom of my sun lounger as Sam is spread out on his.

'Yeah fine.' He nods to Sam, who looks up expectantly, waiting for his usual light-hearted banter.

'Nice run, Josh?' she asks.

'Yeah, yeah.' He doesn't look at her.

'Think I'll head back to the room, do you have your key?' he asks me. I'm disturbed by his abruptness. This isn't like him, but I don't say anything in front of Sam. He clearly doesn't want to share whatever it is that's upset him.

'I'll come up to the room with you,' I say, sitting up and tying the halter neck of my costume.

'Don't leave on my account.'

'No, I want to go inside now, it's getting too hot for me.' I smile, hoping he'll mirror it, but he doesn't. In the corner of my eye, I see Sam watching us like a game of tennis.

'Okay, if you're sure?' he says.

'Yes, this heat is exhausting, I need to rest.' I pick up my beach bag, which Josh automatically tries to take from me.

'I carry it,' I say, pulling away. I wish he wouldn't treat me like I'm unable to look after myself. I know he means well, but he makes me feel claustrophobic, especially in this heat. Plus his mood has affected me. I went from enjoying chatting with Sam to feeling hot and irritated, not to mention worried. I don't know what's happened, and I'm not asking him in front of Sam. It's like a hotbed of suspicion here, everyone is looking at everyone else and we're all letting our imaginations run away with us.

'See you later, Sam,' I say, 'thanks for the coffee.'

She gives us a wave with her fingers as we head away from the pool. It's a suntrap and stifling, and as we walk the heat seems to radiate from the paved flooring. It's surely as hot as Greece. There isn't much relief as we enter the lobby; apparently the rubbish air-con has now broken, and like everything else here, someone from the mainland has to come and fix it. But that won't be for a couple of days. I try not to think about the heat, I just waft a brochure from the lobby table in my face. I'm desperate to get Josh on his own to find out what's happened.

'Josh, what is it? You seem upset,' I ask, the minute the lift doors close and we're alone.

I hear a deep sigh. He's looking down at the floor. I catch myself in the reflection of the jagged mirrors on the lift wall and I'm shocked at how thin I am, how gaunt my face is.

'I don't know where to start,' I hear him say.

I instantly forget how I look. Now I'm seriously worried. I take a deep breath and ask myself how bad can this be given the fact I have possibly weeks to live?

'You're scaring me.'

'Sorry. I came back from my run, and Granger asked to see me *again*.'

'Oh? I think the police are panicking,' I say trying not to panic myself at this news. 'They arrested Daisy last night. Apparently she spent the night in the cells on the mainland, she's back now – and so is Granger by the sound of things?'

'Daisy? What the hell? Why did they arrest her?'

'No one really knows, Sam reckons there's a theory she made up the assault. It might have something to do with that?'

'Well, of course she did. She can't identify anyone, there's no evidence whatsoever, the police have been scouring the area where she says it happened and found nothing. No clues, no weapons, no DNA...'

'You know a lot about it.'

'Yeah, well on the group walks I've been chatting to the officers. I think they doubt her story too.'

'Oh dear, nothing and no one are as they seem, are they? Okay,' I say, trying to sound calmer on the outside than I am inside. 'So why did Granger want to see you?' I hear myself croak.

'I can't talk here.'

'Is it to do with Stella?' I almost whisper this, partly because I don't want to be heard, but also because worry has eaten into my voice box and I can't speak.

I wait for his reply, holding my breath.

He nods. Slowly. I feel like I've been punched; my legs start to buckle under me.

'Are you okay?' he says, reaching around my waist to hold me up.

'Yeah, I shouldn't have sat so long in the sun. I feel like I'm on fire,' I hear myself murmur. Then everything goes dark.

. . .

I wake up in bed in our room, and Josh is sitting beside me.

I sit up, slowly, looking around feeling disorientated.

'You're okay, Becks,' he's saying, as he holds a glass of water to my lips, stroking my forehead with his other hand. 'Just a bit of sunstroke I think,' he's saying. 'I was just about to phone for a doctor.'

'Josh, *why* do the police keep wanting to talk to you?' I ask. It's the first thing that comes into my head and I just say it.

He takes the glass away, puts it on the bedside table then holds my hand with both of his.

'I don't want you to get upset.'

'I won't. Not as long as you tell me. And not as long as it's the truth.'

'Okay, then I'll tell you.'

I nod. I'm unable to speak, I just want to know so I can deal with whatever it is.

I'm composed, I'm back in my default coping mode, back to clearing up Josh's mess. I look up at him expectantly.

He takes a deep breath.

'Just tell me the truth. It's not like you're guilty of anything, are you?'

But the look on my husband's face tells me he is.

NINETEEN

SAM

I'll never forget seeing her that night, the night she came back from the police station. She was perched on a bar stool next to Tom, a beautiful dress, perfect make-up and the big white bandage round her head. I didn't care why she'd been with the police, or what she might have done; I went over to give her a big hug.

She seemed genuinely touched. 'No one seems to want to talk to us, I'm the pariah of Fitzgerald's,' she said, her eyes filling with tears.

'Rubbish, *I'm* here, aren't I? And David, and I'm sure Becky and Josh will be over once they're down. You've been having a really hard time, haven't you, love?'

She nodded. 'It's been horrific.' She shook her head slowly, and I got the feeling she wasn't going to share. It all felt a bit awkward and I was relieved when David appeared at my side and filled the silence with a stupid joke. And after hugging Daisy, he shook Tom's hand. 'Congratulations, mate, you got her back,' he said. 'Let me buy you both a drink.'

Things had been a bit rocky between David and me, but after an afternoon in bed, we were back on an even keel. I was feeling happier and more secure, even if he did touch Daisy's bare back a little too long when he greeted her. But I was aware I needed to chill; being married to a good-looking man who had charisma was never going to be easy for someone with my low self-esteem. But I knew if I allowed it to get to me and gave in to every little paranoid thought, I might destroy what we had. So as long as he wasn't cheating, what harm did some light flirting do? And when he handed me a glass of chilled Prosecco, I pulled him aside and gave him a little peck on the cheek.

'What was that for?' he asked, smiling.

'For being you,' I replied. I then rejoined Daisy who looked lovely, but she'd lost some of the glitter from her eyes, and I couldn't help but wonder what was going on with her and the police. She clearly wasn't going to reveal it, so I'd have to keep wondering.

Even with a great big bandage over one side of her head she still looked like a film star, platinum hair, immaculate make-up and shiny red nails, sitting there in her white silk dress holding a Bloody Mary cocktail in her hand. It made me recoil, because it looked like a glass of blood, and I caught David staring too. I wondered if it had the same effect on him. But if it did, he wasn't showing it, because next thing, he was holding his glass high and announcing to the whole bar, 'Daisy's back, as beautiful and brave as ever!'

Oh, how he loved to praise women, all women – except his wife.

Daisy grimaced and looked uncomfortable. I doubted she'd want her arrival announced like she was some visiting celebrity. I had the feeling she wanted to keep a low profile after being arrested. There'd been a gruesome murder, a suspected assault, and whatever the truth of that, it really wasn't appropriate to celebrate anything or anyone yet. But David was just being kind and charming, and sometimes he didn't read the room.

'He's quite a charmer,' I said, by way of apology to Daisy in case he'd embarrassed her.

'Quite!' She smiled, but her eyes weren't smiling.

'Hey, Tom, I bet you're so relieved to have her back?' I said, trying to move the conversation on.

'Yeah, so relieved,' he said, gazing at her.

'So what are you doing down here, why aren't you two in the bedroom?' David said.

'David!' I looked at him disapprovingly, but he didn't even notice me.

'We're good, thanks for asking,' Tom snapped sarcastically.

'Another drink?' David asked, but of course Tom wanted to buy them for fear of being emasculated, so they both went to the bar to fight it out there.

'I love your dress,' Daisy said, and I was about to thank her when I saw Becky. I called her over and we moved to a large table together.

'Are you feeling okay after the assault, you must have been in deep shock?' Becky said, tactfully avoiding any mention of the arrest.

'Yeah I did... it's happened to me once before, shock I mean. I went into shock and couldn't speak for two days.'

'What caused it the first time?' I asked.

'Oh just... someone hurt me, but apparently these things can recur, like a scar on your brain apparently.'

'How awful,' Becky said.

'Yeah, it's been a tough couple of days,' she said with a sigh.

'She's all good now aren't you, babe?' Tom said, putting his arm around her shoulder and looking into her eyes. 'I can't begin to even think what shape my life would be without her in it.'

They seemed happy, gone was the anger and the blame. This was who I thought Daisy and Tom were, loving and happy, despite their past problems. But I was still really curious about Daisy's police encounter. What was that about? I wondered again if anyone was who they presented themselves to be.

I looked around the table. David was telling a joke (of course he was), Tom was whispering into Daisy's ear and Josh was smiling at Becky. Her revelation that she was living with cancer explained an awful lot. And tonight, when Josh ordered Becky a sparkling water or fruit juice, or discreetly put her meds in her hand, or gently put a cardigan around her shoulders, I knew why. I had totally misjudged their marriage and I'd definitely got everything wrong about Josh. He was warmer and friendlier than I'd realised; he'd been a bit shy to start off with and probably needed to get to know people first. I think Becky took longer, and when Josh leaned over to talk to Tom and Daisy she suddenly seemed lost.

Daisy was obviously telling Josh about the attack, and I could see by his reaction how caring he was, asking questions, and most of all asking Daisy how *she* felt. Daisy seemed to be opening up to him too and I could now see why Becky and Josh were together; they were both sensitive and caring. But I felt a bit sorry for Becky now Josh was involved with Daisy and her story, so I pushed my chair closer to hers and said: 'I *love* your dress, that colour really suits you.'

'Thanks, Josh likes it too, but it's far too big. I've lost a lot of weight.'

'I wish I could lose weight, the food here is so good none of my clothes will fit me by the time I leave,' I said, blowing out my cheeks.

She laughed. 'I envy your curves, I had them once – enjoy being healthy,' she said.

'I would, but David might divorce me if I got fat,' I joked. I saw her face tighten.

'Sam, you are lovely, and no one should be using anyone's weight to threaten them.'

'Oh he doesn't, I was just joking,' I lied. 'We're fine, me and David.'

'Are you? Good. Did you decide not to speak to the police?'

'Yeah, for now,' I said. He'd probably divorce me if I did.

'Well, that's your choice,' she said. 'But just be aware of your value, and if he does ever threaten divorce, know it's him who'd be the loser.'

'Who's getting divorced?' Josh said in a jokey way, turning to join me and Becky in the conversation.

'No one,' I said, 'not tonight anyway, I think all six of us are happily married tonight.'

'I'm happily married all the time,' he said, and I felt the weight of his sadness as he reached for Becky's hand and gently took it, resting it on his knee. As we talked, I was aware of him stroking her palm like you would a child. It was as if he was comforting her, and letting her know he was there. I thought about them meeting at school. Teenage sweethearts with their lives ahead of them, then young parents, and a happily married couple heading into a gentle middle age, grown up children, grandchildren – until this. They must have been terrified of what came next. It made me stop and think as I looked around at everyone else that evening. Who knew what was around the corner for any of us?

When David returned with my Bloody Mary, I sipped it like Daisy had hers, hoping to emulate her glamour and poise – but probably not achieving it. 'I'm coming to sit with the girls, boys are so boring,' Daisy said, manoeuvring Tom out of her way and returning back to her place between Becky and me.

'How are you feeling physically?' Becky asked. 'Has that head wound given you any problems.'

'No, it's just a bad cut, my head hit the ground quite hard.'

'Ouch,' Becky replied. 'And the bruising?' She gestured around her own neck.

'It's tender, but I've had far worse,' she said.

'Do you mind if I ask something about the attack?' I asked.

'Yeah fire away.'

'Were you assaulted, sexually I mean?'

Becky gave an audible gasp at my side. I'd probably gone a step too far.

'God, sorry I shouldn't ask you that.' I was surprised at myself but needed to know the nature of the assault. David's remark about Daisy needing to 'be tamed,' was still bothering me. He wasn't a violent man, but she had angered him; had the 'taming' comment been an indication of how he really felt. Was it a sexual remark?

If she was shocked at my question, she hid it well. She just shook her head and said, 'No. I wasn't raped if that's what you mean, but that might be because he got a knee to the groin. I hope he never has sex again.'

'Ouch,' said Becky, which made us smile.

'When I think about what Stella must have gone through it makes me so angry,' Daisy said. Her voice sounded like she was on the verge of tears. 'I keep thinking about how he must have just thrown her off the cliff, like she was nothing.' Daisy wrapped her arms around herself, a frown forming on that perfect, porcelain forehead.

'We've all got to keep an eye out for each other and be careful,' I said. 'Especially you.' I looked at Daisy.

'I know but how am I going to be careful if some crazy has decided I'm next and he wants me dead? I'm locked up in this bloody hotel with him twenty-four-seven,' Daisy said, rolling her eyes.

'I just think you need to be aware of your surroundings, who you're with,' Becky warned.

'Don't get in the lift with anyone,' I added, scaring myself now.

'It could also be that this guy picks on women who are alone and vulnerable, and both you and Stella were in the same place, at different times, but alone. So stay with Tom or one of us,' Becky offered.

'Of course there's always another theory...' I said, fear catching the back of my throat. 'You and Stella are both beautiful blondes, you're both a similar build, and about the same height. On a dark beach at night you could be mistaken for each other.'

'Shit. I hadn't thought of that,' she said. 'The madman might never have meant to kill Stella, he *meant* to kill me.'

TWENTY

DAISY

Daisy knew that throughout the evening she'd be looking over her shoulder, studying the face of every man in the bar, wondering if it might be him. It didn't help that things weren't good with Tom. As caring as he'd been when she first came out of hospital, the arrest had scared him, and she had this horrible feeling he didn't trust her. They were now circling each other. She was aware of his doubts, his lack of trust, and he seemed wary of *her*, and she had the feeling he wasn't the only one. She could see by the look on some of the guests' faces that they were less than sympathetic. Did they all think she'd made up the assault too? How quickly rumours spread around the place, especially as everyone was stuck on the island. Even the most beautiful luxury hotel palled when you weren't allowed to leave, and when people were seeking some release, what better than a juicy rumour to embellish?

Earlier that evening, as she and Tom got ready for dinner, she'd wondered what the reception would be like.

'Everyone will know about the arrest by now,' she'd said absently, as she gazed into the dressing table mirror, attempting to cover the bruises with Touche Éclat. 'You know what people are like, there's no smoke without fire,' she said in a silly voice. 'I just hope no one asks me about it.'

'What if someone asks *me* about the arrest?' Tom looked up from tying his shoelaces.

'You tell them they made a mistake, no details, no explanation – you just say *that*,' she snapped, applying the magic, nude cream briskly to her stormy purple décolletage.

When he didn't answer her, Daisy stopped camouflaging her wounds and turned to look at him.

'Tom, you *do* believe me, don't you? I mean, you know how the mix-up happened. I had nothing, *nothing* to do with Stella's death.'

'Yeah, of course,' he muttered, and it was like a punch in the stomach; she knew in that instant that he doubted her.

She looked back into the dressing table mirror. He now stood behind her tying his tie. She glared at his reflection.

'You don't believe me, do you?'

'Oh don't start on all that again, babe, I *do* believe you.' But she knew he was lying.

'There's a "but" in there,' she said, feeling her eyes well with tears. 'You don't believe I was assaulted either.'

He let out an exasperated breath of air. 'What do you want me to *say*?'

'That you believe me.'

'It doesn't matter *what* I believe,' he replied. 'It's what the police believe. You can't give them any information about your attacker, there's no forensic evidence, so in the eyes of the police, you were *either* attacked because of a connection to Stella, or you *weren't* attacked at all, and just *said* you were. And whatever the case, the assault puts you right in the middle of the picture as far as the police are concerned, and *that's* why they went through all your social media. And surprise, surprise, up pops Stella.'

'What do you mean, "surprise, surprise"? I was as shocked

as you about that,' she said, angry and hurt. 'I had no idea who she was, you knew her better than I did.'

'That's right, you're in a mess so point the finger at me,' he snapped.

'I didn't say it like *that...*'

'I can't believe how *stupid* you were to run out the other night – all this trouble has come from that!'

She was close to tears. 'Stop it, Tom, stop it!' She covered her ears.

'That's right, cut yourself off, let's not deal with it, just run away like you always do,' he yelled.

'You're the one who runs away,' she yelled back. 'I'm going through hell, someone was in our room, I don't even feel safe here.'

'You had a head injury, you were all over the place, still are if you ask me.'

'I'm fine. I banged my head, I didn't go insane. Stop gaslighting me, it suits you to believe I wasn't assaulted because it makes you look bad. You let me walk out into the dark with a killer on the loose. You never came to look for me, Tom.'

'No, I didn't because you needed to cool off. If I'd chased after you, you'd have screamed and yelled and it would have made things even worse. Yes, I should have run out, I should have stopped you being hurt, I should have stopped James from dying – but I didn't, I didn't.' He broke down, huge great sobs that racked his body. Daisy was shocked; she'd never seen him cry like that before, even when James died.

He cried for a long time, and Daisy sat, emotionally spent, unable to offer him any comfort. He eventually stopped crying, walked over to the bed and wiped his eyes with his shirt sleeve. She watched him in the mirror, remembering what he'd said to her in the hospital. 'What you told me as I was coming round was the most honest you've ever been with me, about your feelings, about James, and that you feel ready to make a different life now,' she said.

He didn't respond straight away, but when he did, he said, 'And that's what I want, a different life than the one we planned. Not worse or better – just *different*. I've accepted that we can't have children, but we can have us, and that's enough.'

She was still watching him through the mirror.

'Yeah. It's enough,' she said quietly. 'But are *we* enough. I've felt so alone, Tom.'

'So have I, my heart was broken too. But I had to be strong for both of us.'

She stood up and walked over to him.

'You don't *have* to be strong. You don't have to carry the weight of this, we can share it. And it's okay to cry about him, to rail against the unfairness and the loss, but what you said in the hospital was so true. It can still be a good life, and the most important thing is us.'

To get back to the people they used to be would take time, it wouldn't happen overnight, they had a lot of stuff to work through – but first they needed to heal.

An hour later they joined everyone in the cocktail bar and no one would have guessed they'd had a huge, emotionally gut-wrenching conversation that left them both fragile and exhausted. But for Daisy there'd been a paradigm shift, she'd seen the old Tom, glimpses of the people they used to be, and in spite of the horrible situation everyone was in, she allowed herself a little glimmer of hope. And over drinks, she went to sit with Becky and Sam, needing some female support, wanting to gauge their feelings about her after the arrest.

She hadn't intended to discuss anything too intimate that evening – everything was still raw – but after a few Bloody Marys, all three women were talking quite openly and honestly, and Daisy was telling them about the conversation she and Tom had earlier.

'I guess I didn't think he was hurting, but the truth was he just didn't want me to see it.'

'Exactly, and he's right to want to move forward. You have to find new goals, new dreams, we're lucky to be alive here and now,' Becky said, 'and I should know. So don't waste precious time wanting something that's too far out of reach.'

'I guess I saw having a baby as my achievement, something I would be giving to the world, leaving my child or children.'

'Yes, but you have other gifts to give to the world,' Becky replied.

'Yeah, you create all those amazing fashion spreads in your magazine, that's your gift,' Sam offered.

'You see?' Becky said. 'Just make them the best bloody photographs you can.'

They all smiled at that, and for the first time Daisy could begin to imagine a world where having a baby wasn't everything. Did it exist? She hoped so.

'You know, when I became a teacher, I did it because I wanted to make the world a better place,' Becky said. 'Sounds corny I know, but that's the truth, I wanted to be there for other kids who were having a hard time. But when I became ill, I had to leave teaching, and leaving my job felt like the first goodbye. I had to give up on that dream of making the world a better place, but I know that some of those kids will remember me for ever, and hopefully they will pass stuff down to their kids.'

'What do you mean, your illness?' Daisy asked, and Becky told her. She was, not surprisingly, shocked. 'I had no idea.'

'Good, that's the best compliment you can give me. And as I said to Sam when I told her – forget it now, just see Becky – not "poor" Becky.'

'I wish you'd been my teacher, Becky, I'd probably be a

doctor now,' Daisy said with a smile, and making like she'd forgotten as requested.

'You're doing just fine as you are. Just be the best you can, that's all you have to do.'

At forty, Becky was just two years older than Daisy, but she felt to Daisy like a parent. She wished her own mother had been just a bit like Becky. How terrible for her children that she'd have to say goodbye to them too soon.

'You still have a lot of life to live, is there no more treatment?' Daisy asked, thinking of Becky's children.

'Josh has set his heart on new trials in America, but they're hard to get onto, and even if I was accepted I don't want to be on and off planes and in and out of hospitals for the last few months I'm on earth.'

'*Tell* him then,' Sam urged.

'I *want* to tell him, but before we came here, he spent every waking hour working on the US trip, calling hospitals, speaking to specialists, planning the logistics, collecting the sponsor money, everything. But the thing is, I've realised, if he didn't have this, he'd have nothing – it's all he has left to cling to at the moment.'

Becky seemed on the verge of tears. 'Are you okay, Becky?' Sam asked.

She nodded, blinking back the tears. 'I'm just worried about him, like I said, he has a lot going on at the moment.' Both Sam and Daisy turned to look at her.

'What do you mean? I could tell he was upset today at the pool when he came over, are there problems with the police?' Sam asked.

Becky looked at the faces of her new friends and Daisy could tell by her face that she regretted saying anything.

Daisy touched her arm. 'The police arrested me, but they made a mistake. They're making mistakes because they're desperate to get whoever did it. If Josh has been accused of something, I had a good lawyer with me today, I could give you her number?'

'I may take you up on that, we just had a difficult talk this afternoon. Stuff I hadn't been aware of...'

'So the police are accusing Josh now?' Sam asked. Daisy winced slightly. Sam was sweet, but a little naïve and said what was in her head instead of considering her words first. And naturally, her forthright questioning often made people clam up, like now.

'Sorry I'd rather not talk about it if you don't mind,' Becky replied.

It suddenly felt a little awkward, and as the three of them sipped their drinks in silence, Daisy was a little wounded by her friend's refusal to share. Sam's abrupt questioning aside, they had all been very open and honest about their lives over the past few days, or so Daisy had thought. They'd been trapped on an island, and the situation had escalated their friendship, but Becky's reaction made Daisy realise that however close they might think they were, they were just people on holiday at the same time. And despite the long talks late at night, the chats by the pool over coffee and the shared suspicions and frustrations about their 'better halves,' they all had their secrets.

'I wonder when we'll be allowed home?' Daisy mused, in an attempt to erase the awkwardness.

'I can't wait,' Becky said, 'I've missed my kids, and my mum.'

'I can't wait to get home too. I'm so tired of looking over my shoulder, imagining him in every reflection; is he here now?' Daisy looked around the room.

'Stop, you're freaking me out,' Sam said, while reaching for her drink, but in doing so, knocked Daisy's Bloody Mary over. The sudden shock of cold liquid through her white silk dress made Daisy scream, and everyone turned around to see the bright red stain now blooming like an open wound on her silk dress.

It was horrific. Sam covered her face with her hands so she didn't have to see the deep scarlet stain slowly growing on the white fabric. When she finally allowed herself to look, her eyes locked, and she stared in sheer terror. Sam couldn't move, it was as if she been bolted to the floor.

Daisy was upset about her dress, but more concerned about Sam; she'd never seen anyone so terrified, her face was so white. Daisy didn't understand why she was reacting like this, but then Sam began to wail loudly, 'NO, NO, NO...' Her voice became louder and louder, more frantic. And the louder she was, the quieter the room, as everyone turned to see what was happening. Glasses stopped clinking, everyone in the bar stopped talking as they watched on in silence, all with the same frozen, horrified look on their faces. By now, Sam was sobbing and clumsily dabbing at Daisy's dress with a napkin, putting her right in the centre of this mortifying mess. Sam was scaring her. Daisy looked down at the poor woman lunging at her dress with the now grubby tomato-stained napkin. She was pressing down on her stomach, rubbing and rubbing, making the huge mark worse.

'It's all my fault, all my fault,' she kept repeating on a loop, through her tears.

'It's *fine*, it was an accident – it's only tomato juice,' Daisy was saying gently. Everyone in the bar was gazing over, and Daisy could only imagine what they were thinking – that she was in the middle of yet another drama. Even Tom was looking at her with a horrified expression. Meanwhile Daisy was desperately trying to push Sam away, make her stand up and stop wailing. She had to stop herself screaming at Sam to stop. Even in her distress she was aware this would make her look crazy and attention-seeking, but by now Sam was on her knees wiping at Daisy's cleavage with a napkin and sobbing in her lap.

Daisy looked around for help, but Tom wasn't moving, he was still staring in horror. Thankfully, David leapt into action and attempted to pull Sam away from Daisy.

'Calm down. She's *fine*, what the hell is *wrong* with you?' he hissed in Sam's face, but she wasn't listening.

'She's not fine! Stop LYING to me David, you're always lying to me. She needs an ambulance, before it's too late! I can't have this on my conscience too...' she cried, still trying to staunch the flow that she seemed to think was some kind of terrible wound. Daisy couldn't begin to understand what trauma Sam was reliving, but realised she needed kindness, not David's abrasiveness. So Daisy tried to reach for Sam, but she was yelling at David, and beyond any kind of reasoning. Grabbing her bag, Daisy left the scene. She ran to the bathroom, where she robotically scrubbed at the scarlet stain on the dress, which just seemed to make it worse. Finally, she looked up at herself in the mirror. Her hair was a mess, her mascara had run, and the dress... the dress was ruined, and she wondered if the same was happening to her life. She started to cry, all the fear and hurt came pouring out, and she cried until she couldn't cry anymore.

Eventually, she left the bathroom, half hoping Tom might be waiting outside, but passing the bar, she could see him still at the table, talking to Josh and Becky. She couldn't face going back in there, so headed upstairs to her room. Standing in the lift, mirrors all around her, she couldn't get away from the stained dress, the bloodstain, the fear that someone might be waiting for her on the second floor.

And when the doors opened, she wanted to cover her eyes and scream. But no one stood in front of her, and she walked out onto an empty hallway and let herself into her room, all the time looking behind her, and waiting for the footsteps.

She entered her bedroom, pulled off her ruined dress and sat on the bed, her arms wrapped around her waist, just rocking backwards and forwards in the dark, when suddenly there was a quiet knock on the door. It was so quiet, she wasn't sure if it actually happened, but a few seconds later the knock came again.

'Tom?' she called. Perhaps he had come to find her after all. Had he lost his key?

Silence, but she heard a shuffling outside the door, which creeped her out a little.

'Who is it?' she called.

'It's me,' a man's voice muttered. She switched on a lamp, grabbed her silk dressing gown slowly and nervously opened the door.

'Oh, it's you!' She had hoped Tom would have come to find her, comfort her, make sure she was okay, but he hadn't, someone else had.

'Hi, I hope you don't mind, I just wanted to check on you... after what happened in the bar,' he said.

'Oh that's so lovely of you, thank you. I'm fine,' she lied, genuinely touched. It was thoughtful of him to check on her, and more than Tom had done.

He was still standing in the doorway, and it felt awkward, so she stepped back and he walked in.

'Lovely room,' he said.

'Thanks.'

He pointed at the standalone bath in the window. 'I bet that's nice, bathing with that view?'

'Yeah, it's lovely actually.' She walked towards it, her back to him. 'You just have to make sure you close the net curtains, or everyone else would be getting a view.' She turned around to smile at this, and he smiled back.

'Yeah, and what a view that would be, even better than the sea,' he said, giving her a wink. She suddenly felt uncomfortable; it was probably an overreaction after what happened to her, but still she felt uneasy in her room alone with a man.

'I think it's time you went back to the bar,' she said, tapping her index finger on his chest in a gentle reprimand.

'Sorry, that was a bit forward of me,' he said. 'I guess it's just being alone with a beautiful woman.'

It was then he reached out, putting his hand inside her dressing gown.

'Hey.' She flinched, moving away a little. God, he'd obviously got the wrong idea. She liked him, but not in that way. She'd been here before, with men who thought that, because you gave them attention, smiled and were polite, you had the hots for them. She'd now have to let him down gently.

'My husband is due back any moment, and he's the jealous type, so I think you need to go,' she said firmly, still keeping the tone light. She didn't want to embarrass or upset him.

'Your *husband* has just ordered himself and everyone else a round of drinks, he's going to be quite a while.'

'Oh, well I'm off to bed, so...' She moved towards the door touching his back, hoping he'd follow.

'But you'll be all alone. Aren't you *scared* to be on your own?' he said, and slowly, almost defiantly lay down on the big bed.

She was starting to prickle with irritation now. Her head was throbbing and she was tired, she didn't need this.

'Come on now, it's time for you to go,' she said, and, walking towards the bed, stood with her hands on her hips, waiting for him to get up and leave.

'Let me look, let me just have one look at your perfect body?' he asked.

She shook her head. 'Can you leave now please,' she said firmly. This had gone beyond a joke.

'And what if I don't?'

'Then I'll call reception and someone will come and remove you.'

'You wouldn't do that to me.'

'I *would!*' she said, marching to the telephone on the bedside table. Reaching for the receiver, she started to dial. But before she could get through, he'd leapt off the bed, and pulled the wire out of the wall.

She gasped, and deciding to make a run for it, she headed for the door, but he was there before her, his back pressed against it. His fingers reached behind and locked it. He now had the keys in his hands.

'Give me the keys please,' she said, trying to hide the tremor in her voice.

'What will you do for me?'

'Nothing, I just want my room keys.' She wanted to punch him, smack him, but she knew there was a good chance he'd just overpower her.

'One glimpse and you can have your keys back, and I'll go. Just take off your robe, Daisy.'

She quickly looked around the room for a weapon, but he wasn't actually attacking her, just standing in front of the door with her keys. If she went for him with a lamp and hurt him, how could she call it self-defence? Would it be an overreaction to a friend just teasing her?

'Your husband's down there drinking, he doesn't appreciate what's up here waiting for him, but I do. I appreciate beautiful women, all I want is to look. I won't touch. And you get your keys back,' he said playfully.

She took a long breath. There was no way she was doing that.

But still clutching her keys, he walked back to the bed, touching her face on the way, and lying slowly down again.

'I'm waiting,' he said, in a sing-song voice. 'Just one look, promise I won't touch.'

'Then you'll go?' she asked. He was far enough away not to be able to touch her, and if it got rid of him, what did it matter if he saw her naked? She was desperate to get him out, or escape herself. It was hot and stuffy and so scary. 'You promise you'll go if I do that?'

'I promise.' His breath was quickening, and he licked his lips.

Slowly, with trembling fingers and tears in her eyes, she allowed the silky material to open.

'More,' he said, 'I want you to drop the robe.'

She pulled it around her. 'No.'

'Oh God you're such a tease, Daisy, go on.' He waved the keys. 'Drop the robe, and the keys are yours, I promise.'

She stood for what seemed like forever, just wishing there was an alternative, but unable to think of one, she eventually opened her robe again and let it slip to the floor. He groaned, and started to put his hand near his groin, so she bent down to pick up the robe. He said, 'No, just a few more seconds.'

So she stood humiliated for a few more seconds, then went to reach for her gown, but before she could grab it, he lunged at her, and taking her by both arms, pulled her down onto the bed on top of him.

'That's enough,' she cried. 'You need to leave!'

'Look, we *both* want this Daisy,' he said, his voice suddenly not so playful. 'You've been teasing me all holiday, you've been asking for it.'

She tried to get off, but he was holding her arms so tightly she couldn't. She was looking down at his face; desire could be so ugly.

'Don't try to deny it, I've seen the way you look at me, you *want* it.'

He flipped her over onto the bed, and was now on top of her.

How stupid she'd been not to see this would happen. What an idiot she was. Her anger and fear were now turning him on; he loved that she was struggling, so she stayed still, and said in an over-bright voice, one that sounded like someone else's:

'Hey, why don't we hook up tomorrow? We can't do this now, *here*.'

'Oh we *can*,' he urged. She saw the need on his face, she saw how much he wanted her, his mouth now pushing down onto her mouth, wet and slimy and unwelcome. She wanted to be sick, hoped she could be. But she doubted even that would put him off. The determination in his voice, his face... she was beyond rescue.

So Daisy did what she'd done many times before, as a child, when her mother went to work and she was left alone with her stepfather. She let go, stopped fighting. She knew from experience, she was likely to be hurt even more if she struggled, so she went to the safe place in her head. She imagined beautiful beaches, high mountains and fine buildings far, far away from there, and she let him do what he had to do. And all the time, he pinned her down, grabbed her by the neck, until she didn't know if it was him, or her stepfather, or if she was thirty-eight, or ten years old and crying for her mother.

For a few moments, he just lay on top of her, spent and sweating. She wanted to kick him, scratch his eyes out, punch his smug, satisfied face, but if he was the killer, he might still have plans for her, so she just lay there. She couldn't breathe for the weight on her chest, but she waited until he was ready, just praying he didn't make her do it again.

Turning her head away from him, she gazed out through the net curtains and the open French doors onto the balcony. Where *someone* was watching them.

TWENTY-ONE

BECKY

Being stuck on this island has made us all pretty paranoid, suspecting fellow diners, the man who swims laps of the pool every morning, even the lovely gardener who waters the plants several times a day in our desert-like climate. We've all gone a little crazy, and last night was proof of that. Poor Sam was in such a state, it was like all the pressure had suddenly been released and a tsunami of fear gushed from her. I tried to help her, but she was in her own world, and when Josh suggested we leave and go to our room, I agreed. It was too painful to watch.

We weren't back in our room long before Josh said he wanted to go running, and though I'd resented him leaving me alone, tonight I was okay with that. I am trying to hold it together, he's been behaving in a slightly manic way for weeks, rushing around, unfocused, pre-occupied. This has happened before, and his high (which last time had resulted in a speeding ticket and a twelve-month driving ban) is often followed by a tremendous low. I can't reach him when he's like that. He behaves differently, he's reckless, lost and nothing I say can bring him back, until he has the crashing low. He's had a hard time, and got himself into such a mess, no wonder he's anxious.

I don't begrudge him some running therapy, after everything he told me yesterday.

Now I'm alone, I can have some time to think about what he told me after he'd been interviewed again by the police yesterday.

'Why did Granger want to interview you again?' I'd asked him. After fainting in the lift, we were now safely in our room.

'Just tell me the truth,' I said. 'It's not like you're guilty of anything, are you?'

But the look on his face told me he was guilty of *something*. I remember feeling horribly sick. He was ashen, and I could see by the way he was tapping his fingers and fidgeting that he was jumpy and on edge.

'Tell me *everything*,' I said gently, like I was talking to one of the children. And like an obedient child, he pulled an easy chair closer to the bed where I lay, and sat down to tell me.

'When I spoke with the police just now, they said that the night Stella... died, I was seen, by two witnesses,' he said.

'Doing what?'

'Running... along the beach.'

'So, you were on one of your night runs.'

'Yeah...' He paused a moment. 'But apparently, there's CCTV at the pool bar, and before I went for my run, I was seen arguing with Stella.'

The room suddenly shifted. 'What? *Arguing?*' I was confused. I knew they'd had a conversation, I'd watched from the balcony as he walked behind the bar and she'd followed him a few minutes later. I couldn't see them behind the bar, so I had no idea what was going on, but the last thing I expected them to be doing was *arguing?*

'What were you arguing about, Josh?' I could hear the tremor in my voice. Now I was just praying he wasn't going to tell me their disagreement had somehow resulted in Stella's death.

'It all started when I got there. It was late, as you know, and on my way to my run on the beach, I saw that the pool bar was still open. It was hot, I was thirsty, so I asked Stella for a glass of water. She served me, we chatted for a bit and then she said she was going for her break and wandered off. She didn't say where she was going, but I assumed she'd go back into the hotel, and after about ten minutes I got up to go down to the beach and do the run. But as I did, I noticed the till drawer hadn't been closed properly. I could see notes sticking out. And I swear my first thought was to go to reception and let them know, but then I thought, why should I do that, when she's gone off on her break and can't even be bothered to lock the till?'

He looked at me, and I could see he was ashamed of what he was about to tell me.

'Go on,' I murmured.

'Okay... so, I looked to see if anyone was around, but it was dark, and late and then I heard a noise and I saw Stella. She was behind the trees on the opposite side of the pool, she was with someone, a bloke, she was kissing him, and they were in a real clinch. I couldn't hear him properly, but he was saying, "Go on, you know you want to," and I don't know what made me do it, Becks, but before I knew it, I'd walked behind the bar, opened the till, and taken some of the notes – well, *all* of them. I didn't even feel guilty or anything. I was surprised at how easy it was. There's me worrying about how we're going to pay the food and drinks bill at the end of the holiday, and here was this gift. There was nearly a thousand pounds in that till.'

'Oh, Josh,' I moaned. I couldn't believe my husband would do something like that. 'This isn't you,' I heard myself say, knowing the stress of my illness had been the major cause of this, and I felt guilty.

'No, it's not me, I promise you, Becks... but everything was caving in, it still is. I feel like I don't know how to cope with the simplest things at the moment.'

'I know, I know,' I said, soothingly. 'Everyone is sympathetic to me, but you're going through just as much.' I tried to smile at him, to make him feel less wretched, but I find it hard to pretend these days.

'So go on, you took the money from the till, and then what happened?' I needed him to stay focused.

'Well, I'd stuffed the notes in my hoodie pockets, and down my T-shirt, I hadn't thought it through because I just didn't have anything to carry it in. So I was stood behind the bar with all this money, panicking, and was about to make a run for it when I heard her say to the bloke, "I'll lock the bar up and see you later, you can walk me home." I didn't know what the hell to do, so I just stood there. Frozen to the spot. And she walked back behind the bar, looked me up and down and said, "What are you doing *here*?"'

'Christ,' I murmured. That fitted in with what I saw. Stella walked behind the bar and joined Josh, I couldn't see them behind the bar, and in truth I thought something might have happened between them. I wouldn't have blamed him for having a moment with a beautiful young girl; why would he turn her down? We haven't slept together in months.

'So at first I told her I'd seen the till open and taken the money out to keep it safe. I said I'd planned to take it to reception, but of course she knew I was lying. "Why didn't you just call me?" she said, "I was only over there, having my break, you knew that."

'God it was awful,' he said, putting his head in his hands, distraught at the memory. 'Anyway, she started threatening to call the police, she was being really loud and I was worried the other guests would hear her from their rooms. I kept telling her to calm down, but she wouldn't and she was getting louder and even more angry with me. You know what I'm like, I hate conflict, so I just stood there while she yelled at me. I was worried that someone was going to turn up and call the police... All I could think of was you, and how hurt you'd be.'

'Oh, Josh.' I was terrified at this point. I wanted to know more, and at the same time, I didn't.

'Then it just came to me,' he said. 'She and the bloke had been so furtive, he'd been waiting behind the trees, he never came to the bar, I didn't see him, only heard him. You'd only do that if you didn't want to be seen, and why didn't they want to be seen? Probably because they shouldn't be together. He was either a member of staff, or a married guest. So, I told her I'd seen her kissing her lover. She was on duty, and I was going to report her to the manager. I was winging it, I didn't know what they'd been doing behind the trees, I just gave an educated guess,' he said. 'She soon calmed down then, and started begging me not to tell anyone, that she'd lose her job and she needed it because she was saving up to go to college. I told her I didn't want to ruin her life, and I certainly didn't want her to ruin mine, so let's agree to *both* keep quiet. I said if she allowed me to put the money back in the till and walk away, I'd never say a word about her lover.'

'And she agreed to that?'

'Yes, she did, but I was all over the place and not sure I could trust her. I came up here, and you were fast asleep, but I couldn't settle, I kept imagining the manager and a police officer knocking on our door; I couldn't put you through that. So just to let off some steam, I went out again, and did another run on the beach. I didn't go anywhere near the bar, just straight to the beach. But I think that's when the witness must have seen me and assumed I was running away from her body.'

'And you told the police all this?'

He shrugged. 'I had to. I decided it was better to be a thief than a murderer, but the way Granger looked at me you'd think I'd done both. "According to our CCTV you were the last person to see Stella Foster alive," she said in that posh voice.'

'Do you think she believes you?'

'I don't know. They asked me about the bloke Stella was with, they might be interested in him, but I didn't see him, he could have been anyone.'

'But he was coming back later to walk her home... sounds like *he* was the last person to see her alive.'

'Yeah, I guess he was, unless she died before he came back? But I swear on our children's lives, Becky, the last time I saw Stella Foster she was alive,' he said.

Thinking back over the conversation, I'm not sure how I feel. I can imagine the whole scenario, Josh doing something stupid and mad on an impulse, and doing it for me. But even when Stella was killed, he never told me or the police about what happened. He thought he could keep it all a secret, and told me he'd just been running, which was a lie. So how can I trust him? The police didn't arrest him, but he reckons they are just looking for one piece of evidence. 'One foot wrong and they'll come down on me,' he said, which made my heart beat too fast because trouble follows him and this won't end well, and I worry what's going to happen.

After he'd told me, he moved from the chair, sat on the bed, and embraced me. He kissed the top of my head, and I felt his pain run through me.

We both hold each other's agony, and I have to stand by him and fight for him if he is blamed in any way for Stella's death. So at a time when I have only months to live, when I should be cherished, and nurtured and saved, my husband has presented me with something so distressing and so complicated, I can't untangle it.

I think back to when we returned from the awful scene in the bar, the way he sat in the bedroom, fidgeting, unable to sit still, desperate once more to run away. And now I lie alone in the dark as he runs on the beach, and it feels like we've already said goodbye.

TWENTY-TWO

SAM

I was mortified! How did I lose it so badly? It was a splash of tomato juice, but at the time I genuinely thought it was blood. Afterwards, I felt so stupid just thinking about it, but there I was yelling for an ambulance, refusing to listen to anyone, accusing David of lying to me and making a total spectacle of myself. I felt awful, especially when Daisy pushed me away and ran off to her room. I waited for her to come back so I could apologise, but she didn't. I'd obviously embarrassed her too. David wasn't speaking to me, Becky and Josh had left, so I also ran out of the bar.

I didn't want to go back to our room straight away, so I went for a wander around the grounds, and tried not to cry too much. It was a shame because I'd been having such a lovely evening with Daisy and Becky until I spilled Daisy's drink. I'm so clumsy.

When David finally came to bed after me, swaying and reeking of alcohol, he said he was disappointed in me. 'You're not who I thought you were,' he said, as he fell into bed. He lay there a few minutes, bubbling away with rage, then had the cheek to ask me if I thought I had a drink problem.

'No. I was a little tipsy,' I replied, 'but that wasn't why I got upset. It's been a tough few days, we're all under pressure and I saw the red on Daisy's white dress and it took me right back to Marie, and that night. I thought I was over it, I thought I'd come to terms with what had happened, but I haven't at all.'

'Well, you need to start trying, because I refuse to lie with it for the rest of my life, even if you want to.'

'I don't, I hate it. But tonight, I was just mistaken, that's all.'

'You can say that again,' he hissed.

I didn't have the energy for another argument, and I also felt embarrassed about the way I'd behaved. I knew if I continued to discuss it with him, David would only make me feel worse, so I got out of bed, and locked myself in the bathroom.

Once he was asleep and snoring, I slept on the sofa in our room. My honeymoon had to be the loneliest one ever.

I was still upset and deeply embarrassed the following morning, and went down to breakfast in sunglasses, vainly hoping no one would realise I was the crazy lady from the previous evening.

David and I were seated at a table in the corner – no warm sunny window for us that morning, he was as eager as I was to hide. He didn't speak to me, and that was fine, because if he did say something I might just have started crying. I was keeping so much inside, my chest felt like a pressure cooker. I just had to get through breakfast.

We ordered our food and I gazed around at the beautiful restaurant, then back at my husband. The previous evening I'd let us both down, and he was right to be angry with me, I'd embarrassed him too, and he didn't deserve that. But instead of his rage, I'd have appreciated his understanding, and not once had he asked how I felt. But then looking back, he'd never been particularly sensitive to my feelings, and though he'd brought me here because it was my dream, it was also somewhere he was at home and I wasn't. And throughout our time here, he hadn't done anything to help me through this, to metaphorically hold my hand and explain things. Consequently, I was still so intimidated by everything here, the other guests, the extravagant décor and especially the hotel staff, who didn't even let me open my own napkin. Napkins were whipped off the table with a flourish and laid on laps, which always made me feel uncomfortable. And on our first night at Fitzgerald's, when David and I returned from dinner, I thought there'd been an intruder in our room, as someone had turned down the bed and left chocolates on our pillow. But throughout this time, David hadn't helped or guided me; he'd simply laughed at me, like I should have known.

One morning I'd ordered a pot of tea, and the waitress asked if I wanted lemon with it. I always have milk, but felt so overwhelmed, agreed to have the bloody lemon. It tasted awful, but when David remarked on it, he made me feel so stupid that I panic-lied and said I often had lemon with my tea and loved it. Since then I'd felt obliged to have lemon with my tea when I was with him, and to me it tasted disgusting.

But that morning after the incident with the Bloody Mary, I ordered milk with my tea, and it tasted like home. And instead of the dry toast that David encouraged me to have for breakfast, 'because you don't want to get fat,' I spread lashings of butter and strawberry jam on my toast and took big, comforting bites.

'Do you have to crunch so loudly?' he said, no doubt attempting to ruin my enjoyment of the delicious, fruity preserve. The absolute disgust on his face made me put down my toast.

'You really hate me, don't you?'

'Not this again. Please don't be high maintenance this morning, I'm not in the mood. Just eat your bloody toast.'

'I can't now, I'm self-conscious,' I said, on the verge of tears.

'Eat it!' He raised his voice then probably realised how it

sounded. 'I'm sorry,' he added as an afterthought; he didn't want a scene.

I tried to crunch quietly, aware that every mouthful was to him the revolting sound of toast meeting teeth and saliva. I realise now, that was his game, to crush me, make me feel worthless, embarrassed, and just when I was down there, he'd tell me he loved me.

'Is this how you treated Marie?' I asked, aware my hand was shaking as I slowly poured milk into my second cup of tea.

'What the *hell* are you going on about now?' he said in a quiet voice, fringed with irritation.

'Did you blame her for every single thing? Did you try and tie her in knots if she defended herself, did you sulk for days if she made the slightest mistake? Did *she* crunch her toast too loud for you too?'

He gave himself a moment to compose something suitably cutting. 'No, because as crazy as my ex-wife was, she never screamed in someone's face and demanded an ambulance if she spilled a drink. Last night you were an *embarrassment*,' he hissed, piercing the membrane of poached egg with his fork. I watched as rivulets of bright yellow yolk trickled through green avocado.

I couldn't answer him, I felt such hurt and fury building inside me. I tried to stay calm. I put two large spoonfuls of sugar into my tea and stirred, before taking a sip. I hoped it would soothe me, and it did – until he spoke.

'Do you have to take so much sugar? You complain about being fat but you do *nothing* about it.' He gave a hollow little laugh. I felt so foolish, not because of the sugar in my tea, or the way I crunched my toast, or even because I'd overreacted to a spilled drink the previous evening. I thought what we had was so precious it had to be nurtured and protected. There's nothing I wouldn't do for David, nothing I wouldn't do for our marriage. How foolish I'd been to ruin my life for a man who wasn't capable of love. I took a sip of my sweetened tea. 'That's yummy,' I remarked.

I could feel the tension simmering across the table.

'Did Marie like sugar?' I asked, my head to one side inquisitively. 'Did she have a little weight problem for you to nibble away at too?'

He was silent for a few moments, probably working out the most economical way with words to wound me as deftly as possible.

'I've told you before, Marie was sick, her obsessive behaviour was down to mental health issues.' He paused. 'I can see the same patterns in you.' He held my eyes for a few seconds, then went back to his breakfast.

I almost laughed. Did he really think he could get away with that? I pushed away the plate of strawberry jam-laden toast, my appetite now eaten up by rage.

'It's hard to hear the words you used about her used against me,' I said into the thick, loaded silence.

He didn't answer, so as we were in a public place with lots of people around, I prodded him a little harder.

'No *wonder* she had mental health issues, she was married to *you*!'

'Do we really have to rehash every little thing?'

'It might be a little thing to you, but it wasn't to Marie, and it isn't to me. You never mentioned her to me when we were first together, and I doubt you mentioned me to her either – because you were *still* together when we met, weren't you? And Marie got suspicious, and understandably jealous... That's why she followed you and that's why she made such a scene in the wine bar. You weren't over, you were still married, and out with me – your bloody mistress!' I'd been thinking a lot about Marie and the hurt she seemed to carry, and of course now it made sense.

He gave a deep sigh and placed his fork down on his plate, like he needed a free hand to explain this.

'As always, you're making a big, bloody drama out of nothing. Our marriage was over when I met you. And yes, I was still *married* to Marie, still living with her but it was over.'

'Yes, she was ill, she was mentally fragile, because you *made* her that way. You flaunted me in front of her to finally push her over the edge.'

He laughed at this. 'Trust me, if I needed to *flaunt* anyone, I wouldn't choose you!'

I ignored his nasty comment. 'She tried to warn me, but I wouldn't listen, I was too brainwashed by you.'

'Sshhh.' He looked around, alarmed at the volume of my voice. 'You need help,' he said earnestly, like it was a real issue. 'At first you were fun and sexy and easy-going, but you're as bad as Marie, no – worse!'

He wiped his mouth on the napkin, and right on cue, I watched as his eyes followed someone across the room. Daisy.

'She looks good, doesn't she? New Mistress material, perhaps?' I asked.

'Oh shut up, keep your jealous little remarks to yourself.'

'I wish I'd realised what a vile person you were before we married,' I said, my voice wobbly with hurt, and disappointment.

'I wish I'd realised what a boring, jealous little bitch *you* were before we married,' he monotoned, while looking around the room. 'I can't take much more of this, Sam,' he said quietly. 'I vowed I'd never be with someone who made me feel like this again. I can't breathe, can't move without being accused of something. I need some air,' he said, standing up, tossing his napkin on the table. I flinched, like he was throwing it at me.

My bottom lip trembled. Tears were coming and I could feel other guests' eyes on me, the nature of his departure made it clear we'd had a row.

Within minutes, Becky appeared at my table.

'You okay, love?' she asked.

I just nodded. I didn't dare speak because if I did I would just start sobbing. I needed the tears to leave my throat, and my heart to stop thudding.

'You sure?'

'I'm fine,' I lied. We both knew that wasn't true, but Becky wouldn't make me talk about it.

'Is that Daisy over there?' she said, peering across the room.

'Looks like it, but she doesn't look her usual self.'

'No, she's in a black kaftan, not like her at all.'

Becky and I waved, and when Daisy saw us, she wandered over.

'Are you alone?' I asked. She nodded; she didn't look right at all.

'I need some nice company, Tom's being a pain.'

I was feeling very raw and fragile, and Daisy looked pretty beaten up too – literally. She was wearing lots of make-up, but the bruises on her neck were still vivid under the flesh-coloured foundation. In fact, they'd really come out, black and purple and blue. They looked worse than they had the previous evening.

'Come on, you sit here,' I said, giving Daisy my seat and getting up to grab a chair from an empty table.

'God, I've had enough of this place.' She rolled her eyes.

'You okay?' I asked.

'I will be, just feel a bit shit today, that's all.'

'I'm so sorry, Daisy.'

'It's not your fault, it had nothing to do with you.'

'But I made such a fuss over the drink.'

'Oh... oh yeah, that was nothing,' she said with a sigh. 'Let's not even talk about it – unless you want to?'

I shook my head.

'I'm not much company this morning I'm afraid,' Daisy

murmured. She looked dead behind her eyes; I'd never seen her like this.

'You're bound to have bad days, you've been through such a lot. The bruises are starting to show now. Actually they look far worse.' I looked more closely. 'They look like fresh bruises,' I said, looking from Daisy to Becky.

Daisy didn't respond; she suddenly seemed to find the menu very interesting, and just didn't look up. Eventually she said, 'Please, let's talk about something other than me and my bruises.' She shook her head and wafted her hand dismissively.

'How are your children, Becky, did you manage to speak to them?' she asked, putting down the menu and changing the subject.

Becky's face lit up. 'I did. It was so lovely. Josh and I had a long chat with them this morning before he went for his run. Mum's enjoying having them too, and my sister's helping when she can. She's got her own though.'

'My sister and I used to love staying with my nan,' Daisy said. 'My parents split when I was very young, so Nan stepped in a lot, if Mum wasn't well or needed a break, you know?'

'That must have been difficult for you, not knowing your dad?' Becky said.

'Yeah, I guess, but he was a waste of time, and so were the conveyor belt of men my mother introduced me to as "Daddy",' she said bitterly, 'until she finally married one, and then life really took a nose dive. I realised at a young age I'd rather have one nana than ten bad dads.'

'Yeah, nans are the best. My mum is brilliant with the kids, but I have to say I worry about Josh when I'm gone.'

'Why?' Daisy asked.

'He just can't cope under pressure. I can't face leaving the kids, but I know they'll be fine – my biggest fear is leaving Josh, because I really don't know what he'll do.'

'That's quite a worry,' I said. 'Would he share their care with your mum?'

She shook her head. 'I don't think so, I wish he would, but he says he feels like he has to step up and be a good dad. I just worry that the kids will end up looking after *him*.' She smiled at this.

At this point the waitress came over to take our order. Daisy couldn't face anything, I'd eaten and Becky just wanted coffee, so that's all we ordered.

But then before she left, I asked for a large helping of toast and strawberry jam.

TWENTY-THREE

DAISY

Daisy felt numb and raw. She'd endured more in the past few days than some people had in a lifetime. She wondered how long she could keep this quiet – or even if she wanted to. Perhaps she should just tell everyone everything, including the police? But who would believe her? Before he left, he told her she'd been flirting, and pointed out there was no sign of a struggle. 'You even took your own robe off for me,' he said, with a revolting wink. Of course there was the other issue of his partner, and of Tom, and though she was sure there was CCTV in the corridors which would show him knocking on her door, it would also show that she let him in. Even DNA wouldn't make any difference; he said if she told he'd admit to having a 'roll in the hay' with her, and she was extremely willing. After that it was her word against his, and at the moment, her word meant nothing.

The police were currently investigating an assault she'd reported which, so far, had produced no evidence at all. She was the one who'd found Stella's body, and Granger believed Daisy had lied about knowing her. Tom thought she'd made up the attack to get his attention, and then thrown him under the bus by saying he knew Stella. She'd had no intention of throwing suspicion at Tom, but now he doubted her. Even Granger had asked her if she'd tried to throw her husband under the bus. On paper she looked like a bitch, and when your husband doesn't even believe you, then you're in serious trouble.

She recalled their spectacular wedding a few years earlier, from the gown handmade in Milan, to the cake flown in from a Parisian patisserie, to the spectacular little church in Portofino. They'd danced until midnight under the stars, and even then all she could think of was the baby they would have, and how they'd give that baby everything. After her own upbringing, it was Daisy's dearest wish to bring a child into the world, and be the mother she'd never had. She would guard that baby with her life, love him unconditionally and in doing so, it might just erase everything that still kept her awake at night. But now, after everything that had happened, she realised how fragile life was. How frayed the thread of her life was that it could tear at the first pull?

Still in shock from what had happened the previous night, Daisy had wandered aimlessly into the dining room, and was now drinking coffee with Becky and Sam. Becky had been telling them about her kids, and the funny things they said when they were little and Daisy was trying to focus, and not feel the weight of him on top, the filthy words.

'Do you think you'll have children?' Becky asked Sam, as she talked of her own kids.

'No, I'm not hell-bent on having children; my sister has three and I love them to bits, I'll make do with them.'

'I envy you not having this horrible pull,' Daisy said, playing with her spoon in the coffee cup.

'Oh, love, it's all so random,' Becky said, reaching out her hand and placing it on Daisy's. 'Don't even try and make sense of it. Look at me with this cancer cloud hanging over my life. I didn't ask for it, it just happened, and instead of thinking why me, I have learned to say, why not me? You can't take responsibility for your infertility, but you can take responsibility for your life. And you owe it to yourself – and to someone like me – to make your life amazing.'

'Yeah, perhaps I need to become a better person,' she said absently.

She saw the other two glance at each other, if she didn't step up, they might guess something was wrong and start asking questions. And any questions about last night had to remain unanswered.

'I need a drink, does anyone fancy a pitcher of something made out of gin?' Daisy asked, realising she had to blank out the previous evening if she was to get through the day, alcohol would do that.

'Sounds good to me,' Sam replied.

Daisy was waiting for Becky to refuse, and she surprised her after a moment's hesitation by replying, 'Yes, I love gin. I told Josh only this morning that I wanted to try every gin there is before I go.'

'Okay, let's start now,' said Daisy, and ordered a pitcher of blackberry gin fizz. She felt hot, and sticky and longed for another shower, but she'd had three that morning and her skin was as raw as her heart. 'It's stuffy in here, let's take it out on the patio,' she said, ushering the other two out onto the sun-drenched decking.

The waitress soon arrived with a huge frosty pitcher of fizz and three champagne flutes.

Daisy sipped on the cold, citrussy cocktail, allowing a little warmth from the sun to meet her face. It felt somehow healing, but she knew that healing was impossible at the moment. And as the other two chatted, she slipped back into her thoughts of what had happened the night before.

She seriously considered just leaving the table and going to find Granger, and tell her what happened, but how could she? Granger wouldn't believe her, and the way things were between her and Tom, her husband might even believe *him* that she consented.

He didn't even believe her that someone had been in their room when she *knew* they had, so what would his reaction be to her 'inviting' one of their friends into their room when she was alone and half-dressed? Would he really believe this man had raped her? There was no sign of a struggle, no ripped clothes or fighting back; in fact, she'd taken off her robe for him. No, she couldn't tell, there was too much at stake, her and Tom, the rapist's wife, who would be devastated and the fact the police wouldn't believe her anyway. No, she'd probably keep the rape to herself and never tell anyone.

Daisy thought now about her husband, and was comforted by that. She was lucky to have Tom. Together they'd walked through deserts, held each other's hand on top of mountains and watched sunsets as hot air balloons filled the sky like confetti.

'You know,' she said as she sipped on cold alcohol and tried to anaesthetise her pain, 'Tom and I had the most amazing wedding, and we've done so much wonderful travel and it's all been so good, but I missed it.'

'What do you mean?' Sam asked.

'We'd been trying for a baby before we married, and on the morning of our wedding my period arrived. I was so devastated I barely remember our beautiful wedding, it was as if I wasn't there.' Daisy and Tom had so many disappointments, including several early miscarriages that broke them in two, and after carrying James for more than six months, she really thought this was her reward for going through so much. But he wasn't their happy ending.

But Daisy was never down for long; she could always rally round even in the worst circumstances, and now was probably one of the worst days of her life. In the aftermath of an attack, she had gone through a rape, and now she was here drinking gin and trying to forget.

'Like Becky said, I can't be responsible for my infertility, but I can be responsible for my life. And what I have is a loving husband, a beautiful home and enough money to get by. So far, I've been chasing something I can't have, and it's eaten up the good years, the good times. Now it's time to take those back, and accept my lot.'

'Acceptance, that's it,' Becky said. 'Once you realise there's nothing you can do about something, you can let go. You're not responsible and it's liberating.'

'I long to be free in that way. I have to if I want my marriage to survive,' Daisy said. 'When we lost James, our baby, everyone said it would strengthen us. But it hasn't, because every time I look at him, I see our baby and wonder if he would have had Tom's eyes, his build, his humour. And coming up against that every single day has taken its toll. But while I was *doing* that, and feeling those things, I wasn't loving Tom and appreciating who *he* is. And all the wonderful times together were tarnished, because I wanted something so much, when in reality I have what I need.'

She thought now about what had happened in her bed, when Tom was downstairs completely unaware, and it made her want to cry just thinking about it.

A little later, when Sam had gone to the bathroom, Becky and Daisy began talking on a deeper level, as people sometimes do when a group gets smaller. Daisy had drunk too much of the gin cocktail and despite holding everything inside all morning, she just started to cry, which prompted Becky to press her on what was wrong.

'Daisy, you're not yourself, last night you seemed to be coming round, but today... I don't know, you look haunted.'

Daisy hadn't intended to tell anyone, but it filled her mind, and the gin had loosened her tongue.

She couldn't tell anyone though, and kept shaking her head and wiping her face with a napkin. It took Becky some time to get her to speak, but after a few more glugs of gin cocktail she calmed down.

'Something happened,' Daisy said, still hiccoughing tears. She was rocking and biting her lip, and looking around like someone might be watching.

Becky discreetly leaned forwards. 'Those bruises on your neck are fresh, aren't they?' she said, and lifted Daisy's kimono sleeve. 'These too.' She revealed more bruises on her arms, deep, purple-black fingerprint shapes around her bare arms, similar to what was on her neck, but deeper.

'Daisy, what happened?' Becky asked, and looked into her face, where there was a shadow of a bruise at the side.

'I can't talk about it,' Daisy said.

'Tell me.' Becky spoke gently, like a mother, and Daisy had always wanted a mother she could talk to.

'Last night someone knocked on the bedroom door...' She stopped talking, and her friend waited for her to continue. But Daisy didn't, she just sat staring ahead for a little while. Becky said her name gently, and she suddenly remembered Becky was there.

'He made me... I'm confused.' Daisy touched the white dressing on her head that covered the injury. Perhaps the head injury was the reason for her confusion? Or was this a delusion caused by the injury?

'I don't know anything anymore, Becky.' Tears stained her cheeks, pink streaks of flesh revealed through creamy make-up, like cracks in alabaster. 'I only had my robe on. He told me to take it off. He hurt me.'

'How?'

Daisy couldn't speak, so Becky spoke for her.

'Are you saying someone broke into your room and *raped* you? Who?'

She paused, shook her head and stared ahead again, like she was reliving this. 'It was like he didn't hear me, like I wasn't there...' She started to cry again.

'Oh, Daisy.' Becky looked like she might cry.

'I didn't want to tell anyone, because I thought no one would believe me,' Daisy said, 'but I think I saw someone watching from outside. So *someone* else must know.'

'Oh?'

'I *saw* someone, he was on the balcony, peering in.'

'Are you *absolutely* sure? How could anyone get onto the balcony from outside?'

'It would be easy, the balconies are connecting, you'd just have to climb across.'

'Oh I just can't imagine anyone...'

'Yes, it was a dark figure at the window, his face pressed against the glass.'

'Did you see who it *was*?' Becky asked.

'No, it was dark outside, and there was only a lamp on inside the room, so I couldn't see him.'

'Are you going to the police?'

'I want to, but I can't – they won't believe me... but now I'm thinking, if I could find the guy who was looking in, he might be a witness?'

'It depends what he saw...'

'That was it. He probably didn't see anything incriminating because I didn't struggle...' she started. 'It's happened to me before, and... if you struggle, they hurt you more.'

'Oh, love,' was all Becky could say, and Daisy reached out and held her hand, wishing she hadn't told her, but overwhelmed by a feeling of relief that she had. Poor Becky seemed to take on everyone's pain.

'Does anyone else wish they were on a girls' holiday?' Sam

asked, rejoining the table and shaking both women into the present.

'That would be fun,' Becky said with a sigh. Daisy was still composing herself, and grateful to Becky for picking up the reins and covering for her by engaging Sam in a conversation. This way she didn't notice Daisy's tears, and ask any awkward questions. 'Josh is a nightmare, he's like a bad-tempered nurse! I told him this morning I don't want to go to America, I want to live until I die,' Becky said, with one eye on Daisy to make sure she was okay.

'Good for you,' Sam said, 'and how did he take it?'

'Not very well, but I think he'll get used to it. I just told him I want to spend what time I have left doing things I want to do.'

'Great,' Daisy replied, not quite sure what she was congratulating Becky on, but trying to give the illusion that she was still with them.

'So, how would you spend your time if you could choose?' Sam asked.

'I'd go for walks on the beach with the kids, spend Sunday mornings reading newspapers, eating roast dinners and falling asleep in the chair. I'd want the four of us to re-watch all the children's films we loved when the kids were young. I'd want to eat too much chocolate and try and drink every single flavour of gin available. It's important that I die safe in the knowledge that I've sampled every make and flavour of gin.'

'That all sounds wonderful,' Sam said, 'but as you're stuck here with us for at least another few days, is there anything here that you'd like to do with us?'

Becky took a breath. 'Okay, blue skies – bucket list? I want to break out, go mad, get drunk, dance with a stranger, throw off all my clothes... and... and... swim in the moonlight.'

'Yes!' Sam made mini clapping gestures with her fingertips.

'Let's all go moonlight swimming tonight then?' Daisy suddenly said.

They both turned to look at her. Becky was nodding, but Sam looked a little doubtful. 'It's a great idea, but I might sit this one out. I can't swim.'

'Oh go on, Sam, you have to do this for Becky,' Daisy insisted, still a little half-hearted but trying to be positive.

'I know Josh will be difficult about it too,' Becky said.

'For God's sake, you two, live a little!' Daisy was beginning to like the idea of this. 'There's going to be a beautiful full moon, we're all together – we can look after each other. Please let's do it, I'll bring champagne?' she offered.

'Now you're talking,' Becky said, 'I haven't had champagne for such a long time. My pills don't mix well with alcohol, so I won't take them today. I'll tell Josh I have, but I'll hide them at the back of the bathroom cabinet.'

'That's the spirit!' Daisy said, feeling vaguely pleased, which she felt was the nearest she'd ever get to happy again after what had happened. She tried to be enthusiastic for Becky, but her back ached from the force with which the man had pinned her down. She'd felt his hot, alcohol breath as he panted in her face, his mouth salty with sweat. It was so disgusting, so horrible, just thinking about it made her want to shower again. As the other two talked, she gazed at the sea, and realised that something repulsed her even more than his sweat, his breath and the sickening words he spattered all over her naked body. It was the look of victory on his face as he left her room; it would stay with her for ever and she wasn't sure she could live with that.

After returning to the conversation briefly, Daisy felt she needed her space now. She was exhausted from everything that had happened.

How foolish she'd been to think she'd escaped, when men like him were everywhere, a beast that refused to die. She could lock all the doors, but the danger was already in there with her. He *lived* inside her, she'd never be free.

TWENTY-FOUR

BECKY

I say goodbye to the girls and go back to my room. It's still warm, but I don't open the windows. I close the curtains and almost fall onto the bed, relieved to have landed before I collapse.

I try not to think about Daisy. It hurts too much, and I can't take it on at the moment. So I think instead about my clandestine drinks with the girls, and marvel at how human beings find a camaraderie in the darkest of places. I'm also finding a strange nugget of comfort that there's stuff going on that isn't about me. For once it isn't just *me* frightened for my life, other people are scared for theirs too, and at the same time, I welcome the sense of community that's been built out of fear.

I find it strange that Stella has become this huge figure in our lives, yet most of us barely knew the scrap of a girl who ran around the hotel, always smiling, always busy. I also find it fascinating how people talk about Stella, like she was a friend, a family member. They allow themselves an intimacy with her that didn't exist when she was alive. Her name's on everyone's lips, and they all seem to be discovering and exploiting tenuous connections to the girl. The overheard conversations are as hilarious as they're macabre: 'she served a good pint', 'always had a smile', 'her mother was a single parent' – weird little scraps of her life gobbled up in death by those who probably didn't even give her the time of day when she was here. I wonder if people will be like that when I've gone? Will people I've barely met and online acquaintances suddenly mourn for me like best friends or lovers? Will they share their 'grief' on Facebook, expecting to be comforted by others who never even knew my name, who also join the dance? I shudder at the thought of it and make a note to ask Amy to delete me when I'm gone. I don't want bits of me left for the grief sharks to feast on in my absence.

God, I haven't drunk in months and my tolerance is so low I felt pissed halfway through the second glass, but it was great to drink cocktails with the girls. I drift off to sleep. I'm so incredibly tired I'm out for a couple of hours, and when I wake, I'm lying on my side, looking at Josh's white pillow next to mine. I'm groggy and trying to open my eyes, when I see a rose on the pillow. I melt inside, and reach for it. Then I see the note. It's been left with the rose, so it's obviously from Josh. I haven't seen him all day, I hope he's forgiven me after our difficult conversation. Suddenly, I want to be sick, so I run to the bathroom, where alcohol and the dregs of my morning medication trigger a session of projectile vomiting on a new level. Exhausted, I eventually emerge and fall across the bed, and after closing my eyes for a few minutes, open them to see the folded note, which I'd almost forgotten about. Fortunately, I'm within reaching distance so pick it up. But it's not from Josh as I'd thought, it's from Sam. Bloody hell, she came into my room while I was asleep. I wonder if that's slightly inappropriate? Nevertheless I open it, and my heart sinks a little.

This is your formal invite to Becky's Bucket List Part One! The Midnight Moonlight Swim. Tonight at 11.30pm we meet by the cliffs which can be reached through the hotel gardens.

Suitable dress is requested: thongs and bikinis for the ladies,
and black ties for the gentlemen. Given recent events on the
beach after dark, husbands and partners are invited for safety
in numbers! Love Sam xxx

I groan inwardly. I thought this was just a fun chat today and that it might happen another day. I'm tired and really don't feel up to it. I'm sure Daisy won't either, but Sam's note is typically enthusiastic and inclusive, and she's so sweet. I remind myself that Sam has done this for me, and I should be grateful. After all, this is her honeymoon, albeit a rocky one. And now, she's giving up her time to help me make my bucket list and swim in the moonlight. I do worry that she's almost too kind for her own good, because men like David take advantage of women like Sam. And then there's Daisy. I'm just emotionally drained after my conversation with her and I know I mustn't get stressed, but it's hard not to.

I slowly start to get ready for dinner, reminding myself not to drink too much with the meal if we're going swimming later. I'm going to break it to Josh that I will from now on be having a drink occasionally, so he's not to be a pain about it. The medicine I'm on reacts with alcohol, that's why he hates the idea of me even having a sniff of a drink. So even if I'm drinking just one glass tonight, I won't take any meds this afternoon. I'm sure Josh will check what I've taken when he comes in, he thinks I can't manage my own tablets, and does a little 'stocktake' of my pills regularly. But he doesn't have a clue; for an accountant, he's not great at counting, there must be far more left than there should be.

I drift off to sleep, and dream again about water. This time it's me that's drowning, which I guess technically is a nightmare, and just as I'm about to die, I wake up. I'm choking and pull myself up to a sitting position thinking, *this is it, the end of my story, it's all over.* That's what it's like being terminally ill, as if death is my stalker, waiting around every corner to get me when I least expect it. Even in this luxury paradise, where the sun seems to never stop shining, the threat of my demise is a shadow across the sun. I feel its presence as I lie by the pool, walk on the beach and sit down to dinner. Even in sleep it taunts me and this latest nightmare has really shaken me, and I suddenly feel uneasy about tonight. Are we being stupid going swimming late at night, when there might be a killer out there on the beach? It's all very well having goals, and so kind of Sam to arrange this, but along with the obvious dangers, I'm a sick woman who's frail. Am I putting my already failing health in danger? I'm relieved Sam suggested we bring our partners along. However I might feel about Josh, there'll be someone there to help me up and down the steps, and stop me from going under.

I turn to see if he's back, and feel a tinge of sadness when I see he's also left a note, only this one's on my bedside table.

Hey, I came back to the room, but you were really in a deep sleep. You must have had a busy morning chatting with the girls, hope you enjoyed it. Sorry things have been difficult, and sorry I've been moody. Let's put it all behind us now and do as you say and enjoy life – at least for the rest of the holiday! I love you, J xxx

I roll over on the bed, wondering where my husband is. I tell myself he's out running, or canvassing for sponsors in the foyer... at least that's what he'll tell me. He's told me so many things, I've caught him out on some, but after the first few years I stopped questioning him; I let things go. But after yesterday, I know my husband isn't who I thought he was, and I can never trust what he tells me ever again.

TWENTY-FIVE

SAM

We arrived in the dining room for dinner at different times that evening. David and I were first. I was always hungry, but tonight it wasn't hunger driving me to the dining room, it was anticipation of the night ahead.

'What's wrong with you, leaving half your starter. On another diet?' he asked.

'I'm nervous, about the swim.'

'Let's not go then?' He picked at his cauliflower tempura with ponzu dipping sauce. 'It's probably the maddest thing you've ever done, suggest we go swimming at night with four fellow guests we don't really know. In the middle of a murder investigation.'

'They're friends,' I insisted, but the way he phrased it did make me think about it.

'It depends what you mean by "friends,"' he said. 'Any one of them could be the killer, because people who kill don't usually mention it over cocktails by the pool. You might see them as friends, Sam, but all they're doing is presenting a version of themselves that's socially acceptable.'

'Rubbish. Could you really see any of them murdering someone?'

'Well, *someone* in this hotel committed murder, and if daft Daisy's to be believed, they also assaulted a woman on the cliffs.'

'Was it even the same person though?'

'If not, that makes it worse,' he said. 'That means *two* guests are potentially dangerous psychopaths – a murderer and some wannabe committing a violent assault. *If* she's to be believed.'

He was making me feel very jumpy. I was beginning to wish someone would call the swim off. 'Stop being so dramatic. I have to go along, it's Becky's bucket list.'

'Would she even notice if you weren't there?' The implication was, of course, that I was insignificant.

'Actually she would, Becky and I have grown close on this holiday. And Daisy too, we had a lovely time together today.'

He looked up to the ceiling. 'The desperate housewives.'

I didn't give him the satisfaction of responding to this. I was still hurting from the way he'd spoken to me that morning over breakfast, and I didn't have the energy for another row. I wanted tonight to go well, it was important to me as Becky's friend that it was a success. I was just scared of being in water.

Even the dessert, a confection of strawberries, vanilla foam and dry ice, didn't seduce me that evening. I couldn't concentrate on anything, I was too nervous, I hated water at the best of times, but in the dark, on a beach where someone had died only days before?

'Why are you putting yourself through this? Becky won't thank you for it, and the other one will no doubt end up in some self-made drama.' David wasn't letting this drop. 'I wonder if that Daisy's on drugs, there's always something going on with that one. They're the type, aren't they, her and him. Both flaky,' he added, dabbing his mouth with a napkin. 'I don't trust them, or that Josh always playing the caring husband...'

'He is!'

'Well, if I looked at Daisy like he does, you'd be nagging me to death.'

'I don't think anyone could look at Daisy more than *you* do,' I replied. 'You told me you want to *tame* her, what kind of a comment is that?'

'I said she needs *taming*, I didn't say I wanted the job. She just needs putting in her place, too full of herself – then again it could be the drugs.'

I rolled my eyes and didn't respond to this ridiculous comment, because just at that point, Becky and Josh came over to our table.

'Ahh, Sam, thanks for organising this, I really appreciate you doing that for me.'

'I haven't done anything, thank *you* for organising it, and for having such a brilliant idea!' I said, reaching out and squeezing her hand. I looked up at Josh, who responded with a tense smile.

'Why don't you join us?' David said, looking around for a waiter to bring a chair, but Josh wasn't keen.

'No thanks, David – Becky is tired, she—'

'Oh, not too tired for swimming?' I asked. After what David said, I'd have been relieved if she'd cancelled; it suddenly didn't feel like a good idea.

Josh started to shake his head doubtfully. 'I don't think—' but Becky interrupted to say, 'Of course we are. We're still meeting at eleven thirty at the cliffs, right?'

'Yes! Can't wait,' I said, faking a full-on smile.

'Have you seen Daisy and Tom?' I asked, peering around the dining room.

'They aren't eating dinner this evening.' Becky looked a little awkward.

'That's not like them.'

'They're having room service,' she said.

'Oh, she never said.'

'Yeah, they just fancied something light.'

I wondered if Becky and Daisy had been in touch by phone. How else would Becky know they were having room service? Were they developing a friendship independently of me? That had happened at school, and in the salon, and it was always hurtful.

After dinner, David and I went to the bar. I'd hoped some of the others might be there, but none of them were. I wondered if perhaps the four of them were drinking together in one of their rooms. I sometimes overthought my friendships; David said I was paranoid.

'More Prosecco, my sweet?' he asked jokingly.

'No. We're going swimming, remember.' He didn't take any notice, just ordered himself another beer.

I would usually have suggested he slow down, but he wasn't in the mood to be told anything, and I didn't want to have an argument. Annoyingly I needed him there that night, if for no other reason than to stop me from drowning. Then again, I was beginning to wonder if he'd save me anyway if I was screaming for help in the water.

At 11pm, we headed outside to the hotel gardens that led down to the sea. I hadn't really thought it through, but the lights in the gardens went out at ten thirty so we were wandering around in the pitch dark. David was behind me complaining, and suddenly yelped.

'Are you okay?' I called out into the darkness. I waited for him to answer, but nothing. 'David?' I called again, but silence. 'David, this isn't funny,' I yelled, now feeling very uneasy. I felt like I was in a scene from the opening of a horror film, where one by one we were all going to die – mind you, I'd felt like that most of the time I'd been here. The silence was eerie, even the sea was quiet that night, lurking inky black in the distance.

Then, I suddenly heard a twig snap, and shot round to try and see whether someone was there.

'David?' I called again.

'What?'

'So you're there, why didn't you answer me?' I said, irritated. I realised now that these were just the sort of games David played. He'd heard me, but decided not to answer to make me uneasy or scared. I just continued walking. It wasn't easy, I walked into several prickly plants, ripping my dress along the way, but there was no choice, it was the only way to the beach.

'I just hope Becky is okay,' I said as he caught up with me.

'Why?'

'Because she's fragile, and I care about her. I don't want her to hurt herself, or get too tired.'

'You should have thought of that when you decided on this ridiculous outing. It's bloody dangerous for someone like her, not to mention someone like *you* who can barely put one foot in front of the other on land, let alone in the sea,' he hissed.

'I do okay,' I said calmly; I wasn't biting that night. 'And as you know it's on her *bucket* list, have you got any heart?'

'Heart? Have you got any *sense*, more like? The woman is at death's door, but you're wasting everyone's time helping her fill her bloody bucket list. Christ, we're going through all this and she might not be here next week!'

I almost gasped at this and was about to respond in no uncertain terms, when I heard someone behind me.

'Sam, is that you?' It was Becky's voice, she sounded quite close by. I felt sick. She must have heard what David just said. I could never forgive him for that. It would have hurt her so much. It was everything she feared – being defined by her illness, seen as a lesser person because her death was on the horizon.

I managed to fill the silences with small talk, but even in the dark I could feel the tension. They'd definitely heard. Josh barely spoke, and David said absolutely nothing, which made me realise what a coward my new husband was.

But being Becky, she didn't let on if she had heard. She was such a generous soul. She put her arm in mine and as Josh called, 'Be careful, Becky,' every ten seconds, we negotiated the prickly plants in the garden. He continued to call to her as we both staggered, laughing down the rickety beach steps built into the cliffs.

'She's fine, I'm with her,' I called to Josh, when we arrived on the beach.

'That's what I'm worried about,' Josh called back. 'You two together on steep stone steps don't inspire me with confidence.'

'He has a point,' Becky said, holding on to my arm. She was surprisingly agile and full of energy.

'You're doing great,' I whispered.

'That's because I've not taken any pills today. I hid them in the bathroom cabinet, and I feel alive,' she confided. 'Just don't tell Josh, he'll only worry.'

The moon was like scattered sequins on the black sea, and I linked Becky's arm again as we walked along the edge of the water. The moon was casting enough light that we could just about see each other's faces, and I looked at her.

'I'm sorry about David,' I said. 'He just shoots his mouth off, says stuff about everyone, I just don't listen to him anymore.'

'You don't have to apologise for him. Besides, he has a point, it's a waste of everyone's time, I *will* probably be dead this time next week,' she said, in her characteristically fair and measured way. It stung me to hear it again. She'd remembered it word for word; how terrible to live with something like that in your final days. And how terrible for me to be newly married to a man that could *say* something like that.

We walked further along the shoreline. The glassy stillness was changing, there was a storm in the air and the sea seemed to be slowly gathering momentum. Dark frills of water whipped at our feet before quickly withdrawing, then coming back, each time a little closer, until we were ankle deep in cool water.

'David was saying tonight that we're all being a bit mad,' I said.

'Why?'

'Well, we've all come down onto the beach, where only days before a body was found. We still don't know who killed Stella and there are all kinds of rumours swirling around still about Daisy knowing Stella, and Tom being friendly with her.' I didn't mention the one I'd overheard in the ladies' toilet where a lady from the spa said Stella had had a huge argument with Josh on the night she died.

'David's right, who knows whether the rumours are true or not? But I reckon if we thought hard enough we'd all have a reason to kill someone.'

'Even you and I?' I said.

'Yeah, I'm a bitter, desperate woman with weeks to live, I might have envied Stella's life, her future – well I did, I guess,' she says, like this has just occurred to her.

'And I envied her youth and her figure and the way David looked at her,' I said with a smile.

'I don't think a nice figure and a glad eye is a good enough reason. If I were Granger, I'd be ruling you out of my list of suspects,' she said.

I was intrigued. 'So if you were Granger, who would be top of your suspect list?'

She shook her head. 'That would be telling, and a good detective never tells.'

I raised my eyebrows, nodding in agreement, but I had a feeling she wasn't telling me because I might not like who her top suspect was. My husband.

TWENTY-SIX

DAISY

Daisy and Tom arrived late for the midnight swim. Daisy had been so devastated about what had happened she couldn't face seeing *him* at dinner, so she told Tom she wasn't hungry.

'Let's just order room service,' she said. 'We don't want to eat too much if we're going swimming.'

She had the feeling Tom didn't believe her, that somehow he knew she was avoiding someone. In fact, she wondered if he'd sensed something the previous night when he'd returned after drinking in the bar. She'd been in such a state, but Tom wanted to talk. 'Daisy, I feel like we were getting somewhere when we talked about... James. But now you've put your walls up again. This was supposed to be our healing trip,' he said, taking off his tie and sitting on the bed where she lay on top of the covers. He was right, this was supposed to be the calm holiday where the two of them regrouped as they moved into the next stage of grief. No work stress, no distant locations for Daisy, no long hours for Tom, just the two of them coming back together, and she too had felt that slow thawing. But now she was back on a horrible, scary ride and Daisy really couldn't take any more. The last thing she wanted to do right now, in the aftermath of a rape, was have a heartbreaking conversation with her husband. Nor did she have the energy to try and convince him of what had just happened; apart from the obvious reasons, there was also the pain for him. She knew now that he had found it hard to talk about their son because he'd felt he had to be the strong one, but he hurt as much as she did. This would be the same and she wasn't piling on any more agony for him.

'I... I don't feel too good,' she'd replied, still trying to get her head round what had just happened. 'I think I'll take a shower.'

'But you had a shower before we had dinner,' he'd said, puzzled.

'Yes, it's hot and sticky and I need a cool shower,' she'd answered defensively.

She'd locked the bathroom door that night, and before stepping into the shower, she opened her large toilet bag where she kept her bottle of disinfectant and wire brush. She lay these things out on the shelf along with her shampoo, soap and conditioner, and stepped into the shower. She took the wire brush and disinfectant, and scrubbed every inch of her body until it stung, and prickles of blood emerged on her flesh. It was agony, but the only way she knew to hold back the pain of what happened to her as a child, and now what had happened that night.

Now, twenty-four hours and ten showers later, she still felt dirty. Tonight, the last thing she wanted was to go swimming in the dark with a group of friends she'd met on holiday – essentially strangers. But she wasn't allowing what that man did to her have any influence on the shape of her life, even the small things, because then she really would be defeated. And besides, this wasn't about her. This was about Becky, who had been a kind friend to her and talked wisely about acceptance and the essence of living for today, and taking back control. She'd made a mark on Daisy's life in ways she'd probably never know.

So after a light sandwich supper from room service, Daisy

and Tom had fought their way through the gardens in the dark, and arrived on the beach. Daisy looked and felt a mess, and Tom was sullen and monosyllabic. She'd brought with her two bottles of champagne and some paper cups, and on arrival, joined Sam and Becky.

'You okay?' Becky asked discreetly.

Daisy rolled her eyes. 'Yeah, just me and Tom, we're not really talking.'

'Have you told him?' she murmured.

Daisy shook her head.

Sam leaned in, she was obviously intrigued but too polite to ask.

Daisy couldn't relax, she was aware of Tom circling the group. She wished he'd sit down, he was making her tense. She knew her mood had affected him, and he'd been hurt the evening before when she seemingly had refused to talk to him about their future. He'd probably assumed she wasn't planning a future with him, and was on the verge of ending things. But Daisy needed time and space to deal with everything that had happened, she just hoped he'd understand.

So, she gave nothing away, just sat with her arms wrapped around her waist, a self-comforting technique she'd used since childhood.

'How lovely that you brought champagne,' Sam said, calling David and Josh over to join them.

'Shall we open it now, before the swim – or after?' Sam asked.

'I think now,' Daisy replied. 'I reckon we all need a drink.'

'Yeah, and I need Dutch courage,' Sam said with a smile, making a big play of the champagne. Daisy was glad someone was trying to make this special for Becky, because Josh wasn't. He didn't say much and sat staring out into the blackness. He was clearly concerned about Becky in all this, but she wasn't so frail she couldn't tackle a swim in the sea, she'd be fine. But like

Josh, David also seemed to be there under sufferance, none of the chatty charm and repartee he usually thought was his brand.

Sam opened the first bottle of champagne and screamed as it erupted. It was now dripping everywhere.

'We can't waste it,' Daisy said and, standing up, she took the still dripping bottle from Sam. 'Bring the paper cups,' she said, 'we'll pour over here, everyone's getting wet through.'

'I don't mind being bathed in champagne,' David remarked, but Daisy and Sam both ignored him and went to pour the drinks.

Daisy poured the champagne and handed each cup to Sam to pass round. 'This first one is Becky's,' she said. 'Becky's bucket list is about to begin,' she announced, handing Sam the first one to pass along. 'Give this one to David, it's a nice full one,' and 'oops, spilt a bit,' 'give this one to Josh,' and so on, until they each had a drink.

Once Sam and Daisy had had their drinks, Daisy gave a toast. 'To the first of many exciting adventures as Queen Becky begins her bucket list!'

Daisy sat down, joining the rest of the group, and Becky raised her own cup to her. 'Thanks for the champagne, Daisy, it was really thoughtful,' she said.

'Well it's not every day someone ticks off an item on their bucket list,' she raised her paper cup back.

Sam was now giving an impromptu speech about how amazing Becky was, and how, 'This woman has changed my life, and we'll be lifelong friends,' which made Becky cry. It made Daisy, and probably everyone else cringe slightly at her choice of words – after all, poor Becky didn't have much time left for 'lifelong friends', but Sam meant well. Daisy was surprised David hadn't used Sam's rather clumsy comment as an opportunity for public humiliation, which was, after all, his speciality. But she could see even in the dark that he wasn't really listening. He rarely listened to Sam, and Daisy could tell by his lack of engagement he just wanted to get this over with.

'Right, everyone,' Sam called out, 'it's now ten after midnight, and Becky's waited long enough. Let's strip off and MIDNIGHT SWIM!'

Becky was the only one who cheered at this. She threw off her dress and underneath was wearing a bikini for the first time on this holiday. In the moonlight Daisy could see her hip bones jutting out, and when she turned her back to walk into the water, she could see her shoulder blades. Her silhouette against the night sky was skeletal, and it brought home to Daisy why Josh had clearly been so against this swim. One big wave and she could be in trouble. 'We need to keep an eye on Becky,' Daisy whispered to Sam as they walked in together.

'Yes, she's ever so frail, isn't she? But Josh is with her.'

Josh, as always, wasn't far away and immediately went to Becky as she walked gingerly into the water, her arms out as if to steady herself.

'If she survives this it will be a bloody miracle,' Daisy heard David say under his breath to Sam as they all entered the water together. Daisy could see he was playing his usual mind games, attempting to scare Sam and spoil whatever she was doing. He was so good at lowering an already rock-bottom esteem.

'Becky'll be fine, the waves aren't big. I'm far more likely to go under than Becky if you don't hold on to me,' she said. But beneath the light-hearted banter, Daisy heard the shiver of fear in her voice.

'You don't *have* to go in, why don't you just watch from the beach?' David was saying.

'No, David. I want to do this for Becky,' and turning to Daisy, Sam said, 'I'm *terrified* of water.'

Daisy was already concerned about Becky, but she hadn't realised how scared Sam was. This could be a big mistake.

'Perhaps it's best if you don't go in the water,' she suggested.

'No she shouldn't,' David snapped. 'She's being stupid, and I can't help, I have a slipped disc.'

'I don't need your help,' Sam snapped. Daisy saw her tweak his ear, then she pinched his bum, but David wasn't amused.

'Stop that, or I'm going,' Daisy heard him say angrily under his breath, but Sam wasn't listening, she was calling to Becky, who was holding on to Josh at the very edge of the water.

'You'll get a cold, Becky,' he was saying. 'I just don't think this is a good idea, guys,' he called.

'It's on my bucket list, Josh!' Becky said, as Daisy ran through the water and started splashing everyone. Tom joined her, and she turned away from Becky to splash him. In the moonlight he looked so handsome, tall and lean, but muscular in all the right places. He was staring at her, and she pushed her way through the water to get closer to him. 'You good?' he murmured.

She nodded, and reached her arm around his neck, pushing her face into his chest, feeling his chin rest on her head. Now she was home. If ever she needed convincing that they were worth fighting for, it was here and now.

'Let's talk later,' she whispered in his ear.

He put both arms around her, pulling her close, and guiding her away from the others, he started to kiss her, and she kissed him back. She loved Tom, she always would. They belonged together, kissing in the ocean, under a big, dark sky. They were there for a long time. They didn't feel the chill of the water, or the rumbling storm approaching. So wrapped up were they in each other, they didn't even hear the anguished cries for help in the near distance. This island had already witnessed violence, and a gruesome murder on that sweltering summer, but now as the storm approached and the cries grew louder, it seemed there was more to come.

TWENTY-SEVEN

BECKY

It all happens so quickly. One minute we're all a bit tipsy, laughing and splashing in the water, and now we've lost Daisy and Tom who have swum out, probably to be alone. God knows what they are up to. Meanwhile Josh and I are swimming, side by side.

'We shouldn't stay out too long,' he says, when we stop for a rest treading water to stay afloat.

'Oh, Josh, why do you always have to put a limit on things? This is my night, you're here for me, not to tell me what to do!'

'I don't want to go out too deep, you don't have the stamina to stay out here. There's a storm coming, and we don't want to get caught up in that. Can't you hear it?'

'I can hear something rumbling in the distance, but it's so far away I doubt it's going to affect our swim. Come on,' I say, and continue the gentle breaststroke through the rippling water, as he splashes behind me. I am loving this, I feel free, I feel more free tonight than I have in a long time. But Josh hasn't even wanted me to paddle, he's so scared of something happening. I keep telling him everything will be fine, and the others are here as support if anything *should* go wrong. I've always been a strong swimmer, and now I'm doing what I want to do, and he doesn't like that. I understand he is that way because he wants to protect me, keep me safe, keep me *alive*. I just wish he'd stop telling me to be careful and treating me like I'm incapable of anything. He is constantly by my side warning me. Then I realise that Josh hasn't shouted out to say 'be careful' for at least a minute, so I slow down and look around. The water's still calm, but a cloud has moved over the moon and taken the light. I can't see anything in the dark. 'Josh?' I say loudly, but all around me is eerily quiet, even the distant thunder seems to have paused.

If this had been pre-diagnosis I'd have guessed he was teasing me, and would leap up like a dolphin any moment. But he doesn't tease me anymore, he doesn't do anything that might hurt me or scare me, he doesn't even make love to me because he thinks I might break. I'm still waiting for him to suddenly appear or answer me. Even if he's swum in a different direction and can't see anything, surely he'd hear me because it's so quiet.

'Josh?' I say louder. Anxiety is curling in my chest like smoke. Just the sound of his voice will quell it, so I wait, and wait. But the only sound I hear is the rippling of water.

I keep telling myself that Josh is a brilliant swimmer, and I didn't hear him splashing around as though he were in trouble, so he must be okay. I'm starting to feel cold now, and hear the shiver in my voice as I call again. 'Josh! Where *are* you? Josh!' I'm shouting now, and suddenly I hear a voice responding, a long way away. It's Sam.

'Becky, are you okay?'

I don't have the strength to swim quickly towards her voice, and the cloud is still hovering over the moon, blocking out light.

It's really scary, I'm worried about Josh, and also myself. I can't stay much longer in the water. I'm beginning to feel tired, and I need to get to the shore. So I head in the direction of shallower waters where I can work out what to do. I call to Sam again, and hope she can hear me, but at the same time, it bothers me that if she can hear me, why can't Josh?

'Keep calling, we're coming to you,' Sam's yelling.

'Over here!' I call, 'I can't find Josh, help!'

'We're coming, Becky,' Sam calls. In between her shouts of reassurance, I wait in the silence for Josh. But the longer I wait, the more terrified I am. Where is he?

'Shit, we've just got to get to her,' I hear Sam calling to David.

'Stay right behind me,' he calls back, as their splashing gets louder and closer.

All I can do is listen. I'm listening for Sam and David, but most of all for Josh. I still can't believe that anything's happened to him. I try hard to look around but the moon still hasn't managed to extricate itself from the thick cloud wrapped around it.

'Becky, where are you?' Sam's voice again.

'Sam, I'm here!' I yell into the rippling silence of the sea. I'm pushing forwards towards her voice, but the weight of water is almost impossible for me to shift.

'Becky, I think we're close,' she cries, and it sounds like she's just a few feet away.

'I'm over here. I'm over HERE! Josh has gone, I can't find him. I don't know where he is.' I'm crying, from cold and fear and exhaustion. I can hear her splashing and wading through the water, and they're soon with me and we're now all calling Josh's name.

'What happened?' David asks.

'I don't know, he was swimming by my side at one point, and I started talking to him. When he didn't answer, I started calling out for him.'

'He's a good swimmer, I've seen him lapping the pool,' David says. 'He'll be around here somewhere. Has he gone underwater to swim?'

'I don't know, I haven't seen him for at least ten minutes now, he wouldn't be able to hold his breath.' I also knew he wouldn't be able to take his eyes off me, he wouldn't just leave me by diving under the sea.

'He's here somewhere, Becky, we'll find him,' Sam says as she clings to me, shaking with fear. This night was supposed to be about friendship and moonlight swimming, and instead it's turned into something frightening.

'There wasn't anyone else in the water, was there?' David asks suddenly.

'Not as far as I know, why?'

'I just wondered if...' His words hang in the air like a fret over the ocean. And it suddenly occurs to me that we may not be alone. What if there was someone else in the water? What if they swam towards us, and stealthily pulled Josh under? Like David says, he's a strong swimmer, there's no reason he would just disappear. I can't allow my mind to go there, so I just huddle with Sam. We're still in the water but our feet are on the ground.

'I'm going to swim further out, see if I can spot him,' David says. And we both watch him until he disappears into the darkness. We're now on our own in the hushed sea in the cold night, two women, one who can't swim, the other too weak and exhausted to swim. I am shivering with fear, because if there *is* anyone else out here, Sam and I are not going to stand a chance. I know she's thinking the same. She's sobbing quietly. 'Should we wade to the beach?' she asks. 'It's not like either of us can do anything.'

'I can't leave him here, in the sea, I have to stay and wait for him,' I reply.

'Of course,' she says.

I know it doesn't make sense, but my instinct is to stay as near as possible to where I last saw him.

I hear someone in the distance, a voice, some movement.

'Josh, are you there?' I call. But he doesn't answer, so I call again, and still he doesn't answer. The only sound is Sam whimpering.

We stand in the stillness, both of us listening for a sign of life other than our breathing, and Sam's sporadic whimpering. I turn around and see nothing for miles. 'Where are Daisy and Tom?' I say, and Sam clutches me.

'Oh God, Becky, what if something's happened to them too?' We look at each other in utter horror.

Suddenly, into the silence, a huge whoosh of water.

'Is that Josh?' she says.

'I bloody hope so. JOSH?' I call.

'It's me,' David replies.

'Any sign?' Sam asks.

He doesn't answer. He doesn't need to.

It occurs to me that if Josh had been in trouble, with cramp or something, he might have swum to the shore. 'He could be out there on the beach?' I suggest, trying to stay as calm as possible.

We suddenly hear voices. Daisy and Tom are calling us, they must have heard the noise. 'Are you guys okay?' Tom's shouting.

Sam and I respond, and eventually they find us in the dark and we explain what's happened.

'Shit! You guys need to go and get help,' Tom says, so we head for the beach, while Daisy and the men stay behind. They're all strong swimmers and can keep searching, they can dive underwater too in case he's there.

Meanwhile, Sam and I head for the beach. Fortunately, she has her phone in her bag, and we go to the signal spot and call the police.

Eventually the three of them emerge from the sea and collapse on the sand, wet and exhausted.

While we wait for the police and the coastguard, I wander to the edge of the ocean and pace backwards and forwards. I feel like a puppy who knows her owner is out there somewhere, and thinks if she walks back and forth long enough he might turn up.

After about half an hour, we see activity at the top of the cliffs – flashing lights and voices – and we all breathe a sigh of relief. 'Help at last,' Daisy says, shaking her wet hair and looking up at the gardens. We stand and start waving and calling so they know where we are and we're joined by four police officers, who ask us all the obvious questions to establish the facts.

I am a mess by now, and burst into tears. It's finally hitting me that Josh might actually have drowned. 'I don't understand, he's a good swimmer, it doesn't make sense,' I say over and over again.

'Now, love, until we find him, we don't know *anything*,' the older police officer says kindly. He bends down lower to talk to me, 'Coastguard Rescue are on their way, meanwhile my colleagues and I are going to do a thorough search, the caves, the rocks, we will literally leave no stone unturned,' he says. 'Now I know this is hard, but—'

'He isn't on land, he was in the water!' I say.

'Yes, but there are strong currents here,' he replies. 'He may have been swept in a different direction, even strong swimmers can get into trouble if they get caught in a current.'

'If something's happened to him, how do I tell the kids...?' I burst into huge, heaving sobs, while Sam puts her arms around me, rocking me like a baby.

'Let's not jump to conclusions just yet, we'll stay down here until the rescue arrives and an air ambulance is standing by,' the officer adds reassuringly.

'Where are they?' I ask through sobs.

'On their way.' He looks at Sam. 'Perhaps it might be better if you could take her up to the hotel, get her a warm drink, she's shivering.'

We all slowly head back up the beach and haul ourselves up the rickety steps back to the hotel. I stand on the cliffs looking out, like there's a chance I might just see him swimming back to shore, and it's all been a big drama for nothing. But the sea is calm, the moonlight is back, I can see for miles, and he isn't there. Everything's quiet. Even the waves are calmer, like their hunger has been sated now.

TWENTY-EIGHT

SAM

By the time we'd all got back to the hotel, the weather had started to turn. We sat in the lobby with hot drinks as the threatening storm moved swiftly towards the island. The sea was suddenly energised, and though in the dark we couldn't see it, we could hear the beginnings of its roar. David was exhausted and went off to bed as there was no point all of us staying up through the night. But Daisy, Tom and I stayed with Becky, and when a police officer came into the lobby and told us that the oncoming weather meant the coastguard couldn't start the search until morning, we all feared the worst.

'Why don't you go and get some sleep?' I said to Becky. 'I'll wait here for news, and the minute there is any, I'll come straight up to you.'

She reluctantly agreed, and Daisy and Tom walked her to her room.

I sat for a while staring out of the lobby window where sun loungers hurled themselves across the patio area. The pool was swirling in anticipation of what was to come, and the sky was lighting up in the distance. If I hadn't been with him in the water, I might have suspected David of hurting Josh. He didn't like him, I think he saw Josh as weak. But Josh wasn't weak, he was kind and gentle and he cared about his wife – whereas my husband was an egotistical macho man who didn't care for anyone but himself. I'd realised by now that I'd misinterpreted his arrogance as confidence, and his brashness as charm. Josh was popular with women because he was a good person and women could sense this. But it didn't matter how many drinks David bought, or how much he bragged about his car or his business, people still preferred Josh and David was jealous.

I sat for a long time watching the storm, thinking about my marriage. It felt like a watershed.

I stayed with Becky in her room for most of the following morning, just sitting by the window, watching, looking out at the sea. 'Is he still out there somewhere?' she asked.

She didn't want to tell the children just yet, but she'd called her mum and sister, and cried a lot during those calls.

'I made them promise to leave it until I get home before I tell Amy and Ben,' she said. 'It's the worst part of all this. But I want to be the one to tell them.' She was looking out at the cliffs and I wondered if she was hoping she'd see him, doing his morning run along the beach. It broke my heart to see her, and now she seemed more frail than ever. She'd lost what little spark she had left and I just kept thinking about the night before and how, in just a few moments, a midnight swim with friends had turned into something else.

I stayed with Becky when the manager and the police came to take statements. No body had been found as yet. Later, we sat on her balcony drinking coffee and tearing at bits of croissant, and she said, 'Do *you* think it was an accident?'

I gave it a moment, of consideration, and replied, 'Yes, what else *could* it be?'

'Someone drowned him?'

'Who? I can't see how. David and I weren't anywhere near, and Tom and Daisy were miles away. You two were completely alone out there. Besides, Josh was one of the nicest guys I've ever met, I can't imagine he had enemies?'

'Oh, he had his demons,' she said quietly.

'Demons?' I was expecting her to elaborate.

But instead, she looked up at the sky. 'It's chilly today, we complained about the heat and now we're sad it's gone.' Becky was snuggled up in a big cardigan. It wasn't that cold, but she felt it more than me, she was so frail. She looked like a little old lady in a shawl. How tragic that her mind was so sharp, and meanwhile there was Mum, with a healthy body and a sick mind. I gazed at the thick grey sludge moving slowly across the sky, and dreaded what the day would bring.

We left the balcony to sit inside. 'The weather's really coming in, isn't it?' Becky said.

'Yes, it really is end of the holiday weather,' I murmured.

Just then there was a knock on the door, and when I answered it Tom and Daisy were standing there with their suitcases.

'Oh you're going home?' I said sadly.

'Yeah, the boat's back and the police have no choice but to let people go, so we thought we'd get out of here while we can,' she was saying, walking towards me, her arms open.

She looked lovely, in a summer dress and her floppy Gucci sun hat.

'You look fab, you're wearing my favourite hat,' I said, hugging her. Becky was getting up from the armchair by the window.

'Is there any news?' Daisy asked.

Becky shook her head. 'I'm just waiting so I know what to tell the kids.'

'So sorry, Becky,' Tom said, as Daisy hugged Becky.

'Oh, love, I'm sorry this happened, you don't deserve this,' Daisy murmured, still holding her.

'Anyway, he still might turn up,' Tom offered optimistically.

And in a rather futile attempt to give Becky a flake of hope, we all agreed.

'Hey, who knows, he might even be in South America by now,' Becky said.

I looked at Daisy, then Tom, and both of them seemed surprised at this. It was hardly the time for joking, especially from Becky.

'You don't think he's faked his own death, do you?' Tom was frowning, clearly intrigued by this.

'No, not Josh,' Becky replied. 'He wouldn't know where to start. He's hopeless, couldn't have got to Devon without me, never mind South America.'

Saying goodbye was really, really sad because when you've been through what we'd all been through, you feel the pull. These people were so much more than friends you meet on holiday, we'd held on to each other in a big storm, and had been through so much.

'I'll miss you,' I said, hugging them both. 'Do you have to go now, surely you can stay and have lunch?'

'No, no we really do have to leave,' Daisy said. And with that they left. It felt abrupt in light of what had just happened, but they had their lives to return to.

Once we were left alone, we continued to sit together by the window. The storm clouds were still rolling in and despite it being daytime, the sky was brooding and dark.

I thought about our very first night on the island, David and I sitting in the beautiful ballroom. I'd never been anywhere so luxurious, and everyone was so glamorous and worldly. I'd changed so much since that first night. So much had happened to me and I knew my life would never be the same again.

'We were due to leave tomorrow,' Becky said, 'but I've

called my sister to come and get me. I have to see the kids. I need to have that conversation with my children.'

'If he... doesn't come back, how will you cope without him?' I asked.

She gave a hollow laugh. 'I've told you before, love, I'm fine, the question is, how would he cope without me?' She was smiling at me. I could tell she wanted to say something, and after a moment she did. 'Sam, I hope you don't mind me asking,' she started awkwardly.

'Yes, anything. What?'

'You and David, will you stay together?'

I wasn't going to say anything, Becky had her own nightmare to live through.

'He left, this morning. We're getting a divorce.'

'No!'

'I'm still processing it, but we both know it's for the best. I did stupid things when I was with him. I thought if I held on, fought off any threats, he'd stay with me for ever and I'd be happy. But I was wrong. I changed from the moment I met him, and hated who I became.'

'I'm sorry, Sam.'

'No, don't be, this holiday has been difficult for everyone, some couples survive it, some don't,' I said, suddenly realising how that sounded. 'Sorry, I didn't mean...'

'It's fine, but you're right, look at Daisy and Tom, they've come through their own storm by the looks of things.'

'Yeah, and I'm sure they'll be fine.'

'Do you think David would ever go back to his ex-wife?' she asked.

I shook my head. 'She's dead.'

'Oh, I didn't realise.'

'Yes, it was very difficult. She didn't accept mine and David's relationship, but recently I began to understand why... They were still together when we got together. He said they were estranged, but it seems she wasn't aware of that, so she saw me as the other woman – I guess I was, I just didn't know it. Anyway, she asked if I'd go and visit her for a chat. I felt like this might be the answer, we could clear the air, she'd see I wasn't some evil homewrecker and we could all get on with our lives. David warned me not to, but I went anyway, and when I arrived at her cottage, the front door was open, so I walked in. I was half-expecting her to run at me from inside with a knife.'

Becky's hand flew to her mouth.

'I called her name but after no one answered I walked into her living room...' I paused, I found it so hard to talk about. 'I walked into the living room and... and saw two feet suspended in the air. At first my mind couldn't work out what it was. Then I realised, she was hanging from a beam.'

'Oh, Sam,' Becky moaned.

'It was horrific, there was so much blood. She'd tried to slash her wrists first, but presumably it wasn't quick enough for her. She was wearing a thin white nightie, and the blood...' I tried to push it away. 'God, I shouldn't be thinking about stuff like this, not today.'

'Bad things can inspire bad memories,' she said gently. 'If it helps you, just talk about it. Bring those memories out into the daylight, you've obviously been hiding them inside, and that isn't good.'

'I haven't talked to anyone about it, but at night I go to sleep and see bloodstains on her white nightdress, and her face. That's why I reacted like I did to spilling my drink on Daisy's white dress, it just triggered me – and David knew, he *knew* why I reacted like that, but still hated me for embarrassing him. I can see her face, mouth open, eyes in the back of her head.' I shuddered. 'I couldn't go near her. I called an ambulance, and then I called David who berated me for going round there when he'd warned me against it. But now I know she staged it for me, because I wouldn't listen to what she was trying to say to me.

Now I know that David is toxic, and any woman stupid enough to fall for him will ruin her life.'

'But you've got out now, Sam, you saved yourself.'

I shrugged. 'It's too late for me, I've already ruined my life. I might as well have done what Marie did.'

'No, no you have your life before you...' Becky was saying, but of course she'd think that.

'It's like I never left her that night, and she's still with me.'

We both sat for a while in our own worlds as the afternoon grew darker, and the storm moved in. A heavy, navy-blue sky fringed with smoke grey bore down on us, as we allowed our minds to go wandering through the dark clouds filling our heads.

Becky's sister arrived later that day to help Becky pack and take her home. She was lovely, and it was good to know Becky had someone like that to take care of her in Josh's absence. The day after she left, his body was found washed up on the beach. It was terribly sad, but Becky wasn't strong enough to make the journey back to the island, so I didn't see her again. Guests were then suddenly allowed to leave, which started the rumour that Josh had been the killer all along, and the police had no need to keep us at Fitzgerald's. But I had no reason to leave, I called home, asked my mother's nurse to stay on and extended my stay by ten days.

I had a lot to think about and some important decisions to make about my future, and besides, I'd taken the time off work, David had already paid for some of it in advance. So I hung around, along with a few straggler police officers, and Granger, who was apparently in the process of packing up and moving the investigation to the mainland.

I asked Elizabeth, the lady whose nephew was on the investigation team, if she knew what was happening. She was changing my bedsheets and I was helping her. It was against hotel regulations, but the poor woman had a bad back and I couldn't see her struggle.

'Apparently they found drugs and alcohol in Mr Andrews' blood,' she said. 'It seems he had some issues.'

'Wow!' I was stunned. 'Josh was the nicest guy, I never imagined anything like that. God, you just never know the people you meet on holiday, do you?' I said, forcing the pillow into a clean pillowcase. But it all made sense now. 'Josh must have taken drugs and drunk too much champagne and just drowned.'

We tucked in the under sheet on either side of the mattress as I contemplated this.

'Yes, so that's one death solved, Miss Marple, but we still don't know who killed Stella, do we?'

'I wonder if we ever will, Elizabeth?'

I finally leave Fitzgerald's after two extra weeks, and it's been bliss. I'm sad about the marriage, but not about David. I've been so much happier since he left, and it's harder to say goodbye to this place than to him. But sadly, the day has finally come when I have to check out, and as I pay what's left of the bill and say my goodbyes, the receptionist asks me to wait. She disappears into a back room and emerges with a carrier bag. 'With all the police comings and goings this ended up in the office,' she says, 'but I remembered that one of the guests, Daisy Brown, left it for you.' She hands me a plastic carrier bag, and inside is Daisy's beautiful Gucci sun hat that I'd admired. I'm not sure I'll need it where I'm going, but it makes me so happy to think that Daisy liked me enough to give it to me. It's a precious memento of our friendship, and a lifelong reminder of a cruel but beautiful summer.

EPILOGUE

DAISY

A week later

Daisy and Tom returned from their holiday like different people. He was more open and talked through things, and she was beginning to work towards a new future, but before she could totally embrace this, she had to see someone. So she made a call.

'I feel like you and I need to talk,' Daisy said.

'I guess we do,' Becky replied. And so it was agreed that Daisy would travel the eighty-odd miles to visit with Becky. She arrived the next day at the neat little suburban semi where Becky and Josh had lived with their children.

Becky's home was just as Daisy had imagined: a neat little garden, fresh paintwork, clean white window shutters that kept the world out. And even in the middle of a tumultuous struggle to stay alive, it seemed like Becky had found the strength to decorate the frontage with a full hanging basket.

Daisy knocked on the door and was greeted with much

warmth by Becky's mother, Margaret, a bustling, older version of Becky, who informed her she'd moved in, while guiding her down the neat little hall into the front room where her daughter waited. Daisy tried not to show her surprise when she saw how diminished Becky now was. The cancer had ravaged her body, leaving the forty-year-old shrunken and grey, looking twice her age.

'Lovely to see you,' she said, smiling weakly, her breathing laboured. She seemed welded to the sofa, unable to move. Even talking seemed to suck all the energy from her.

Daisy had brought flowers which she handed to Margaret, who took them to put in water and rushed off to busy herself making tea, but not before closing the door, 'so you girls can have your privacy.'

Becky watched her mum leave the room with a smile on her face. 'She used to say that when I had school friends over for tea. Things don't change, do they? Relationships just carry on, the dynamic stays the same, it's just the settings that change. Mum was here at the start of my life to usher me in, and now she's here to help me go.'

Daisy didn't know what to say to this. It was too sad, too raw.

'I owe her such a lot,' Becky said, pausing for a gasp of breath. 'I can die in peace knowing that she's here for the children. I often think of something you said about one good mum being worth ten bad dads?'

Daisy smiled. 'Yeah, I think parents are overrated, but what do I know, never really had any to speak of.'

'You pulled yourself up by your bootlaces, Daisy Brown,' Becky said. 'You've done all right on your own. I guess that's why you always fight your own battles, you've had to?'

Daisy shrugged.

Margaret returned with tea and cake and stayed for a few minutes before leaving, with the same comment about privacy as she closed the door. The women looked at each other and smiled.

'I'd have given anything for a mum like yours,' Daisy said, when she'd gone.

'She's a good one, you can borrow her if you like, she's going to have some time on her hands soon.' Becky almost tripped up on this, but managed to swallow back the tears.

'I'd like to stay in touch with her, and the kids,' Daisy said. She paused a moment. 'Look, Tom and I both have decent salaries, and I'd like to put some money in a trust for Amy and Ben. It will help with their university education, or weddings whatever?'

'That's very kind,' Becky said, putting her cup and saucer on the coffee table. '*Too* kind, some would say.'

'It's the least I can do.'

Becky looked at her. 'You mean because you killed their father?'

Daisy swallowed; she hadn't expected this. 'You *knew* it was me?'

Becky nodded slowly. 'I had an invite from Sam, left on my pillow, but when I saw her at dinner she thanked *me* for organising it. I saw her invite on the table and it was from me. I was confused, but didn't really think about it; only later did I realise that someone must have really been keen to get us – and our husbands – in the sea that night.'

'I realised after we'd talked about going swimming that it was my chance to do something. I was still disturbed and in shock from the rape and I wasn't thinking straight, I just wanted to kill him, Becky. So in order to make sure he came swimming I made formal invites, but I wasn't sure anyone would come if the invite was from me.'

'I'm sure we would have,' Becky said.

'I knew he'd try to talk you out of it, and I knew Sam might back out because she was scared of water, so I had to make sure you all came along. I knew that you and Sam had a bond, you'd spent more time together, and you were more likely to feel obligated if Sam invited you, and Sam would feel she had to turn up if you wanted her there.'

'Perhaps,' Becky conceded. 'And you were right, Josh didn't want to go swimming, he was concerned about me. I think he was also concerned about you being there, and if you might say something.'

'Exactly, that's why I wanted him to think it was Sam's invitation. He might have been suspicious if it was mine.'

'So it was *you* who came into my room when I was asleep and left the rose and the invite?'

'Yeah, I thought it was just the kind of thing Sam would do, and I wrote her invite in your style too. Security was so tight I had to bribe the maid that cleaned your room,' Daisy said. 'I was sure you'd wake up when I put the invite on your pillow, and I nearly dropped the pills on the floor in your bathroom, but you slept through.'

'Yeah, when I came to leave the hotel room I discovered my anti-depressants were missing from the back of the bathroom cabinet where I used to hide them so Josh thought I'd taken them.'

'You'd told us where you hid the anti-depressants, and I knew mixed with alcohol they could be lethal. So I ground them up into powder and had to time it so that I could put the powder in his drink and make sure he was in the sea when they took hold.'

'I know as well as anyone that too much alcohol, and too many anti-depressants at midnight in the sea is quite a cocktail.' Becky took a deep breath. 'So, when the police said large quantities of anti-depressant had been found in Josh's blood, I just knew. So I lied and told them he was depressed about my illness, was careless the way he took anti-depressants with alcohol and that must have been why he drowned. They accepted this readily. I think they were just relieved to solve at least one murder.'

'You knew it was me who killed him and yet you saved me?' Daisy said in an almost whisper.

'I guess I did,' she replied.

'You know why I killed him, don't you?'

'Yes.'

'*How* do you know?'

'It was me watching from the window, I wore one of Josh's black hoodies. I'd been watching him all holiday. I'd watched him chatting to Stella the night she died, I watched him running every night – all from our balcony. But that night I couldn't see him, so I climbed across next door's balcony. You were next door but one, and as you will recall, the balcony walls were low. I knew something was going to happen, and I'd seen the way he looked at you. I knew Tom was downstairs, because we'd left him there, and I had a feeling Josh might have gone to your room. He was manic... but I never expected him to rape you. I couldn't tell that night what was happening, I even thought it might be consensual sex.'

'Because when you saw us, I wasn't struggling?'

'Yes, and I thought perhaps you two had an attraction, and given my situation, I didn't feel I could stop him if it made him happy. I had no idea until the next day when I saw your bruises and you told me what had happened. I knew it was him, and wanted to kill him myself.'

Daisy took a breath. 'God, it was so awful. I didn't want to hurt you, and I never intended to tell anyone, I've never even told Tom. I just wanted to keep it to myself. I didn't want to destroy you or your kids. I didn't want to destroy myself either, because while it was locked inside me I could pretend it never happened. But that morning I felt so alone, so wretched. I used to feel like that as a kid sometimes, and I had no one to talk to... but that morning I had you.'

'I'm just so sorry he put you through all that Daisy, and then there was the assault...' She paused. 'When my sister and I packed his stuff at the hotel, we found muddy clothes, a face mask, gardening gloves. It was Josh who'd assaulted you on the cliffs too, love.'

Daisy nodded. 'I didn't know, but I'm not surprised.' She tried not to think about it.

'You see, he wasn't even capable of hiding evidence.' Becky rolled her eyes. 'If the police had searched our room they'd have arrested him on the spot, he was hopeless. Even after twenty years of marriage, I had no idea my husband was capable of rape, I didn't know he was capable of violence of any kind. But I was shocked at what I found in his stuff along with the gloves and the muddy clothes. There were condoms hidden in a zip lining of his jacket, photos of women on his phone, including some of you. There was poetry on texts he'd written to girls he'd presumably become obsessed with. Oh, and a pink, silk nightdress.'

Daisy groaned. 'Short, strappy?'

'Oh, was it yours?'

'Sounds like it.'

'I'm sorry. It was unnerving to find all that. But he wasn't who I thought he was, I don't know if he ever had been.'

'I'm so sorry, Becky, in some ways it might have been better not to know about him?'

'I think subconsciously I knew things weren't right with Josh and hadn't been for a long time. I just kept blaming my illness. But I had been making excuses, and the rape ended any residue of feelings I had for him.'

She poured more tea for them both, and handed Daisy a steaming cup.

'And Stella, did you ever find out what happened to Stella?' Daisy asked, taking a sip of the tea. 'I heard her death is still "unexplained."'

Becky put her head in her hands. 'Granger spoke to me. She knows my situation, knows I have two kids, and I have to think of them.' She paused and took a breath. Daisy heard the rasping sound and ached for her. 'Granger says someone saw Josh running away from the body. Josh said he was just running along the beach, but he probably lied. Stella was just his type – as we discussed, blonde, slim and a bit like you. We know for a fact he attacked you on the cliffs, so it would make sense that he did the same to Stella. She wasn't sexually assaulted, so she probably struggled as you did. Granger said her killer was rough with her, she was bruised on the upper arms just like you. They can't say for certain if she was pushed off the cliff or if she slipped, but it's immaterial, the poor girl lost her life at the hands of my husband. I just hope it never comes to light and the children never find out.'

Despite all the trauma she'd been through, Daisy found her visit to Becky was healing, and with help from Tom, she knew she could now close this chapter and move on. Even if Becky hadn't died the following week, she and Daisy would never have met again. They were from different worlds. Like any other holiday friendship, the only thing they had in common was their time at Fitzgerald's. But what happened there had impacted their lives in ways they could never have imagined. In the final days of Becky's life, she'd seen her husband for who he really was, and who, without her, he would become. In lying about the nature of his death, she'd given Daisy her life back, and Daisy was grateful. She would live with the guilt of murder, it was a small price to pay; she'd lived with the injustice of abuse from her stepfather for the first half of her life. She wasn't going to let her rapist free and spend the rest of her life without justice.

That night on the beach, she'd poured the champagne in the moonlight, and added Becky's strong anti-depressants into one of the paper cups. She then handed that cup to Sam saying,

'Give this one to Josh,' and as Sam gave the cup to him, Daisy watched him drink it down like water. And with every gulp he took, she remembered what he'd done, and what her stepfather had done, and felt the weight of years lift from her shoulders.

When the women parted that day on Becky's doorstep, they knew they'd never see each other again, but they were bound together for ever, and they would take their secret to the grave.

EPILOGUE

STELLA

He seemed like a nice guy, when he hung around the beach bar. He even came to watch my yoga class with his wife once or twice. It was obvious he had a thing for me; on the day they arrived, he caught my eye at the bar. He was fun and attractive and on that first night, he and his wife came to the pool bar. As the weather was so hot we stayed open until late, and when she left, he stayed behind and we talked.

On the Sunday evening, he turned up alone at the bar just as I was closing, said he couldn't sleep because of the heat. Apparently his wife was out like a light, but he'd been sitting on the balcony for ages trying to cool down. I'd seen him watching me from there, just a shadow in the dark, but I knew it was him. Anyway, I didn't have to be anywhere, my shift was over, so I poured us both a large one and we got talking. I liked him – turned out he had a property business, bought and sold places, and also rented them out. I think he was quite rich – well, when you're twenty-two with nothing, a guy with a *car* is rich! So when he started asking me about my future and my hopes and dreams, I was there for it.

'Look, Stella,' he said, 'I don't know you, but just talking to you, I feel like we'd be a great fit, professionally speaking. You're a good-looking girl, great with people and I bet you're great with social media. If ever you fancy taking the property business by storm, you should look me up. I need someone to do our marketing and you'd be perfect.'

It was August, and I was starting to wonder where I might go next. I'd tried to get in with a couple of big influencers hoping they might give me some leads, but wasn't getting anywhere. I also had a vague idea about going back to art college, but this felt like an opportunity to make money and live in a big city for a change.

'I'd love to think about it?' I said.

'Let's drink to thinking about it?' he said, as I poured us another couple of drinks.

The next night was the same, he couldn't sleep, came out to the bar late, and we sat and drank until late. We got along really well, he said he could start me on a great salary, and I would be a millionaire by the time I was thirty. I knew a lot of it was talk, he was a bit full of himself, but he was inspiring and exciting, and I was ambitious. But the following night, the Tuesday, was when it started to get a bit weird, he turned up slightly earlier and there were a couple of people still at the bar. He seemed a bit pissed off about the other guests and said, 'Come for a walk with me.'

I explained I worked until eleven thirty and couldn't leave the bar, but he was very persuasive and convinced me to come out from behind the bar and have a quick chat in private. So I agreed, and we walked over to the far side of the bar behind some trees and started talking. He said he'd been in touch with his accountant. 'I can pay you £30k starting salary, and that would include your apartment rent-free.'

I couldn't believe it. 'Thank you, where do I sign, I'd love to take you up on that,' I said. But before I could say anything else, he's suddenly pressing me up against a tree, and I wasn't too sure about that. I know I shouldn't have, but I let him kiss me. And when I said I had to go back to the bar, he said he'd walk me back to the staff house and we could talk some more when my shift finished.

I went straight back to the bar, wondering if I was doing the right thing agreeing to a job with David, when I saw the running guy, Josh, stealing money out of the till! I couldn't believe it, the poshest hotel in the area, and one guest's trying it on behind the trees and the another one's robbing the till. They're nothing but scum. So I had a few words with Josh. He said he was sorry, begged me not to call the police, and when I said no, he got funny. He said he'd put the money back in the till and keep quiet about me with my 'lover' if I kept quiet about the money. He obviously didn't know it was David I'd been with but kept saying, 'You've been kissing him behind that tree, I saw you, and I'll tell the manager.' I didn't have a choice, I needed that job, at least until I could go back to college, or start at David's company, but who knew when that would be? And I was beginning to wonder what I might have to do to keep the job he was offering me; if it involved sleeping with the boss, that wasn't me at all.

So I agreed with Josh that we'd both keep quiet. He put the money back and when he'd gone David emerged from the darkness, and said he hoped I hadn't got the wrong idea. 'I just find you so incredibly bright and attractive, and I had to kiss you. That was the first and last time it will ever happen,' he said. So I washed the glasses while he talked about how amazing I was and how he could give me such a bright future, but I just wasn't so sure anymore. And after I locked up the bar, he walked me back to the house where I was staying.

When we got to the door and he tried to kiss me again, I pushed him away and politely told him to go back to his room where his wife would be waiting. I told him I wasn't going to be his mistress in a flat in Manchester even for £30k a year, and he tried to get round me, but eventually left. I walked to the cliff area and watched him walk back through the gardens and to his room to make sure he was gone. When I turned around to go back to the house, someone was standing right behind me.

'I've been waiting for you,' she said, walking towards me. It was David's wife, standing in the darkness.

She made me jump, but the look on her face terrified me, and for a moment I froze.

'Please don't take him away from me, Stella, you could have anyone, but he's the love of my life.'

'I'm not, it's not like that, we're... friends,' I said gently.

Tears were streaming down her face. 'No, he's been hanging around the bar all night, he walked you back here, and I see the way he looks at you. I don't know what to do, what shall I do?' she whispered in my face.

Before I could say anything, she'd gripped my arms with her fingers and was shaking me, and in a loud, staccato whisper said, 'Please, I'm begging you, leave him alone. Don't ruin this for me. It's my honeymoon. You can have your pick of men, but I can't. He's my husband. I love him.'

I tried to explain but she didn't want to hear. She'd convinced herself that her husband and I were together.

And all the time, her face was right up against mine. I was terrified and trying to pull away. I eventually managed to extricate myself from her grip and ran through the gardens away from her. I shouted for help, desperately hoping someone would hear and come to my aid, but not at the resort; everyone is so genteel, polite, they keep themselves to themselves. But suddenly, I tripped slightly on the stony path, and hurt my ankle. I was hobbling now and she caught me up. She was right behind me, and I started screaming, but she put her arm around my neck, and her hand on my mouth to quieten me. But I kept trying to scream and was struggling to escape her grip. She was bigger than me, and quite strong and as my ankle was now hurting I knew I couldn't run away.

'Stop it, Stella, and I'll let you go,' she was hissing, so I stopped screaming, and she released me. I turned around and the horror on her face matched mine. It was like she couldn't believe what she'd just done.

'Oh God, I'm sorry, I'm so sorry,' she was saying, walking towards me with her arms outstretched. But I didn't trust her and as she walked towards me, I walked backwards, still facing her so she couldn't grab me from behind again.

'Look out!' she yelled and leapt towards me, but I leapt back away from her, and my ankle completely gave way. Suddenly I was falling. The world slowed down. I was weightless in the dark silence, there wasn't even enough time to scream. The last thing I saw was her silhouette looking down at me from the top of the cliffs, and the last thing I heard, were her sobs. Twenty-two years blown away as I hit the ground with a horrible thud.

EPILOGUE

SAM

Now

As I step onto the boat, a sudden breeze catches my hat and though I try to grab it, I'm not quick enough. With tears in my eyes, I watch the beautiful Gucci boater tied with grosgrain ribbon, as it floats further and further away.

I try not to cry as I take my seat on deck, opposite a woman with searching eyes and alarm in her voice.

'Oh no, is that your hat?' she asks.

I nod, avoiding her searching eyes.

'Was it expensive?'

'Very,' I reply, wishing she'd shut up.

I take my phone from my bag in an attempt to avoid speaking to her. I'm surprised to see a signal. We've been shut off from the rest of the UK for the past few weeks, and it feels strange now, almost scary to be able to speak to the outside world. I don't know what to say. What can I say? Impulsively, I decide to call my sister; I'm tired and tearful, I need to hear a familiar voice.

'Hey, you,' she says. 'Are you okay? I heard what happened, it was in all the newspapers. Are you finally coming home?'

I'm moved by my sister's voice, and the sound of home, but her words are like a hammer in my head, a reminder of how life was before this trip.

'Are you there, are you okay?' my sister's saying, and a wave of huge, loud sobs emerge from somewhere deep inside me. The woman opposite is staring at me.

'No, to be honest, I'm not okay.'

'What? What is it?' My sister's voice has turned to panic.

'Sis, can you do me a favour?' I say. 'My signal's dying. Will you call the police and ask them to meet me on the mainland? I have something to tell them.'

Still clutching the phone to my ear, I move further down the deck, so I can't see my departing hat, or the woman's beady eyes. I stand alone at the far end of the boat, surrounded by the ocean for the last time. I allow the salty sea breeze to ruffle my hair, and cool my cheeks. It has been the hottest summer the UK had ever known. As the mercury rose, and storms rolled in, secrets were spilled and lives were lost in that beautiful white palace overlooking a turquoise sea. And as the boat cuts through the now choppy waters, I see Fitzgerald's grow smaller and smaller in the distance, until it looks like a glittering diamond standing proud in the middle of the Atlantic Ocean. Only then do I turn to see the mainland, where an uncertain future awaits. I pull my shawl around me, and brace myself for what happens now.

A LETTER FROM SUE

Thank you so much for choosing to read *The Resort*. If you enjoyed it, and want to keep up to date with all my latest releases, just sign up at the following link. Your email address will never be shared and you can unsubscribe at any time.

www.bookouture.com/sue-watson

The setting for this book was inspired by a day on the beach in Devon with my family last summer. We were at Bigbury-on-Sea, a lovely beach that looks out onto a small island, home to the most beautiful art deco hotel. It's a place I've always wanted to visit, a white palace and writer's paradise. Agatha Christie wrote two of her books – *And Then There Were None* and *Evil Under the Sun* – while staying at the hotel's beach house in the 1930s. The island and the hotel together are called Burgh Island, and apart from its loveliness, I was intrigued by the way the tide cuts it off, which means, at times, no access and no escape. As a writer I was captivated by the idea of a mix of guests being stranded on an island, and I had to set a book there. So, earlier this year I stayed for one very special night at The Burgh Island Hotel, and though Fitzgerald's isn't totally faithful, it's clearly inspired by the real-life hotel. During my short stay, I was seduced by this wonderful place, and it will stay with me for ever, and I've tried to capture the glamour, luxury, and mystery in Fitzgerald's just for you.

I hope you loved *The Resort* and if you did, I would be so

grateful if you could write a review. It doesn't have to be as long as a sentence – every word counts and is very much appreciated. I love to hear what you think, and it makes such a difference helping new readers to discover one of my books for the first time.

I love hearing from my readers – so please get in touch! You can find me on my Facebook page, Instagram, Twitter, Goodreads or my website.

Thanks so much for reading,

Sue

www.suewatsonbooks.com

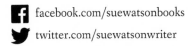 facebook.com/suewatsonbooks
twitter.com/suewatsonwriter

ACKNOWLEDGEMENTS

As always, my huge thanks to the wonderful team at Bookouture who are amazing, and never cease to amaze me with their professionalism, enthusiasm and brilliant author care.

Thanks to my wonderful editor Helen Jenner, who has helped shape this seed of an idea from a visit to a beach in Devon, into something really special. Her energy, her ideas, her professionalism. And thanks even for those big edits that keep me up late into the night and make my books so much better.

Special thanks to my American friend and reader Ann Bresnan who was as amazing as ever, sharing ideas and discovering vital clues I'd missed. Huge thanks also to the brilliant Harolyn Grant, for casting a forensic eye across an early copy of the novel, finding the devil in the detail and making a real difference. What a star! Big thanks also to Sarah Hardy, who gave this book an early read, and added some extra polish, and to Anna Wallace, whose final read-through put everything to bed beautifully! You are all amazing and I'm so lucky to have you on my team.

As always, a big thank you to the wonderful book bloggers who read my books and take time to write reviews. I'm so grateful for everything you do. And finally, to family and friends, not forgetting Poppy our cat who sits next to me on the sofa when I write – thank you for always being with me on my journey, inspiring and supporting me every step of the way!

Made in the USA
Middletown, DE
02 August 2022

70415764R00163